SEA OF SCOUNDRELS

J. C. Thompson

Cover art by Jennifer Grumbles
info@uptowncountryhome.com

ISBN-13: 978-1977699824

This book is dedicated to my beloved Grandma Edith. I miss you every day.

And to Delryn Fleming of Brookhaven Community College in Dallas, Texas. Thank you for your excellent teaching and words of encouragement so many years ago.

Acknowledgments

I wish to thank Patty McBratney for her thoughtful and thorough editing, Erik Reinecke for his expert technical support, and Suzy Tatum and Bobbie Topp for their unflagging moral support and helpful advice.

I couldn't have finished this book without you.

SEA OF SCOUNDRELS

Prologue

It was well past midnight, but the pedestrian plaza behind the world-famous Monte Carlo Casino was brightly illuminated by sodium vapor lights. Her gown iridescent and shimmering in the diffuse bronze glow, a woman walked with sad determination to a chest-high, concrete guard railing that had been constructed to keep unwary tourists from plunging one hundred feet into the Mediterranean Sea below.

She stood on tiptoe and peeked over. Razor sharp rocks grinned up at her like the bared teeth of a hungry wild animal. Wave after implacable wave pounded against the support pilings that sustained the structure beneath her, the thunder of their sheer power calling to her from the dark maelstrom. She shivered at the nightmare visions that flashed through her thoughts like shooting stars as she contemplated her final moments, picturing her body impaled on the jagged rocks or carried off by the icy waves to be eaten by predators from the deep.

It really didn't matter which grim fate would choose her. She was out of options and out of hope. Resolute in her decision, she forced aside her fears, kicked off her shoes, and started to climb over the railing.

PART I

Chapter 1

Twenty Months Earlier

An old Toyota Celica pulled to a stop in front of the Glenrose Hotel in Dallas, Texas, and a uniformed valet jogged over to help Anna Thornbury out of it. She hand-combed her blonde, shoulder length hair into weak submission and walked briskly into the hotel, her high heels tapping a businesslike staccato on the shiny marble floors. Five feet seven inches tall and still svelte in middle age, most would consider her pretty, especially when she smiled. Her eyes changed color depending on the weather, her mood, and what she was wearing. Today they matched her blue blouse and lit up when she spotted her childhood friend, Nicky Morgan, standing by the door to the bar.

He saw her walking toward him and grinned, his irrepressible spirit beaming through a smile that took up half his face. Prematurely gray in college, he was now completely bald. At six feet two inches tall and crisply dressed in a dark gray pinstripe suit, he looked every bit the successful New York financial wizard, notwithstanding his Texas roots.

Nicky and Anna lived on the same street when they were children. They attended grade school and middle school together, becoming the fastest of friends along the way because of their intellectual compatibility and love of science. The saddest day of Anna's young life was when the Morgans moved to a different school district shortly before Nicky's freshman year of high school.

Once a straight "A" student and nerd like Anna, Nicky had gone to college at Yale, then on to business school at Harvard. After getting a master's degree, he returned to Dallas to work for a small local investment banking house, ultimately moving to New York City when the Dallas financial markets could no longer contain his career aspirations.

They hugged in greeting, then Nicky held Anna at arm's length to get a better look at her. "You look fantastic," he said.

"And you look prosperous," Anna said, blushing at the compliment.

They entered the bar and found an empty table tucked into a corner by the massive oak bookcases that lined the walls. Candles in crystal holders illuminated the small tables scattered around the room, the large mirror behind the bar reflecting their flickering flames and filling the air with dancing fireflies. A muted buzz of conversation hovered around them while a tuxedoed musician tickled the ivories of a baby grand piano on the far side of the room. They settled into plush leather chairs, and when their drinks arrived, they raised their glasses and toasted in unison, "Pinkies up!"

Nicky had coined the phrase after once attending the Cattle Baron's Ball at Southfork Ranch. He had been highly amused to see Texas society mavens of both sexes dressed in pricey cowboy chic and drinking champagne with their pinkie fingers pointed straight up like British dowagers at high tea. He took a sip of his eighteen-year old scotch and looked lovingly at his friend. "So, counselor, how's my favorite corporate lawyer?"

"Exhausted," Anna replied, tucking a few wayward strands of hair behind her ears and sitting back wearily. "Sometimes I think the stress and long hours are going to kill me. It doesn't help that I'm working on two different deals with the biggest jerk in the corporate section. This afternoon, he got upset with a first-year associate, hurled a string of filthy epithets at the poor guy, then went into the supply room and kicked the crap out of the copier. He's a misogynist too."

"Do I need to get the van?" Nicky asked, a mischievous twinkle in his eye.

"No, sweetie, we don't need the van." Anna replied, chuckling at the old inside joke. "Not yet anyway."

Back in high school and college, Nicky was a geek and rock star wannabe who drove a beat-up white panel van to hold his musical gear and advanced calculus books. He and his math camp buddies played covers of 1970s and 1980s dance hits, calling themselves "Nicky and the Brainiacs" and achieving marginal success in the wedding and Sweet Sixteen musical markets before Nicky decided to grow up and go to graduate school. As a nerd who could never have gotten laid on brains alone, Nicky quickly concluded that members of rock bands had no such problems, and he put his mobile love nest to prolific use proving the point.

According to Nicky, the van had other uses as well. He always claimed to know certain nefarious characters that, for a fee, would deliver warnings to, extract money from, or exact brutal revenge upon, all manner of deadbeats, thieves, and scoundrels. Professing innocent non-involvement in the dastardly deeds, he hinted broadly that the shadowy crew used his old van for such clandestine outings. Anna was never quite sure if he was joking or not, but whenever she had a grievance, she'd call him and ask him to get the van. To her knowledge, it had never actually been deployed on her behalf, but it was always good for a laugh.

She took a sip of wine and said, "Now it's your turn. Tell me everything about your big city adventures and glamorous life in the caravans of Wall Street commerce."

Nicky relaxed back into his chair, twirling the ice in his glass. "I'm here to work my Texas connections in furtherance of a big financing deal," he replied, "which, if fruitful, will yield yours truly an obscenely large fee." After succinctly updating her on his activities since their last phone conversation, he abruptly changed the subject.

"Enough business talk," he said. "How's your love life?"

"Non-existent," Anna sighed. "I'm always working and too tired to go out; besides, no one wants a forty-four-year-old girlfriend—not in this town."

"Well, if you want to change that, there's a very distinguished man on the other side of the room who hasn't taken his eyes off you since we got here." He nodded subtly in the man's direction. "He looks like he just stepped off a Feadship."

"What's a Fed-ship? Some *Star Wars* thing?"

9

"Not a Fed-ship. A *Fead*-ship. F-e-a-d-ship. It's the name of a yacht builder."

"I didn't know you were into yachts."

"I'm not, but I have many affluent friends and clients who are."

Indulging him, she peered through the dimly lit room and saw an elegantly dressed gentleman chatting with another, visibly inebriated man. The handsome stranger was over six feet tall and weighed around one hundred eighty-five pounds. He looked to be in his early fifties, his jaw square and his nose aquiline. His thick black hair was combed straight back from his forehead in the style of a 1960s Mediterranean movie star, and although it was hard to see in the twinkling gloom of the bar, she could tell that his suit was expensive by its elegant cut and perfect fit. The two men stood next to a table upon which sat an ice bucket holding a bottle of Dom Perignon and around which sat two generously endowed women with unnaturally big, unnaturally blonde hair, their massive balloon breasts barely covered by spandex tube tops.

Not one to mince words, Anna turned back to Nicky and said, "Forget it. You just like him because he dresses like you."

"I think being a lawyer has made you cynical." Nicky said, arching an eyebrow.

Reverting to her childhood, Anna stuck her tongue out at him. "What about *your* love life, my horny friend?"

"Active, varied, and noncommittal," he replied, always reticent when it came to his romantic conquests. "Let's order another drink and then I have to hop. I'm meeting some investors for large steaks, old scotch, and fat cigars." He glanced back at the Feadship man and stood up. "The spandex twins just headed to the ladies' room," he said. "I'm going over to check this guy out for you."

Anna rose halfway out of her chair, snatching half-heartedly at his jacket sleeve. "Don't you dare."

Nicky nimbly dodged her attempt to stop him and threaded his way around the tightly packed tables, walking right up to the tall man. "Hello, I'm Nicky Morgan," he said. "The first thing I want you to know is that I'm not gay, and I'm not hitting on you."

Taken aback by the unusual introduction, the man looked at Nicky aslant without responding. Nicky forged ahead, undeterred. "I couldn't help noticing that you were staring at my friend over there. She's always been shy, so I took it upon myself to come over and talk to you on her behalf."

The man laughed. "Well, that's the most interesting non-proposition I've ever received," he said, smiling and shaking Nicky's hand. "I'm Jonathan DeLuca. I admit that she did get my attention, but I really can't talk to her right now." He nodded toward the table where the others were starting on Dom 2.0. "I'm here with my friend to celebrate his birthday," he explained. "We all came together in a limousine, so I'm stuck here with them. I would love to meet your friend, though."

"Do you have a business card on you?"

"I'm afraid not."

"I'll be right back." Nicky turned to leave, then stopped abruptly and turned back to Jonathan. "You wouldn't happen to have a Feadship, would you?"

"A what?"

"Never mind."

Nicky sauntered back to the table where Anna had been surreptitiously watching the entire exchange. "I cannot believe you did that," she scolded when he sat back down.

"Well, his name is Jonathan DeLuca, and he doesn't have a Feadship," Nicky said.

"Is he dating one of those girls?"

"I don't know."

"Is he married?"

"I don't know."

"What does he do for a living?"

"I don't know."

"Well, what *do* you know about him?"

"I know that he wants your business card." Nicky could tell she was not enthusiastic. "Come on," he chided. "Even corporate lawyers need love. What's the worst that could happen?"

11

Considering the thought briefly, Anna grudgingly agreed. "Fine, but I'll bet you ten dollars he never calls." She took a business card from her purse and handed it to him.

Nicky took the bet and the business card and walked back over to the debonair man named Jonathan. Discreetly handing him the card, he walked back to the table and motioned to the cocktail waitress to bring the check. While he and Anna were waiting for it, Jonathan and his friends got up to leave. The inebriated foursome made its way toward the bar's exit, the women teetering precariously on their stilettos from too much champagne. Jonathan brought up the rear of the drunken parade, turning to look at Anna as the group reached the door. He smiled broadly and flashed the universal "I'll call you" sign. She smiled back but doubted that he would.

Nicky paid the check when it arrived, and they retrieved Anna's car from the valet. She drove him the short distance to Dick and Stan's Steakhouse, a well-known gathering place for Dallas' wheeling and dealing carnivorous crowd. As she eased the car to a stop under the awning in front of the entrance, Nicky leaned over from the passenger seat to give her a brotherly kiss on the cheek. "Love you, babe," he said, getting out of the car.

"Love you too," she said, pulling her car out of the bustling driveway.

Nicky sighed wistfully as he watched her drive away, then put on his game face and went into the restaurant.

Ten minutes later, Anna was in the kitchen of her split-level apartment in the bustling Uptown neighborhood north of downtown. She chose a frozen dinner from the freezer and popped it in the microwave. While invisible radio waves bombarded her mystery meat the red cyclops eye on her Blackberry started flashing, the little black box vibrating and bumping itself across the kitchen counter as if possessed by the demanding demon of a sleepless senior partner.

After reading dozens of new emails that had arrived after she left the office, she opened her briefcase, took out the latest version of a two hundred-page merger agreement, and sat down at the kitchen counter to work. A few hours later, her eyes bleary and her body begging for sleep, she checked her watch—it was already 1:00 a.m.

With merger matters on her mind, she shuffled to the bathroom and got ready for bed. Setting her alarm for 6:30 a.m., she was soon fast asleep, having completely forgotten about Jonathan DeLuca.

Chapter 2

Jonathan DeLuca awoke at 8:00 a.m. the next morning to a raging hangover and a missing wallet. He searched unsuccessfully for it everywhere, cursing his negligence out loud until he remembered having taken it out to tip the limousine driver when he was dropped off at 1:00 a.m. He picked up the phone and called David, his lawyer and drinking buddy.

"Hullo," David answered sleepily on the third ring.

"David. Jonathan."

"What's up?"

"My wallet's missing. Did one of your bimbos take it?"

"I'll ask."

Jonathan heard him shout to unseen third parties, "Hey, Cricket, Dusty. Did either of you find my buddy's wallet in the limo last night?" Unintelligible murmurings filled a brief pause before David came back on the line. "The girls don't have it."

"Maybe it's still in the limo."

"I'll call the car company and ask them," David mumbled and hung up.

Jonathan's phone buzzed ten minutes later. It was David with encouraging news. The wallet had been located and would promptly be delivered to the concierge desk of David's condominium building, where Jonathan could pick it up on his way to work.

"Some night, huh?" David said, regaining a modicum of consciousness and clarity as the drunken haze left lingering from the previous night's revels began to clear. "What was up with that guy who came over and told you he wasn't gay?"

14

"It was just somebody wanting to fix me up with his friend," Jonathan replied.

"The blonde in the corner?"

"Yeah, that one. I could go for some of that, but it's really bad timing for me right now."

"No shit," David said. "Speaking of which, about my bill . . ."

"I have to leave right now if I'm going to pick up my wallet and get to work on time," Jonathan said, cutting him off and hanging up brusquely. He grabbed his Ralph Lauren double breasted jacket from the back of an armchair and let himself out, hurrying down the stairs that led to the parking lot and beeping awake a late model champagne gold Cadillac Seville with his remote-control key. Thirty minutes later, he pulled up in front of David's condominium building in the chic Turtle Creek area and left the car running while he ran into the lobby to collect his wallet from the concierge.

Not surprisingly, when he got back in the car and reviewed the wallet's contents, all his cash was gone. At least the unknown petty thief had left his driver's license, along with the blonde's business card that the bald man had given him the night before. He threw the wallet on the car seat in frustration and continued his drive to work, stopping at the local organic market on the way to buy a bouquet of fresh pink roses. A few minutes later, he arrived at GEM Motorcars.

Named for its corporate patriarch, Garrett Everett Mason, GEM was the largest Cadillac dealership in the southwest and Jonathan's current employer. Jonathan's prime sales targets were widows and married couples in their late sixties to mid-eighties. The women loved him because he was a polite, well-dressed man who opened doors for them and stood up when they did. Many of that generation's men were military veterans, so they liked Jonathan because his father had been a paratrooper in the Korean War.

Fred and Harriet DuPree were his first appointment of the day and were just such a couple. Even though the DuPrees were from New Orleans, Fred drove all the way to Dallas to buy their cars because Harriet liked to shop at the Galleria up the road. Jonathan had won their business a few years earlier after their regular salesman retired, and they had been so pleased with him that they were coming back for the third time.

Jonathan had barely settled in behind his desk when he glanced up and saw them enter the showroom. Harriet was wearing a prim and proper baby blue pantsuit and a hairdo favored by southern women above and beyond a certain age. Heavily styled and sprayed to near petrification, it encircled her face like a pale blue corona. Fred was dressed like a fruit stand with white shoes, unashamedly sporting yellow and citrus green plaid golf pants topped off by a watermelon-colored golf shirt.

Jonathan walked over to greet them, shaking Fred's hand and giving Harriet the roses he had bought earlier as they all sat down at Jonathan's desk and got down to business. "Have you been happy with your car this past year?" Jonathan asked Mrs. DuPree.

"Oh yes, very," she replied, daintily patting the ends of her hair helmet. "It's very comfortable."

"I like the fact that it's big and heavy," Mr. Dupree said. "Priced right too."

"Well, the price has gone up this year. Inflation you know," Jonathan said.

Like so many of his generation and the one that preceded him, Fred was painfully tight with money. He loathed parting with a single penny of it unnecessarily, despite having amassed a small fortune running cargo ships up and down the Mississippi River. "You don't have to tell me, son," he grumbled. "The interest I'm earning on my Treasury Bills doesn't even keep up with inflation, but I'm too damn old to risk money in the stock markets."

"I understand, sir," Jonathan said. "My father feels the same way."

After all the papers were signed and the sale amicably concluded, Jonathan handed Fred the keys to his new car and escorted the DuPrees to the tank-sized sedan. He helped Harriet into the passenger seat and saluted Fred sharply. "I'll see you in six months for your first scheduled maintenance," he said, opening the door for Fred. "Drive safely, sir."

Eight hours and three more sales later, Jonathan tidied his desk, turned off the desk light, and headed toward the back door that led to the employee parking lot. He stopped by the customer lounge along the way to get a bottle of water, spotting the latest issue of *The Robb Report* on the glass coffee table. Needing something kill the time, he glanced around to see if anyone was watching and snatched the magazine from the table, spiriting it away inside his briefcase.

Despite a lucrative day at work, he drove home bemoaning the fact that he was still selling cars for a living at the age of fifty-two. Attempting to talk himself out of his glum mood, he thumped his hands on the steering wheel, making affirmations that he'd learned in a sales training course that GEM Motorcars required of all its employees. "Everything's going to change soon," he said out loud to the thin air. "I know it will. I can *feel* it. This next deal is going to be huge. Huge!"

His mood was much improved by the time he got home, and as soon as he let himself in, he poured a tall glass of Crown Royal and took it into the other room. He took off his jacket and settled into in a chair by the bed to read the purloined *Robb Report*, savoring his drink while leafing through the glossy magazine. The current issue featured yachts, and when he noticed an advertisement for a Feadship, he suddenly remembered the lady lawyer from the bar. He got her business card out of his wallet, studied it for a few seconds, and decided to call her when he had time. Some of his best customers were attorneys after all.

* * *

Jonathan hadn't always been a car salesman, having come from a long line of entrepreneurs on two continents. His paternal grandfather, Antonio DeLuca, was a descendant of generations of olive growers from the fertile lands surrounding Sicula, Sicily. Antonio immigrated to the United States in the 1930s, shortly after the authorities were tipped off to a mass grave in the back hectare of the family's olive grove. After three days of excavation, the local police discovered fourteen bodies and assorted unrelated body parts. Protesting his innocence loudly in the matter and blaming the bodies on a neighbor, Antonio nonetheless decided to hedge his bets and disappeared into the teeming immigrant community of New York's Little Italy.

Resurfacing as Tony DeLuca, he opened a butcher shop as a cover for his less savory enterprises, brutally carving his way to success—figuratively and sometimes, literally. Along the gory way, he fell in love with Sophia Marconi, the raven-haired youngest daughter of a neighborhood wise guy who was high up in the local mafia hierarchy. Tony's blushing and fertile bride became pregnant with Jonathan's father, Ricky, shortly after the wedding. The news of the blessed event prompted Sophia's father to ask his new son-in-law to move his budding family to New Jersey and run the Marconi family's trucking, gambling, and prostitution businesses there. Tony wisely accepted the offer.

Over the years, Sophia gave Tony two more sons and a desire to forge a different kind of life for them. All three boys went to college, but the oldest son's path to a non-criminal career was destined to detour. The Korean War erupted, and having grown up to be an impulsive and headstrong young man, Ricky enlisted in the army without consulting his parents and without graduating from college.

Though heartbroken when Ricky left for war, the DeLucas rallied lovingly around him after he received devastating injuries during his second tour of duty. Both of his legs were grievously injured when a gust of wind caused his parachute to drift, snagging on a tree and depositing him behind North Korean lines. Miraculously, he survived and earned a Purple Heart for his ordeal.

After recovering from his injuries, he finished college and entered Columbia Law School on the G.I. Bill. While out for beers with his law school classmates one night, he met Gina Bianchi, a petite strawberry blonde who was attending the Barbizon School. They married within a year.

It soon became clear that Ricky wasn't taking to law school and it wasn't taking to him. When Jonathan was born during Ricky's third year of law school, Ricky used the new bundle of baby joy as an excuse to drop out of law school, having already decided to go into the concrete and construction business with a buddy from his old paratrooper unit.

Although Tony didn't approve of Ricky's choice, he couldn't refuse his wounded war hero son. He fronted Ricky the money to get started and greased the local political and law enforcement wheels to get things off to a smooth start for his boy.

The new company specialized in pouring concrete foundations for housing developments and office buildings, and although Ricky tried to tread the straight and narrow, the DeLuca apples never fell far from the tree. Ricky's partner easily convinced him to cooperate in beefing up their bottom line by turning a blind eye to the occasional corpse that popped up in a cement mixer. This type of enterprise required some creative accounting techniques, and Ricky's partner copiously employed them to their joint benefit.

Unknown to either of them, they were under investigation by the Internal Revenue Service. Armed agents stormed the office one afternoon, wielding search warrants and seizing the company's business records, easily identifying numerous irregularities, including multiple sets of books. Capitalizing on the incriminating evidence, the feds put pressure on Ricky, hoping to turn him and get information leading to a much bigger fish—his father. Swearing that he had done nothing wrong, Ricky refused to squeal on family, earning three years of hard time in federal prison for tax evasion and the seizure by the IRS of everything that he and Gina owned.

The unfortunate circumstances forced Gina and Jonathan to live with relatives in New Jersey until Ricky got out of prison a year early for good behavior. The one-year reprieve was little comfort to any of them, for in just two years, he had aged decades, or so it had seemed to young Jonathan.

A chastened man, Ricky moved his family to Pennsylvania. Using wartime connections and calling in favors, he started another construction business, this time building shopping centers and other commercial projects. Determined to run his fledgling enterprise on the up and up, he did—for a while.

In the meantime, little Johnny was growing up and proving to be a handful. The DeLucas worked very hard to get him through middle school and high school, which was no small feat. Despite a higher-than-average intellect and a savant-like facility with numbers, Johnny was generally a lousy student and a troublemaker. Expelled from military school and three institutions of higher learning, he finally settled down for a few years and earned a degree in business and finance from a small private college in Ohio. After graduation, he went back to Pennsylvania to work for his father, and the business took off, growing in just two years to twenty employees and annual revenues of twenty-five million dollars.

Their success was fleeting. A year after contracting with a small hamlet in Pennsylvania to build a community recreation center, the pace of the construction started to lag, drawing the attention of the city auditor. The accountants tasked with investigating the matter quickly discovered that the taxpayer funds paid to Ricky's company for construction of the center had vanished into thin air, the project barely half-finished. Rather than spend his days dodging subpoenas and criminal charges, Ricky closed the business and used a substantial portion of his savings to pay off the city fathers. He and Gina moved to Texas to be near their extended family and to avoid state income tax.

Jonathan struck out on his own for ten years, but eventually joined his parents in Texas. He didn't like Dallas, but he liked his job with GEM Motorcars—at least until his next big opportunity came along. He hoped something would break his way soon because he was already getting bored with selling cars. Jonathan craved excitement like his car craved gasoline, and he had been running on empty for a while. But he sensed that something spectacular was waiting for him just beyond the horizon—he just needed to get there faster.

Chapter 3

Anna arrived early at her office on the 43rd floor of Waterfall Plaza, a bluish-green, mirrored glass structure in downtown Dallas that housed the firm's two hundred attorneys on seven floors. She was just sitting down at her desk, a fresh cup of coffee in hand and her computer booting up, when her administrative assistant popped into the office and dropped a stack of messages on her desk.

A middle-aged brunette from Odessa, Texas, Becca was a no-nonsense single mother of two young boys. Highly organized and efficient, she was an absolute whiz on the computer. Each administrative assistant worked for three attorneys, so Becca's time was valuable, and she never wasted words when she was under multiple deadlines. "The F-Man is looking for you and he looks pissed," she said.

Anna felt her stomach muscles go tense. "Is his face all red?"

"Like a big ole' apple," Becca replied, rushing back out the door to answer a ringing phone.

"Thanks," Anna mumbled after her, wondering what awaited her at the hands of the F-Man.

F. Grayson Smith, Esq. was called the F-Man behind his back, partly because of the first initial of his name, but primarily because of his unrestrained and creative use of the "F" word. A newly-minted partner, he was a misanthrope with a ferocious temper, a filthy mouth, and a troglodyte's view of women. A micromanaging, narcissistic perfectionist, he reveled in screaming at anyone junior to him in the law firm's pecking order. When merely annoyed, his face turned bright red. When he worked up a genuine rage, it would turn eggplant purple, and Anna fully expected him to have a mid-rant stroke or heart attack one day. Although there were other partners at B&V who were friendly, helpful, and a pleasure to work with, the one bad apple-faced F-Man always managed to ruin her day.

Expecting the worst, she gathered up a stack of files and walked resignedly down the hall to his office to talk about a merger they were working on. One of B&V's large public company clients—a silicon chip manufacturer—wished to acquire a high-tech company that specialized in data storage. Mergers of public companies are highly secret until the proper forms are filed with the Securities and Exchange Commission, the parties subject to fines and imprisonment for the slightest leak of information. To avoid such transgressions, the business deals were usually given code names until they legally became public knowledge. This corporate marriage had been dubbed the "Nerd Merger" by one of the investment bankers.

The F-Man was on the phone when she got to his office, and he motioned for her to come in and sit. She complied, glancing idly around his cluttered office while she waited for him to finish the call. He hung up and moved some papers around on his desk until he found a yellow pad. He scanned it and scowled at Anna. "Where are we on the due diligence for the Nerd Merger?" he growled.

"I'm still waiting to receive the final shipment of documents to review," Anna replied.

"They need to get here faster. The disclosure statements have to be filed with the SEC no later than the end of business the day after tomorrow."

"I'll call my contact there again and ask, but they're already working around the clock."

"Call that stupid bitch at the company and tell her to get them here by 8:00 a.m. tomorrow." The F-Man's face darkened and turned scarlet, apoplectic. "Get it together and grow some fucking balls goddamit."

"I'll take care of it as soon as I get back to my office," Anna replied, not commenting on the physical impossibility of the F-Man's suggestion.

After ten more minutes of haranguing, The F-Man screamed at her again for no apparent reason, until a new target for his unwarranted vitriol arrived for a conference call. Anna left his office and walked as calmly as she could back to hers. Throwing her papers on her desk, she shut her door and fell into her chair.

She hated being yelled at. It brought back memories of high school bullies who despised her for her 4.0 grade point average and scowling ballet teachers who constantly berated her for the slightest inadequacy in her body or her dancing. The incessant ridicule and criticism had left her self-esteem in a molten puddle, and she spent years cleaning up the emotional messes that the relentless, omnidirectional berating had left behind.

* * *

Anna was the only child of Thomas and Caroline Thornbury, who met at the University of Texas at Austin, where black-haired, blue-eyed Tom was studying advertising and marketing, and brown-eyed, ash blonde Caroline Swenson was studying fashion design and ballet. By the end of their freshman year, Caroline had fallen in love with Tom's roommate, a handsome acting student and part-time pilot who was drafted into the Korean War, then tragically killed in action just a few months later.

Tom was comforting and kind in the aftermath of Caroline's heartbreak, and his friendship eventually turned to love. Caroline professed to share his feelings, and they married shortly after he enlisted in the Marines, also as a pilot. Tom's military star was significantly luckier than that of Caroline's first love, and he never saw active duty due to a heart murmur that had escaped notice during his preliminary physical. When he completed his service as a stateside pilot instructor, they moved to Dallas to start their post-war life.

Tom came to be a hard-working, hard-drinking, traveling insurance salesman, frequently away on business and staying out late in bars when he wasn't. He also cussed like he was still in the service, causing his disapproving wife perpetual consternation. But despite his many flaws, he loved his wife and daughter fiercely.

Caroline Thornbury lacked her husband's emotional range and was never happy with her lot in life, no matter how hard her husband

and daughter tried to please her. A frustrated ballerina who suffered from bouts of depression, Caroline evolved into a stern-faced, emotionally absent housewife, becoming the world champion at giving the silent treatment to anyone who displeased her. Her own future sidetracked by war and marriage, an embittered Caroline insisted that Anna follow in her toe shoes, using her daughter as the vessel into which she poured her unfulfilled dreams of standing ovations and thunderous applause.

The stars in Anna's eyes were much different from those in her mother's. Having become fascinated with astronomy and space travel in grade school, Anna was tired of dancing and dreamed of studying astrophysics at M.I.T or Caltech before going on to work for NASA. Caroline had other plans for her daughter, threatening to throw teen-aged Anna out onto the streets penniless if she quit ballet. Instead of enrolling her in college after she graduated from high school, her parents sent her to New York to study dance.

When she finished her studies two years later, she landed a role as a minor principal dancer and understudy with a regional ballet company. Less than a year later, she was on tour when her parents were tragically killed in a car accident. After settling the modest estate, she said goodbye to her parents forever and went back on the road until a freak backstage accident left her with a shredded ligament and a pin in her left kneecap. Neither her knee nor her dancing career ever fully recovered, so she moved back to Texas and rented a small apartment, teaching ballet at a nearby strip mall to pay the bills.

After a brief marriage and ten years of struggling to make ends meet, she realized that her future was going to look very much like her present if she didn't get her life together and get a college degree. Private universities were out of the question because of her financial situation, so she enrolled in community college at the age of thirty-seven.

Hard work and a heavily loaded class schedule earned her multiple scholarships, enabling her to transfer to Southern Methodist University, where she earned degrees in political science and law. A job in the corporate law department of Brown and Vincent, LLP and seventy-hour work weeks were her reward.

24

* * *

At the moment, Anna was having difficulty discerning anything rewarding about the F-Man's insults, but enduring them went with the job and she needed the paychecks. Inhaling and exhaling for a few seconds to compose herself after his latest barrage, she opened her office door and peeked around the corner where Becca's desk was located. "Any messages?" she asked.

"One," Becca replied, handing her a pink slip with one hand, never taking her eyes off her computer screen. "A man named Jonathan De-something called. Said he knew you."

The name didn't ring any of Anna's bells. "Did he say what company he was with?"

"Nope."

Anna went back to her desk, reading the message and wondering who Jonathan DeLuca was when something clicked and she remembered. *Damn. Now I owe Nicky ten dollars.* Adding the message to a pile of others stacked high on her desk, she turned back to her computer and worked through the day without a lunch break, snacking on junk food and downing diet colas to get her through. It was after 5:00 p.m. when she finally had time to return the call.

He answered after a few rings, his voice deep and husky. "Jonathan DeLuca."

"This is Anna Thornbury at Brown and Vincent," Anna said. "My secretary told me you called."

"I'm so glad you called me back," he said, sounding relieved. "I've wanted to call you for weeks, but I lost my wallet with your card in it and I just recently got it back. I left it in a limousine the night your friend came over to talk to me. I called the car company and told them that I didn't care if there was any money in it, that I only cared about your business card. I was afraid I'd never get to see you again because I had no other way to contact you."

Surprised by the urgent intensity in his voice, Anna wasn't sure how to respond, so she took a professional path. "How can I help you?"

"Would you be interested in meeting me for coffee some afternoon?"

She found herself accepting the offer without reflection or hesitation, and they were working out the details when a loudspeaker voice in the background said, "Jonathan DeLuca, to the customer lounge. Jonathan DeLuca, to the customer lounge."

"Sorry, I have to run," Jonathan said. "See you Saturday."

Wondering what she was getting herself into, Anna hung up and turned her attention back to the piles of documents that infested her desk like a paper plague.

* * *

Anna shut down her office computer at 2:30 p.m. on the Saturday of her appointment with Jonathan and dropped her edited draft of the Nerd Merger documents in the F-Man's inbox before he could torment her. He would no doubt have made some inappropriate comment about the fact that she was dressed too nicely for a Saturday at the office, wearing a green long-sleeved dress that turned her eyes emerald, instead of her usual weekend working attire of jeans and a sweatshirt.

Fifteen minutes later, she pulled into the parking lot of Highland Park Village, the oldest shopping center in the United States and one of the most exclusive in Dallas. Circling until she found a spot, she parked and walked briskly to the center's popular coffee shop, spotting Jonathan sitting at a tiny table in a far corner.

He stood when he saw her, smoothing his tastefully patterned red Hermès tie with his left hand as he did. Nattily attired, he wore a dark blue double-breasted sport coat and a sky-blue shirt with white collar and cuffs. His pants were impeccably creased, his bearing regal, and his back ramrod straight. He smiled warmly as he moved from behind the table, never taking his eyes off Anna as he pulled out her chair in a gesture that once was considered chivalrous, but now is derided as a sexist microaggression.

Neither of them said anything for a few awkward seconds until Jonathan broke the ice. "Would you like something?" he asked.

"Yes, please," Anna replied, "Just a regular coffee. Nothing fancy."

"Done." He walked to the counter to place the order and returned to the table to chat with Anna while they waited. "I'm so glad you came," he said. "I was afraid you wouldn't want to see me because I waited so long to call you."

"Well, my friend Nicky made such a fuss that I thought I owed you the courtesy of apologizing in person for his behavior."

"I admit I was somewhat perplexed by his opening line, but I also have to admit that I couldn't take my eyes off you."

The comment took Anna by surprise and made her blush. She was tongue-tied and searching for words as a voice called out "DeLuca!" above the buzz of conversation, prompting Jonathan to go pick up their order and saving her the embarrassment of an awkward response.

When he came back and handed her the coffee, she noticed his cardboard-stiff, monogrammed shirt cuff displaying the letters "JDF." The "J" was obviously for Jonathan, and the "D" was obviously for DeLuca. Anna had never been very adept at small talk, so she pointed to one of the cuffs and asked, "What's the 'F' for?"

"Frescobaldi," Jonathan replied, his face deadpan.

"Oh?" Anna remarked diplomatically, trying not to choke on her coffee.

"I'm Italian," Jonathan explained. "Third generation on my mother's side, two generations on my father's. Mom is nostalgic for the old country, so I got stuck with her favorite family name."

"I sympathize with you completely," Anna said, smiling. "My middle name is Cornelia." She paused before asking the question she had wanted to ask since Jonathan had first called her. "It occurred to me that you know what I do for a living because you already have my card. What business are you in?"

"I sell Cadillacs for GEM Motorcars," he replied, then raised a hand to interrupt her before she could react. "I know what you're thinking. 'Oh, crap, a car salesman.' Given all the stereotypes, I wouldn't blame you for walking away right now."

"No need to defend your profession," Anna said. "I'm familiar with unpleasant stereotypes too. I can't tell you how many times I've been introduced to someone at a party or in a bar, and a total stranger will immediately say, 'Oh. I hate lawyers,' without bothering to find out anything about me or what I do.'"

"What do you say back to them?"

"I say, 'Then this going to be a short conversation.'"

Jonathan laughed. "Well, we definitely have two things in common—embarrassing names and professions that are equally reviled by the general public."

Anna laughed too and asked, "Have you always wanted to be a car salesman?"

"God no," Jonathan said, shaking his head adamantly. "Selling cars is just a way to earn a comfortable living while I put my next business deal together. I'm pulling down six figures these days, but I might move over to Rolls-Royce and make even more money." He paused to take a sip of coffee. "Of course, I'm only selling cars until my next deal comes through," he continued. "The luxury car business is lucrative, but it requires a lot of hours, making it hard to put other business ventures together."

Having encountered quite a few superficial braggarts over the years, Anna was always annoyed when a man talked about how much money he made. She decided to see if Jonathan was all hat and no cattle. "What kind of business ventures?" she asked.

"Mostly real estate and the occasional international bank investment," Jonathan replied. Anna looked interested, so he told her his story.

"My dad was in the construction business, and it was always expected that I'd go to work for him after college. When I graduated from Columbia University, I went home and tried the business for a few years, but discovered that Pops is incredibly difficult to work for. Anyway, we landed a contract to build an office building in Denver for a man named Hamid Halabi, the nephew of a Saudi Arabian prince. Hamid was impressed with our work, so he hired me full time. He decided to headquarter in Denver, so I moved there for a while after my parents moved to Texas."

"Hamid invested his family's money a lot of the time, but when he wanted to spread their risk around, my job was to locate potential investors and negotiate with banks and other financial institutions to get the project funded. We financed and built some shopping centers in Colorado and a couple of office buildings in Los Angeles. When the real estate markets crashed and bank financing dried up, Hamid went back to Saudi Arabia. I quickly discovered that he had embezzled the money from our company without paying me the finder's fees he owed me. I had to do something to earn a living, so I moved to Texas to be near my parents and started selling cars."

"I'm sorry your business partner cheated you like that," Anna said, concern in her eyes.

"All water under the bridge," Jonathan said. He paused and looked at her intently. "Tell me about you." Was becoming a lawyer your lifelong dream?"

"No, not at all," Anna replied. "I got a very late start in academia and figured out early in my sophomore year that the law would be the fastest way to make a lot of money, given that I would be entering the professional work force at age forty-two. My legal career was born out of sheer necessity. Nothing more." She gave a small shrug and drained her cup.

"What kind of cases do you work on?"

"I don't work on cases, and I never do courtroom work. That's what litigators do. Corporate lawyers like me do mergers and acquisitions, venture capital financings, public offerings, SEC filings—things like that."

"Sounds complicated."

"It can be, but most of the time it's just tedious document drafting and editing."

"How many hours a week do you work?"

"Sixty or seventy, frequently more."

"Ouch. I hope you get paid by the hour."

Anna had always been circumspect when discussing her finances. "I wish," was all she said.

There was a pause in the conversation, and Jonathan glanced at his watch. "Well, I have to get back to work," he said, standing up. "I really enjoyed getting to know you, Anna."

"I enjoyed meeting you too," Anna said as he escorted her to the door, opening it with one hand and ushering her gently through it with the other. She waited expectantly for a signal of some kind, but his intentions—if any—were unreadable. They reached her aged Toyota, and she pointed to it, her cheeks reddening with embarrassment. "Well, that's my car."

Jonathan looked at the decrepit heap and threw his head back in laughter. "I didn't come here to sell you a car, but after seeing yours, I hope you'll keep me in mind when you finally get a new one." He pulled a business card from his breast pocket and handed it to her.

"I doubt I could afford a Cadillac," she said, taking the card.

"All you need is a job and good credit," he said, opening the door for her. "Lawyers almost always get credit approval immediately." He smiled again and shut her door.

She watched in the rearview mirror as he strode off, his long legs carrying him nimbly and gracefully away. Buckling her seat belt and driving home to do the weekly laundry, she sighed at her silly optimism and muttered under her breath, "Well that was a complete waste of time."

Chapter 4

A few days later, Anna was filling out a stack of arcane forms that had to be filed with the SEC on behalf of a client when Becca poked her head around the corner of the door. "Are you expecting a big package?" she asked.

"No, why?"

"Well, a guy from shipping and receiving just called. They're sending something up the freight elevator for you."

Becca filled her doorway again a few minutes later, nearly bouncing up and down in girlish glee. "You have *got* to come see this!"

There was a commotion out in the hallway, and Anna went out to see what the fuss was all about. Next to Becca's desk was a three-foot tall flower arrangement atop a mail trolley. An eight-person line of secretaries from the surrounding work stations trailed behind it as if it were a float in the Rose Bowl Parade.

"Who's it from?" the gaggle of onlookers asked and demanded, almost in unison, "Who's it from?"

Searching through the dense floral foliage for a card, Anna found one attached to a single Bird of Paradise that soared like a jungle parrot above a canopy of roses, daisies, Calla lilies, and white hydrangeas the size of cantaloupes.

The gaggle chanted in chorus, "Read it out loud. Read it out loud."

Anna blushed the same color of the roses as she read, "You stand out in a crowd. Warmest regards, Jonathan."

The chorus ooohed and awwwed. "How romantic. Who's Jonathan?"

"Just a guy I met," Anna replied, there not being much more to say.

The sudden diaspora of the support staff had attracted the attention of several partners, and Anna saw them coming down the hall as the group began to disperse. She whispered to Becca, "Help me get this thing inside my office before everybody gets in trouble."

The two women maneuvered the gargantuan arrangement off the trolley and onto a tiny table between Anna's two guest chairs. It teetered precariously, the table's spindly legs wobbling unsteadily under the unaccustomed weight. The exotic aroma wafting from the fragrant blooms was intoxicating, filling her office with its overpowering scent.

Then, as if searching for witnesses to its beauty, the bouquet of smells wafted out her door and into the hallway, inevitably drawing the attention of the F-Man. He walked into her office and saw the brightly-colored behemoth. "So, what did you have to do to get those?" he asked, sneering.

Anna considered lodging a sexual harassment complaint against him with the firm's human resources department, but instead merely replied, "Nothing. I just had coffee with a guy the other day."

The F-Man mocked her. "Right, coffee. So, *that's* what you single people call it these days." He wrinkled his nose and screwed up his face in obvious distaste, as if the flowers carried the scent of carrion. "Jesus, it smells like a fucking funeral parlor in here."

In a hurry to get rid of him, Anna asked, "Did you need something?"

"Yes. Where are we on the response to the SEC's questions on the Nerd Merger filing?"

"The first comprehensive draft will be ready by the end of the day."

"Make sure it is," he said, turning away and going down the hall to harass some other associate for a while.

Anna didn't finish her day's work until 8:00 p.m. Suddenly remembering that she had forgotten to thank Jonathan for the flowers, she called him at the dealership. He had already left, and with no other way to reach him, she left a message, gathered up her things, and dragged herself home for a frozen dinner and a hot bath.

* * *

The telephone jarred her awake around 7:00 a.m. She sat up groggily in her bed and answered it. "Hello."

It was Jonathan calling. "I'm so sorry, did I wake you?"

"Yes," Anna replied as the fog of sleep began to clear. "But it's good that you did. I should have been up an hour ago." Now wide awake, she remembered the flowers. "I just wanted to thank you. I've never seen anything quite like the arrangement you sent. Neither has anyone else in the office, for that matter. You created quite a stir."

"Excellent," he replied. "I wanted to get your attention."

"You got everybody's attention."

"Great, so now you can't possibly say no to this proposition."

Anna felt an unexpected twinge of anticipation. "A proposition?"

"Yes. I have to work a promotion for the dealership out at the polo club this Sunday and would love it if you could come out and watch the match."

"I really would like to, but I have plans with my best friend. I haven't seen her in weeks, and I really can't cancel."

"Then bring her along. I'll be working most of the time, but we can visit before and after the match."

After Jonathan filled her in on the details, she thanked him again and went into the kitchen to put the coffee on. Her thoughts percolated along with the coffee maker as she puzzled over whether Jonathan wanted to date her or sell her a car. Either way, there were certainly worse ways to spend a rare day off than being surrounded by beautiful people and beautiful horses. She dressed and poured herself a to-go coffee, calling her best friend Cindy Webster on her cell phone as she ran down the stairs to the garage.

"Hi, sweetie," Cindy answered. "I can't wait to see you on Sunday."

"Well, that's why I'm calling," Anna said.

"You are *not* canceling on me again!"

"No, no, not that," Anna assured her, explaining about the polo match.

Always up for an adventure, Cindy whooped, "Boy howdy, I'll go. I love watching all those gorgeous, sweaty men in tight pants astride

tons of rippling horse flesh, leather whips in hand. Yummmmmmmy."
Switching subjects at the speed of light, as was her habit, she asked,
"Who's Jonathan?"

"I'll tell you when I see you," Anna replied. "I'll pick you up
around 2:00 p.m. on Sunday."

"I'll be ready with bells on," Cindy chirped, clicking off.

* * *

As soon as she got home that night, Anna remembered her bet
with Nicky. She kicked off her shoes, poured a glass of white wine, and
called him. It was already 11:00 p.m. in New York City, but she knew
that he and his investment banker buddies worked even stranger hours
than she did.

He answered on the third ring. "Hey, gorgeous!"

"I'm calling to let you know that I owe you ten dollars," Anna
said.

"What for?" Nicky asked, apparently having forgotten about their
extemporaneous bar bet.

"That guy from the bar called."

"Oh yeah—the Feadship guy. And?"

Anna told him about the coffee date and the flowers. When she
finished, Nicky asked, "So what does he do for a living?"

"He's a car salesman," Anna replied, adding before he could say
anything sarcastic, "But it's not like you think. He sells Cadillacs at
GEM Motorcars. Lots of them, apparently."

"You can't seriously be considering dating a car salesman."

"This whole thing was your idea, Mr. Matchmaker. Remember?"

"*Mea culpa*, counselor. Do you want me to check up on him?"

"I already did an internet search and found absolutely nothing."

"I guess nothing turning up is better than something bad turning
up," Nicky mused. "Don't big law firms like B&V have ways to do
background and credit checks?"

"Yes, but we can only use those resources for legitimate, billable
matters; besides, corporate lawyers like me rarely have a need for that

kind of information. I doubt I could slip a search past the powers-that-be without getting into trouble."

"Why don't you hire a private investigator?"

"Isn't that a bit extreme after just one coffee? I couldn't afford a private investigator anyway."

"Well, sweetie darling, you just be sure to let Nicky know if he needs to get the van."

Anna laughed. "I promise."

"So, what are you up to tonight?" he asked, changing the subject.

"The sad usual—a frozen dinner and a movie. I'm vacillating between *Dirty Rotten Scoundrels* and *Dangerous Liaisons* for the cinematic portion of the evening."

"Well, try to avoid both in real life. Gotta hop. Pinkies up!"

Anna hung up and chose chicken and fettucine from her frozen food selection. She opted for *Dangerous Liaisons* as the movie to go with her meal, falling fast asleep on the couch before John Malkovich could successfully deflower Uma Thurman.

* * *

Anna was standing in her closet deciding what to wear to the polo match. It was sunny and already over eighty degrees, so she put her hair in a ponytail and settled on a tasteful floral print sundress and some comfortable sandals. She drove to Cindy's townhouse to pick her up, and as soon as she pulled into the driveway, her flamboyant friend opened the front door with a spokesmodel flourish and flounced down the short sidewalk to the car.

A petite redhead with abundant curls and pale greenish-brown eyes, Cindy managed a highly successful modern art gallery in the Uptown art district. Possessed of both a piquant wit and a creative wardrobe, she deployed both unabashedly and without a tinge of irony.

She said she'd be there with bells on and she meant it. Her brightly patterned gypsy skirt was hemmed with tiny bells that made a melodious, ethereal noise when she walked. A red leather bustier, a black Resistol cowboy hat, and red and black cowboy boots embossed with white stars and longhorn steer heads completed the colorful ensemble. She climbed into the car, her skirt tinkling merrily.

"Wow, nice outfit," Anna teased. "What are we today, a cowgirl dominatrix?"

Cindy sniffed with feigned insult. "This ensemble is perfect for polo, especially the boots." She lifted a foot and waggled it at Anna, who rolled her eyes and started the car.

Wasting no time in going for the gossip, Cindy said, "So, girlfriend, tell me everything about your date—in excruciating detail."

Anna obliged, and by the time she finished her short story, they had reached the main entrance to the polo club. "Where to?" she asked.

"That way," Cindy replied, pointing to a wide dirt road that led to a narrow wooden bridge.

Anna followed Cindy's directions, and they found themselves in a slow-moving line of Mercedes Benzes, Cadillacs, Rolls-Royces, Range Rovers, and stretch limousines as far as the eye could see. "This is mortifying," Anna said. "All these gorgeous cars and here we are in my old bucket of bolts."

The brass and silver bracelets covering Cindy's arms up to her elbows jangled merrily as she fluffed her hair. "I wouldn't worry about it, honey," she said, checking her lipstick in the side-view mirror. You know how many poseurs there are in this town. That guy in the Bentley over there may very well live in it." She looked at the line of cars, then back at Anna. "Speaking of cars, you're still not sure whether this Jonathan person wants to date you or sell you a car?"

"Exactly."

"And this is the same extravagant suitor who sent you the tower of flowers?"

"The very one."

Ever the optimist, Cindy said, "Well, I've been thinking about it, and I've decided it could be both."

Anna hadn't thought of the situation quite that way and said, "Well, we're about to find out."

They were waved to a stop by a perky ticket taker who located Anna's name on the guest list and told her where to park. After crossing the bridge, they spotted a tent with a giant banner that greeted them in large gold and black letters: "Welcome to GEM Motorcars Day at the Polo Matches!"

Anna drove past the tent to the parking area and found an empty space, reluctantly parking next to a white Rolls-Royce Silver Shadow with a baby blue top. As the two friends walked toward the tent, she asked Cindy, "Can a car salesman really make six figures a year?"

Cindy's father had owned a car dealership in the Midwest when she was a young girl, so she was an unofficial expert in such matters. Her father had literally driven himself to an early grave with drink one night, crashing his car into a guard rail going eighty miles per hour on his way home after an eight-hour bender. Cindy was only twelve years old when he died, but her uncle inherited the dealership. She learned a lot about selling cars while she was growing up and still used those skills in her daily business dealings.

She winked at Anna. "Assuming you mean Cadillacs, yes. The top producers earn six figures and then some."

"I had no idea," Anna said, genuinely surprised to hear that a car salesman could make that much money.

* * *

Jonathan arrived at the GEM Motorcars tent an hour before the match, sharply and professionally dressed. He checked in with his immediate boss and went to work with his dealership colleagues, setting up tables covered with business cards, color brochures, and marketing trinkets bearing the GEM Motorcars logo. Garrett Mason sponsored the event every year because the polo fields were fertile grounds for the marketing of high-end must-haves to the polo enthusiasts and social butterflies who attended the matches hoping to see their photographs in the society pages the following Sunday.

GEM always set up a large tent, under which the elite invitees would feast at tables heaped with hors d'oeuvres. Waiters passed trays of expensive champagne in crystal flutes, the better to lubricate the captive potential car buyers. The guests were usually jovial and receptive by the end of the match and often eager to take test drives.

They were only permitted to do so as passengers of course, there being obvious and numerous legal ramifications posed by handing a plastered polo fan the keys to a brand-new Escalade for a post-polo romp up and down Stemmons Freeway.

The guests were just starting to arrive when Jonathan located his friend, Bob Peterson, a fellow salesman and the only co-worker Jonathan liked. Short, wide, and in his late fifties, Bob had a balding head and a growing belly that yearned to escape the confines of his sport coat. Ever since his wife made him quit smoking, he had taken to chewing toothpicks like Winston Churchill chewed cigars.

They talked cars and sports until Bob nodded toward the parking area and took a toothpick out of his mouth. "Here they come. Let's go cover the door."

As they stationed themselves on either side of the main entrance, Jonathan turned to Bob and said, "Happy hunting."

A laconic man, Bob merely replied, "Yup."

They were meeting and greeting when Jonathan spotted Jack Garrison approaching the tent. Jack was a business partner and personal representative of Lamar Buchanan, a Fort Worth billionaire and global business legend. Lamar's companies bought fleets of cars annually, and he could have bought the entire GEM dealership ten times over had he wanted to.

A short, nondescript man in his mid-fifties, Jack was a multi-millionaire in his own right. As Lamar's advance man and deal screener, he was always on the prowl for investment opportunities. Polo was a rich man's game in which a stable of horses could cost well over one hundred thousand dollars with overhead and upkeep to match. People who could afford to play at that level had money to burn, and Jack had made some lucrative connections at the polo matches in the past.

Wanting to introduce himself, Jonathan placed himself directly in front of the entrance, blocking Jack's path and greeting him like a long-absent friend. "Jack!" he called out with breezy familiarity. "I'm so glad you could make it again this year." He extended his hand in greeting. "Jonathan DeLuca."

Jack shook Jonathan's hand and looked at him inquisitively but without recognition. "Good to see you, too," he said.

"Please, come right on in," Jonathan said. "There's plenty of food and champagne. The match starts at 3:00 p.m. You can watch it from here or go to the box seats reserved for our special guests."

Jonathan escorted him to the buffet table, bade him goodbye, and turned back to the stream of incoming prospects. He spotted Anna and a bizarrely dressed little redhead approaching the tent and waved them over.

* * *

"Oh. My. God!" Cindy gushed as they neared the tent and she got a closer look at Jonathan. "He looks like an Italian count!"

"Shush! He'll hear you," Anna whispered.

They arrived at the entrance, and Jonathan bent down to give Anna a courtly kiss on the cheek. "I'm so happy you came," he said. He turned his attention to Cindy. "And who is your lovely companion?"

"This is my dear friend, Cindy Webster," Anna replied.

"Jonathan," Cindy said, stretching out her hand.

"Cindy," Jonathan said, kissing it. He turned back to Anna. "I have to mix and mingle," he said, escorting them into the massive tent. "Make yourselves at home." He winked at Anna and went off to greet more arrivals.

Cindy suddenly squealed "Ooh, shrimp!" Tossing her thick mane of red hair, she trotted off, her skirt chiming joyfully. Anna caught up with her at the buffet table, where fifteen feet of smoked salmon, caviar, shrimp, cold cuts, fresh fruits, and a dozen different cheeses nestled among mounds of leafy lettuce that covered an inch of crushed ice like lichen on a frozen tundra. Accepting champagne from a passing waiter, they crunched on crustaceans and took in the rarified air of high dollar polo.

Cindy wiped her fingers daintily on a white linen napkin and said, "I hope there are Argentinians playing today. Argentinian polo players are the *hottest*."

39

Anna was shaking her head in amusement at her incorrigible friend when Jonathan came back into the tent to tell them that the match was about to begin, suggesting they go find a seat. Along the way, Cindy poked Anna in the arm. "The Italian count has the love eyes for you," she said.

Anna stopped short and looked at her friend as if she had grown a second head. "The what?"

"You know," Cindy said, making cross eyes and bobbling her head. "The luuuhhhhhhvvvvve eyes."

"He's not a count, and he doesn't have 'the luuuhhhhhhvvvvve eyes' for me," Anna insisted. But by the time they reached the spectators' area, she was thinking that love eyes from someone like Jonathan would be a welcome change from her lonely, workaday existence.

They found seats in the GEM Motorcars box, the viewing area affording them a panoramic vista of the polo field spread out before them like a green carpet. The sun was butter yellow and blazing, but an occasional breeze brought a welcome coolness and the scent of freshly mown grass from the manicured lawns of the mini-mansions lining the east side of the field.

The hum of conversation around them turned to cheers as the players took the field. The crowd sang the national anthem, and when it was over, the referee introduced the teams. The players gathered around him, reining in their high-strung horses until he threw down the little white ball, and a scrum of players and horses burst into action. The riders battled furiously for control of the ball, their mallets clacking and clattering like bamboo swords until one of players finally captured the ball. In a flash, five tons of horseflesh carrying one ton of human flesh took off in a flurry of dust and thundering hoofbeats.

Anna was just beginning to grasp the rules of the sport when an air horn abruptly interrupted the action. She watched as a sinuous line of spectators filed antlike onto the field where a gleaming black Escalade festooned with GEM Motorcars banners on each side was parked. Two buxom lasses wearing T-shirts, cutoff jeans, and cowboy boots were serving the thirsty polo fans cheap sparkling wine in plastic cups before sending them off to stomp divots.

Cindy didn't want to sully her boots and wandered off to visit with some clients she had spotted earlier. Anna decided to meander past the luxury cars parked beside the field before making her way back to the tent to visit with Jonathan and allow her champagne buzz some time to dissipate before the drive home.

* * *

While Anna and Cindy were enjoying the match, Jonathan had been diligently working the tent, making sure that Garrett Mason saw him talking up lots of potential buyers. When his boss finally left to watch the rest of the match, Jonathan wandered casually over to Jack Garrison, who had just finished talking with a local real estate tycoon. He was standing by the buffet table, snacking on smoked salmon and caviar when Jonathan sidled up to him.

"I'm sure you're not interested in hearing any more about cars today," Jonathan said. "Would you like to step outside and join me in a cigar?" He pulled two Cohibas from his pocket and offered one to Jack.

"Sure, why not," Jack replied, wiping his hand on a napkin and taking the cigar.

They walked around the north corner of the tent where only a handful of people were milling about. Jonathan lit Jack's cigar and got straight to the point. "I just wanted to tell you that selling cars is just a sideline for me. I have significant experience in real estate and banking deals. I'm always looking for new opportunities." He launched into his elevator speech, encapsulating his business history and wrapping up in thirty seconds. "I know you represent Lamar Buchanan, and I'm sure you must hear this all the time, but I really would appreciate it if I could present to you any appropriate investment opportunity that I might encounter."

Jack was by nature skeptical of such uninvited solicitations, but he was familiar with the real estate projects Jonathan had described. It never hurt to network, so he gave Jonathan his business card. "Call me if something in the thirty-five million-dollar range comes up," he said, knowing that the amount usually weeded out the amateurs right away.

41

If the guy was a phony or a dilettante, the number would scare him off, and he would never be heard from again.

They stubbed out their half-smoked cigars and went back into the tent just as Anna returned. Jonathan made introductions and talked up Anna's association with B&V, the three of them talking business for a while until Jack wandered off to speak with the owner of the *Dallas Morning News*.

As soon as Jack left, Jonathan suddenly took Anna by the arm and rushed her around the same side of the tent where he and Jack had just been. He glanced around and found the coast clear. "My God, you're beautiful," he said, pulling her to him and kissing her passionately on the mouth.

Anna didn't protest and was starting to melt into the kiss when the nerve-shredding blast of the air horn signaled the end of the match and the return of the other guests. Ushering his flustered guest back to the tent, Jonathan said "I have to help take the cars back to the dealership, but I should finish up around 8:00 p.m. Can we meet for a drink somewhere afterward?"

Near breathless from the kiss, Anna sincerely wanted to accept the invitation, but she had work to do back at home and a 6:00 a.m. conference call the following morning. She asked Jonathan for a rain check and got one, along with a GEM Motorcars key chain.

A few minutes later, Cindy bounced back into the tent, and the two women said goodbye to a disappointed Jonathan. He turned back to scan the crowd for any guests that might be sufficiently loosened up and in the mood for a test drive.

Anna's best friend spent the ride home chiding her for picking profession over passion. "Have you absolutely lost your mind?" Cindy scolded. "Why didn't you go for it? I thought your motto was *carpe diem.*"

"It is," Anna said. "But until the merger I'm working on closes, my motto is *carpe sleep*; besides, if he's interested, he'll call."

Chapter 5

Jonathan called the very next day. They went on a real date, then another, and another after that, getting to know each other and on the cusp of falling in love. They had been dating for a month when one night, over veal picatta at their favorite Italian restaurant, Jonathan got serious.

Gazing at Anna from across the table, his green eyes piercing hers, he took her hands in his and asked, "How many times have you been in love?"

Anna thought about the question for a few seconds. "Twice," was her answer.

"Who was the first?"

"Mikhail Baryshnikov."

Jonathan didn't laugh at her joke, so Anna said, seriously this time, "Actually, just once—my ex-husband."

"What happened? If you don't mind my asking."

The topic of conversation made Anna uncomfortable. "I thought the first rule of dating is not to discuss former romances."

Jonathan's look was serious, almost stern. "We're too old to waste time following archaic dating rules," he said. "We're middle-aged adults, and we've both had prior relationships."

His points were valid, so Anna put down her fork and told him. "As you can imagine, life on the road with a professional dance troupe isn't exactly conducive to romance—the traveling dating pool is very shallow, and you're never in one place for very long. I had never been in a serious relationship and wasn't expecting to be until I retired from dancing. But one night during a performance here in Dallas, a local

43

ballet aficionado was so taken by me that he returned for the remaining five performances, sending me roses backstage every time."

"We maintained a sporadic, long-distance relationship for a few years until the ligament in my left knee disintegrated once and for all. My dance career was over, so I came back to Dallas to live. Things got serious between us and we eventually married. My husband was the manager of a boutique menswear store and turned out to be a bisexual with a compulsive spending habit. Less than a year into the marriage, I caught him *in flagrante* with his dentist—male—when I got home early after teaching a ballet class. By the time the divorce was final he was dating a model—female."

"What happened after that?" Jonathan asked, seemingly intrigued.

"Well, since he spent most of his paychecks on clothes, and my earnings were a pittance, there were no assets to split. I left the marriage a little older and a lot wiser, but definitely not richer."

Jonathan unknowingly brought up a sore subject. "Why didn't you have children?"

The topic of offspring always took Anna painfully back to a time when she was only five years old, watching soap operas and cartoons on their old black and white television while her mother cleaned the house. A perspicacious child, Anna had seen and absorbed enough of the daily television dramas to put two and two together. One afternoon, she asked her mother an innocent question.

"Mommy, why do people always have a baby after they get married?"

Her mother shut off the vacuum, a shocked look on her face. "Where did you get that idea?"

"From the television. The television people get married first, and then they have a baby after. Does getting married make a baby come?"

Not wanting to have a conversation about sex with her very young daughter, Anna's mother gave her a non-answer. "When two people love each other very much, first they get married, and then they have a baby."

"So, you and daddy loved each other very much, and that's why I'm here?"

"No, not at all. You were an accident. I never wanted you. I tried to abort you like the first two by jumping off the kitchen counter, but it didn't work."

Little Anna didn't know what an abortion was at the time, but being told that she was an unwanted accident changed her view of herself in ways she was too young to notice or understand. Present day Anna shifted uncomfortably in her chair. She wasn't yet inclined to share those feelings with Jonathan just yet.

"I've never had much of maternal instinct, so I never really wanted children," she said, her explanation flippant and without a tinge of regret. She said nothing further on the subject and steered the conversation onto a new course. "How many times have *you* been in love?"

Jonathan took a sip of his after-dinner cognac. "Just once," he replied. "I was just starting out in the car business at a dealership out in Garland. My ex-wife, Mary, was the receptionist there. One thing led to another and we got married." He shook his head at the memories. "Big mistake," he said. "I don't know what I was thinking. She's nothing but trailer trash, and I had to fix her up a lot." Jonathan's face clouded momentarily, then his features softened. "But I love my nine-year-old daughter, Gina. She's named after my Mom."

"Do you get to see your daughter often?" Anna asked.

"Unfortunately, no," he replied. "Mary has custody. She and her new boyfriend are living in a trailer park on the outskirts of Corpus Christi. He's a roughneck on an oil rig in the Gulf of Mexico. Mary won't drive Gina to Dallas, and she won't put her on a plane alone."

Anna wondered why Jonathan didn't go to Corpus Christi himself, but she saw the pain in his eyes and didn't say anything.

* * *

Their talk of love over dinner that night led to their first lovemaking. They had already been on six dates, and Anna had five years of pent-up desires that remained unsatisfied. Jonathan's honesty and emotional vulnerability at dinner—along with two bottles of wine—convinced her that it was safe to let her guard down. Instead of giving him a goodnight kiss on her doorstep, she asked him to come in for an after-dinner drink. Jonathan accepted, of course.

She was reaching into a kitchen cabinet for a bottle of cognac when she sensed his presence mere inches from her. She could smell the masculine scent of his after-shave, his closeness overwhelming her with sensations more intense than any other she could remember. The heat from his body radiated through his tailored shirt in sensuous waves as he put his hands around her waist and kissed her behind her right ear, whispering "I love you."

She felt tingles in long-neglected places, her body melting as she turned to face him. He drew her to him, kissing her hungrily and encountering no resistance. Raw passion toppled the last of her defenses and she surrendered as he took her hand and led her silently to the bedroom. They undressed each other with feverish urgency and fell onto the bed in a frenzy of naked skin and animal desire. Jonathan's skilled fingers quickly brought her to the brink of an orgasm, and she could feel his erection throbbing against her thigh. Amid the carnal mayhem, she somehow managed to whisper, "I want you. Now."

Jonathan needed no further encouragement, entering her forcefully, ravenously. His unaccustomed size made her gasp with each powerful thrust until the first of several orgasms began to wash over her, each more intense than the one before. She lost all sense of space, time, and reason, riding the waves of forgotten pleasures with Jonathan until he too lost control and exploded inside her.

Collapsing onto the bed, he pulled her close. His long legs felt cool against hers, but his embrace was warm as he whispered again, "I love you."

Anna nestled in his arms and said the words she never thought she would say again to a man. "I love you, too."

Jonathan held her closely, kissing her hair and stroking the curve of her back until her breathing grew steady and she fell asleep. Still wide awake, he put on his shirt, poured himself a cognac, and spent the next hour roaming Anna's apartment, examining every nook, cranny, closet, and cupboard until he finally tired and joined her in bed again.

* * *

At the beginning, they ate out as often as three times a week, but Anna started to feel guilty about how much it was costing. Jonathan always insisted on paying for dinner, and he always paid in cash. She finally convinced him that they should eat in more often to save money, but admitted with coy chagrin that her cooking repertoire consisted of sandwiches, omelets, and pasta with canned sauce. Although Jonathan would be saving cash, he would be doing most of the cooking. He agreed to the plan without complaint because he loved to cook, often bragging that his prowess in the kitchen equaled his prowess in the bedroom. Anna didn't know where he had learned to make love, but she did know that he learned to cook from his mother. If his boasting were true, Anna knew she was in for some fantastic meals.

One stumbling block to the plan was that Jonathan needed a kitchen in which to cook. He had reluctantly admitted to Anna one night that he was living in a room in the Bedford Suites, thanks to his profligate ex-wife. Anna wasn't bothered by the fact that Jonathan lived in an extended-stay motel. She had met quite a few divorced men over the years who had been relegated to cheap motels and efficiency apartments by their divorce settlements. She also knew they usually didn't have decent kitchens.

Logistics won the day, and they agreed that Jonathan would exercise his culinary expertise in Anna's kitchen several nights a week. She would pour him a large scotch on the rocks and try to get some work done while Jonathan chopped, boiled, baked, and sautéed, living up to his self-bestowed reputation.

Most evenings, after one of his delicious meals, they would sit on the sofa and watch old movies together. Jonathan loved movies, especially the *Godfather* series, *Scarface*, both versions of *The Thomas Crown Affair*, and anything featuring James Bond. He had once told Anna that he had developed his sartorial style by emulating his childhood movie heroes.

Anna preferred comedies and science fiction, but they always managed to reconcile their differing cinematic tastes and find a movie that suited them both. Jonathan would rub her feet while they watched, then he'd start rubbing other things. Anna would reciprocate, and they almost always missed the end of the movie.

On the rare Sundays that neither of them had to work, the lovebirds would take long walks along Turtle Creek. Strolling hand in hand, Anna would show Jonathan the twists, turns, and sudden discoveries the rambling paths had to offer as they wound through some of the most expensive real estate in Texas. Sometimes they'd take a picnic basket and a bottle of wine, basking by the water in the dappled sunlight and reading the Sunday paper until it was time to go to his parents' place for supper.

Ricky and Gina DeLuca rented a small patio apartment in Mesquite, living on T-bill interest and Ricky's social security and veteran's benefits. The once strapping, black-haired paratrooper had never stopped walking with a limp, and his hair was now sparse and white. His vision was failing, and advancing age added to his long-ago wounds left him with little to do but watch blurry television and go to doctor appointments.

Jonathan's mother devoted her time to cooking for her DeLuca men. Gina's ancestors hailed from a small village near Florence, Italy, where their roots had been traced back to the 1600s. Unverifiable but long-accepted family lore held that they had ephemeral ties to Florentine royalty and had been bankers in competition with the Medicis. Although Gina didn't know anything about banking, she did know a lot about cooking, and all her dishes were dripping in sauce and stuffed with cheesy love. It wasn't surprising that, after decades of such traditional delights, the former wasp-waisted, trophy wife was now shaped like a pear with a droopy bosom, favoring shapeless housedresses over Halston and Chanel.

The DeLucas welcomed Anna warmly into their home and hearts, and she felt safe and protected there. Chatting with Gina in the kitchen while Ricky and Jonathan grilled steaks on the back patio was very instructive. She learned a lot about her new boyfriend as Gina regaled her with stories about the time little Johnny tried to flush his father's only pair of dress shoes down the toilet when he was four years old, and how he had painted the neighbor's cat pink when he was six.

As the weeks passed, Gina had many more tales to tattle. "One time when Johnny was fourteen," she said, "he found a dead squirrel and stuffed it in my oven—right on top of the five-pound pot roast I was cooking for company."

Anna nearly lost her appetite after that story and assumed it was the worst of Jonathan's pranks—until Gina told her one evening that Jonathan's victims weren't limited to small animals. As he got older, his favorite pastime was hiding in the broom closet at the top of the stairs and waiting for her to come up to the second floor. As soon as she reached the landing, he'd jump out of the closet with a blood-curdling "Boo!" He scared her so much that one time that she fell down the stairs backwards and broke an ankle.

Anna's eyes grew saucer-sized as she listened to the unsettling story. "What did you do?"

"What could I do?" Gina replied, shrugging. "I'd chase him around with a broom sometimes, but he always got away. I could never stay mad at my Johnny for long, though. Boys will be boys and mine was a handful." She looked heavenward, crossed herself twice, and handed Anna a tray of penne a la vodka to take to the table, where Jonathan was pouring Chianti, and Ricky was dishing up freshly grilled T-bones and corn on the cob.

They ate and talked until the late spring sun dipped behind the rooftops. By the time supper was over, Anna had decided to put aside Gina's revelations about Jonathan, attributing his disturbing past behavior to youthful male exuberance.

Chapter 6

The temperate spring passed into torrid summer as their passion for each other rose with the mercury. Anna felt as if Jonathan could read her mind, and even though she found the concept of a soul mate to be silly new age blather, she was beginning to wonder if Jonathan was hers. A well-rounded and determined suitor, he waxed rhapsodic in poetry during the week and waxed her car on the weekends. He somehow knew exactly where all her erotic buttons were, and was clever and creative in the many ways he pushed them.

Even after months of dating, he still sent monthly flower arrangements to her office to commemorate the anniversary of their first date. One such creation was round, comprising two dozen pale pink roses encircling one large red rose in the center. The card said, "You're one in a million, Love Jonathan." The always tasteful F-Man said, "It looks like a giant boob."

Summer arrived, bringing with it law firm recruiting season and a small horde of aspiring lawyers. For three months, the big commercial law firms compete for the best and brightest of the country's law schools, spending lavish amounts of money to entice the budding counselors to spend a few weeks pretending to work while collecting hefty and generally undeserved paychecks.

Anna invited Jonathan to several recruiting events, proud to have such a suave escort on her arm. Always stylishly dressed, he behaved accordingly. A skilled raconteur, he could chat with ease on a myriad of topics, but his favorite subject was always how proud he was of Anna. Her female co-workers and the partners' wives called him "charming," "witty," "urbane," and "charismatic."

The F-Man weighed in one morning following a recruiting dinner at founding partner Harry Vincent's house. "This Jonathan guy is making us husbands look bad," he groused. "My wife has been on my case about it ever since she met him last night." He put on a whiny voice, trying to mimic his spouse. "Why don't you treat me like Jonathan treats Anna? He doesn't just *love* Anna, he *cherishes* her." The F-Man pretended to stick his finger down his throat. "Makes me want to barf."

"I have no idea how to respond to that," Anna said, too in love to let the crass comments bother her.

* * *

GEM Motorcars held an awards dinner in July for its top producers. Jonathan was one of them, and he took Anna to the dinner with him. They sat at the same table as Garrett Mason, along with Bob Peterson and his wife, Mona. Garrett told Anna what a great job Jonathan was doing and told Jonathan what a lucky man he was to have such a pretty date. When awards were given after dinner, Jonathan received a check for three thousand dollars and an acrylic commemorative trophy that looked a lot like Anna's office building.

Acting dutifully on orders from his wife, Bob told Jonathan the next day, "Mona says you'd better snap that girl up before she gets away from you, and I agree."

Agreeing with both of the Petersons, Jonathan said, "I'm glad you mentioned that. Anna's birthday is in a couple of weeks, and I plan on proposing to her."

"Congratulations."

Jonathan hesitated for a moment. "I'm embarrassed to have to ask you this, but can you spot me three thousand dollars until payday? I want to get Anna an engagement ring, but my ex-wife is bleeding me dry."

"What about the bonus you just got?"

"That check went to cover back child support. Come on, buddy, you know I'm good for it."

Bob considered the request for a few seconds. "Well, I don't know, Jonathan. That's an awful lot of money for an engagement ring."

"I know, but I want Anna to have a ring as beautiful as she is."

"Don't you have a credit card?"

"Shit, no. Mary ruined my credit. I swear I'll pay you back when I get my next paycheck—with interest."

Bob hemmed and hawed, grumbled something unintelligible, then yielded and wrote a check.

Jonathan drove to his parents' apartment after work to tell them the happy news in person. They were so excited to hear about the imminent betrothal that Gina hopped up and down at the prospect of impending nuptials, and Ricky was delighted to loan his son the money he needed to buy a suitable engagement ring for his fiancée.

"Anything to make you and Anna happy, son," he said, handing Jonathan a check for five thousand dollars.

* * *

Anna answered the doorbell on the evening of her forty-fifth birthday to find Jonathan standing on the doorstep holding forty-five red roses. He kissed her passionately, then let her go, waiting patiently while she put the flowers in water and finished getting ready for dinner. He had repeatedly refused to tell her where they were going, but he had told her to dress up, so she chose a black linen halter dress that turned her eyes gray and showed off her lithe dancer's body.

They pulled into the driveway of The Manford Estate on Turtle Creek half an hour later. One of the most prestigious and iconic establishments in Dallas, everyone who was anyone knew that "The Estate" was the place to go for a sensuous, romantic evening or a high-powered business dinner.

After a short wait in the entry foyer, the maître d' arrived, greeted them effusively, then guided them along a path of pink rose petals strewn from the entrance of the main dining room to a private nook known as the Reading Room. The cozy alcove ordinarily held tables and chairs sufficient to fete twelve people, but tonight it held only one table and two chairs. More rose petals dotted the white linen tablecloth, and a forest of crystal stemware sprouted from the table. A silver bucket next to the table cradled a bottle of Taittinger Rosé champagne in a cocoon of crushed ice.

The headwaiter winked conspiratorially at Jonathan, initiating a flurry of chair moving and napkin fluffing that preceded the entrance of the sommelier. An imposing man, he was a minor celebrity around town due to his vast knowledge of oenology and attentiveness to his clients. He took the bottle out of the ice bucket, wiping it dry with a linen towel and ceremoniously displaying the label to Jonathan. After popping the cork, he partially filled Jonathan's glass. Jonathan took a sip and nodded in approval, whereupon the sommelier filled both glasses to the brim and withdrew with a gracious bow.

His green eyes glistening, Jonathan looked adoringly at Anna, raised his glass, and toasted, "To the most beautiful woman—inside and out—that I have ever been blessed to know."

Anna blushed the same shade of pink as the champagne, too overwhelmed with emotion to respond in words. Instead, she gave him a very long kiss, oblivious to the curious patrons from the restaurant who kept peeking in to see where the trail of rose petals ended.

When they finished dinner, he came around the table and took her hand, leading her into a multi-level, cave-dark room that served as the bar. A trio of musicians was mid-way through a romantic rendition of *How You Look Tonight* as he walked her to the dance floor and took her in his arms.

Slow dancing with Jonathan reminded Anna of when she was a child. Her parents loved to dance but couldn't afford babysitters, so on Saturday nights, they'd dress her up and take her with them to the local dance hall. She'd sit primly on one of the chairs lining the wall, her tiny legs dangling off the edge of her seat while she waited patiently and watched her parents dance to Benny Goodman and Glenn Miller. Every two or three songs, her father would come over, take off her black patent leather shoes, and carry her to the dance floor. Placing her tiny feet in their frilly white socks on top of his big, shiny black shoes, she'd hold on tight as her father swayed back and forth, twirling her around the dance floor to the music of the 1940s and 1950s. Those were happy times, and Jonathan made her feel the same way again.

When the song ended, he let her go and said, "Wait here, darling." He walked over to the band leader, handing him twenty dollars as they exchanged a few words. Returning to the dance floor, he got down on one knee, and with at least thirty people watching, presented Anna with a red box from Chartrier's. Hopeful expectation filled his eyes as he opened it, revealing a three-karat, round-cut diamond that glinted and glimmered in the candlelight, its facets throwing off rainbow-colored sparks and casting tiny dancing prisms throughout the dimly lit room.

Taking her left hand in his, he kissed it gently and placed the ring tenderly on her finger. "Anna Thornbury," he said, his eyes pleading, "I love you more than life itself, and I would be the happiest man in the world if you would consent to be my wife."

Having spent most of her life overworked, undervalued, and routinely berated, at long last Anna felt safe, loved, and appreciated. Without hesitation, she threw her arms around his neck and said, "Yes, Jonathan, I will be your wife."

The bar patrons and the band erupted in congratulatory applause, and the trio began playing *What Are You Doing the Rest of Your Life?* Anna melted into Jonathan's arms, crying silent, happy tears. She had never told him that it was her favorite song. She looked up at him, grateful love in her eyes. "How did you know?" she whispered.

Jonathan simply held her closer and kissed her hair.

* * *

Anna couldn't wait to tell Cindy the news, but when she called her best friend, they had their first argument. Cindy thought Anna was being impulsive. "Anna, honey," she said, "you know I'd rather kiss a two-headed water snake than do or say anything to hurt you, but are you sure you aren't rushing into this? Maybe you should run a background check on him or something. I've only met him twice, and he seems nice, but . . ."

Anna was offended. "You sound just like Nicky," she snapped. "Anyway, I've already told Jonathan that I want to wait at least a year to get married, and he's fine with it." Anna saw a hurt look in Cindy's eyes and immediately tried to assuage her. "Please don't worry," she said soothingly. "I already did a basic internet search and nothing came up; besides, I don't need to check his background. He has a steady job and earns a comfortable living. I've met his boss and co-workers, and he's met my colleagues, including several senior partners. All of them speak highly of him. Most importantly, his parents are wonderful, and I finally have a family again." Anna sighed. "I thought you would be happy for me."

"I *am* happy for you," Cindy insisted. "I just think you should get to know each other better. But now that I know that you're waiting for a year, I won't worry about it. Something else has been bothering me, though. You never seem to have time for me or your other friends anymore."

"I know," Anna said. "I'm sorry. With work, travel, Jonathan, and Sundays with his parents, there's no time for anything—or anybody—else. He doesn't get to see his friends very often either."

As soon as she said it, Anna realized that she'd never met any of Jonathan's friends, other than his lawyer David and Bob from the car dealership. Now that she thought about it, Jonathan had never mentioned any other friends. An inchoate concern flashed through her thoughts, but it passed just as quickly as it had arrived. She smiled at Cindy. "I promise I'll try harder to get together with you."

"Good," Cindy said. "And you absolutely *must* have the wedding reception at my gallery—whenever it is."

Anna promised her that they would when the time came.

She called Nicky later that night and was both surprised and disappointed by his tepid response to the news of her newly affianced status. He was very big brother-y.

"I'm really happy for you," he said. "It's just that you barely know the guy."

Anna explained about the plan to wait at least a year to get married, and Nicky relented. "Well, that's ok, then—I guess," he said, not inclined to talk about the engagement further, but promising to come to the wedding.

Chapter 7

As Jonathan had hoped, his penny-pinching fiancée suggested that he move in with her to save money. "There's no reason to throw money away on a motel out in the suburbs," she said the morning after their engagement, and Jonathan couldn't help but agree.

Most of his worldly possessions were in storage where Mary couldn't find them, but he still needed to get the rest of his things from the motel room and check out. Less than a week after he proposed to Anna, he left work and drove to the Bedford Suites for the last time. He had just enough money left from Bob's loan and the check from Pops to pay the back rent on the room and recoup his deposit. He bounded up the breezeway stairs and let himself into the room. As soon as he turned around, he exploded in anger. "What the fuck are you doing here, bitch?"

The barrage of foul language was aimed at a petite blonde with a pretty face freckled from the same Texas sun that was giving her premature worry lines. She was standing in front of the room's only closet, loading a few pieces of girls' clothing and some toys into a cardboard box. "I'm here for the rest of little Gina's things and to tell you that I'm filing for divorce," she said in her distinct Texas twang.

"Fuck if I care. You moved out on me, remember?"

"You expected me to raise our daughter in a motel room while you worked on one of your so-called deals? What kind of life is that for a nine-year-old—or for me?"

"If you really loved me, you would have stayed with me until I finished my next deal. You're my wife for god's sake!"

Mary ignored him and finished filling the box, wrestling it to the door while her husband made no attempt to help her. Balancing the

56

box between her chin and her left knee, she finally managed to get the door open. As she passed through it, she delivered a parting shot. "I'm going to ask for a lot of child support, and you'd better pay it or you know what'll happen."

With her last salvo lingering in the angry air, she slammed the door shut with her foot so hard that some starving artist's painting almost fell off the wall.

* * *

A very large moving van hissed to a stop in front of Anna's apartment two weeks later. Four muscular men unloaded a small showroom's worth of expensive furniture and a small storeroom's worth of boxes packed almost to the point of bursting. Jonathan had pointed out that the mid-century modern furniture she inherited from her parents had devolved from vintage to shabby chic to just plain shabby. He was absolutely right, so she kept only a few treasured family antiques and made room for his belongings by donating most of hers to a local organization that assisted battered women.

Everything that came off the truck was designer quality, except a couch that had once belonged to Jonathan's dead great-grandmother. It's dark green velvet upholstery was lumpy and worn, looking every bit as old as his decomposed ancestor. Gold tassels the size of Anna's fist hung on elaborately carved oak support posts that stood sentry at each back corner, striving to hold the crumbling relic together. Anna thought it looked like a moldy pickle with earrings, but she kept that observation to herself and relegated it to the upstairs bedroom that had once been her office, but was now Jonathan's "dressing room."

She sat on the dusty gherkin and watched as Jonathan unpacked twenty suits, thirty pairs of shoes, and at least one hundred expensive silk ties. When she remarked on the sheer volume of his stylish accoutrements, he became defensive. Evidently a committed devotee of the "dress for success" philosophy, he said, "If you want to sell anything to anyone, you have to look like you don't need the money. No one will take you seriously if you look like you're broke."

57

The validity of the concept aside, she was still surprised by how much expensive clothing he had. She headed down the stairs just as one of the movers was carrying the last load upstairs, giving a sidelong glance at a box labeled "Documents" and hurrying downstairs to finish arranging her beautiful near-new furniture.

* * *

The next few months passed rapidly, the two of them busy with their jobs and their budding life together. Other than the occasional spat over little things that all couples inevitably engage in, Anna marveled at how well they got along and how much they had in common.

Reality must eventually intrude upon romance, however, and one evening they sat down at the dining room table to talk about money. After promising each other that there would be no secrets of any kind between them, they spent two hours reviewing their individual financial circumstances.

It rapidly became apparent that Jonathan had significantly more assets than Anna, earning over one hundred fifty thousand dollars a year and carrying no debt. He didn't have a car payment because he drove a dealership demo car, and he had no credit card debt because he had no credit—thanks to his shopaholic ex-wife.

Anna's financial picture was significantly less rosy. Despite her age, she was only a third-year lawyer on a fixed salary that was better than average, but it wasn't partner money. She earned half of what Jonathan did, and even with her many academic scholarships, she still owed over twenty-five thousand dollars in student loans. Her life's savings totaled only slightly more than that. On the plus side of her ledger, her old car was paid for and still running. Her only credit cards were a Newman Marvis card that she used once a year to buy her favorite perfume and a strictly-for-business American CreditCorp card issued through her law firm.

Jonathan was visibly surprised to learn that Anna didn't earn more money than she did and was at least four years away from making partner. She sensed his discomfort, and given the large disparity in their individual prosperity, her lawyerly inclination was to suggest a prenuptial agreement to protect his pre-marital estate.

He was adamantly against the idea. "Everything I have is yours, my darling," he protested. "Why start our life together under the shadow of a foregone conclusion?" He leaned over the table and gave her a loving peck on the forehead. "I want you to handle the family finances. You're so much smarter than I am, you'll do a much better job of it. I'll give you my paychecks, and you can do all the banking and bill paying."

That was fine with Anna after what had happened with her first husband.

"Now then," Jonathan said "do you have any other debts or liabilities that I should know about? We promised each other no secrets—remember?"

Mona Lisa-like, Anna smiled demurely but said nothing, because she did have a secret. It was a secret she had shared with no one and would never share—not even with the man she was going to marry.

* * *

Jonathan was at work one afternoon a few months later when his cell phone rang.

"Hey, Jonathan," David said in an unhappy monotone. "I have good news and really bad news. The good news is that your divorce is final. The really bad news is that the judge awarded Mary seven hundred and fifty-six dollars per month in child support."

Enraged into oblivious disregard of his surroundings, Jonathan blew up. "Are you fucking kidding me?" he screamed into the phone. "I can't afford that on top of everything else."

The showroom was full of customers and staff, all of them turning to look at the source of the high-decibel outburst. Seeing the astonished stares all around him, he sat down and pretended as if nothing had happened.

"Well, you'd better pay timely or you know what could happen," David warned.

"Yeah, yeah, I know."

59

"Sorry to do this to you, but there's more bad news. I can no longer act as your legal counsel. You still owe me twenty grand from last year, and I'm out of options. Nothing personal, but I'll have to turn you over to a collections agency if you don't pony up soon."

"Don't bail on me now, David," Jonathan pleaded. "I'm on the verge of closing Lamar Buchanan on a fleet of Escalades. My commission on that will take care of everything I owe you five times over. I swear I'll make it worth your while if you just stick with me a little longer."

David hesitated. "Okay, okay" he finally said. "I'll hang in with you—but only for another thirty days."

Jonathan slammed the phone down and looked up to see Eric Adams, his sales manager, glaring at him from across the showroom floor and giving him an "in my office now" signal. Jonathan rose from his desk and headed over. *This was going to suck. Hard.*

* * *

Jonathan started pushing Anna to get married sooner rather than later. She didn't like the idea, but he was insistent. "Why do we have to wait until next year to get married?" he protested. "I want to start spending the rest of my life with you as soon as possible."

He seemed genuinely hurt that she wanted to wait so long to marry. She felt guilty for causing him pain and acquiesced to his first request. As soon as she did, he told her that he was an old-fashioned, Italian male and insisted that she change her last name to DeLuca when they married. Anna had never been a radical feminist, but she didn't want to legally change her name again. It was a bureaucratic swamp that she had slogged through before, and she did not want to do it again.

Jonathan was incensed at her demurral, as if insulted to the core. "Don't you want to share my name?" he accused, his eyes filled with recrimination. "We're going to be a family. Families should share the same last name."

He wouldn't take no for an answer and forced the issue every night over dinner. Not wanting to argue with him anymore, Anna reluctantly agreed to his second request. They chose December 23rd for their wedding date, but would postpone the honeymoon until after Christmas because they both had to work.

Several weeks before the scheduled honeymoon, Jonathan drove to the offices of Bennington Travel Services on Preston Road and Northwest Highway. He entered and asked to see the owner, casually mentioning to the receptionist that he was Anna Thornbury's fiancé.

Helen Bennington came into the foyer a minute later and showed him into her office. After some obligatory small talk, he explained that Anna had recommended Helen's agency because it handled B&V's travel.

A black-haired, matronly woman in her forties, Helen had never met Anna personally, but they had talked on the phone from time to time, and she had seen Anna's picture in the firm directory that B&V had given her when Bennington Travel became the firm's official travel agent.

Jonathan showed Helen a copy of the marriage license as proof of his honorable intentions, then handed over his father's credit card for payment. When she balked upon seeing the wrong first name on the card, he explained that his parents were paying for the entire trip as a wedding present.

Naturally, Helen was sympathetic when he told her the heart-wrenching story of the poor old wounded veteran waiting out in the car, his legs too shattered to come in to sign for the charges in person. Thinking that no one that well-dressed and engaged to an attorney at B&V could possibly be lying, she insisted that the aged war hero needn't go to the trouble and promptly put the charges through on Jonathan's signature.

The very next day, she received a lovely flower arrangement of red roses with one white rose in the middle and a card that said, "You're one in a million! Thanks, Jonathan."

* * *

Thanksgiving came and went as the weeks blew by with the chill north winds. Anna was scrambling to close year-end mergers and acquisitions, and Jonathan was scrambling to close out the year with another big bonus.

The day of the wedding soon arrived. In the interest of time and in deference to Anna's thriftiness, they married in a civil ceremony at the downtown courthouse. The bride wore a winter white Dior evening suit that she bought at her favorite consignment store, the groom donning a new black Ralph Lauren suit with a white rose in his lapel that matched Anna's small bouquet. Jonathan's parents, David, and Cindy were present for the brief ceremony. Everyone cried, including Jonathan.

The dinner reception at Cindy's art gallery that night was simple, tasteful, and small. Nicky flew in from New York a few hours before the reception, adding one more to the group of celebrants. Anna hadn't invited anyone from work, given the political perils inherent in doing so. Bob and Mona Peterson attended as the groom's guests, and Garrett Mason put in a brief appearance to offer his congratulations. After chatting briefly with the newlyweds, he bought a twenty-five-thousand-dollar sculpture, sending Cindy into paroxysms of holiday glee.

The gathering was joyous, but brief, because almost everyone had to work the next morning. Nicky stayed behind to help Cindy clean up the gallery. They drank the rest of the champagne and caught up on each other's lives, neither of them saying much about the recently concluded union because, being such close friends, neither of them had to.

* * *

Having procrastinated on his Christmas shopping, Jonathan left work at 3:00 p.m. on Christmas Eve and battled rush hour traffic all the way to NorthPark Center. Stopping first into Newman Marvis, he went to see his friend Stella in the perfume department.

Stella thought Jonathan was such a considerate man, always coming in to buy presents for his sweet mother and his pretty wife. He was so thoughtful that he even brought Stella flowers once, just to thank her for being so helpful. His father was a genuine war hero, too.

Jonathan supervised as she loaded a gilded gift basket with six hundred dollars' worth of soaps, lotions, bath salts, bath powder, perfume, cologne, and scented candles. When she finished ringing up the fragrant purchase, Jonathan asked her for a favor. She graciously obliged, going to an in-store telephone that sat on the counter next to the cash register and made a call, speaking into the phone for a minute, smiling at Jonathan the entire time.

Her mission accomplished, she went back to him and said, "Just head to the second floor and ask for Jackie." Jonathan did, and Jackie of the second floor was most solicitous of his shopping desires, patiently spending over two hours with him in the vortex of the Christmas Eve crush.

Jonathan absolutely hated that his wife insisted on buying her designer suits from consignment stores. It didn't matter to him that no one could tell the difference. No spouse of his was going to wear used clothes. Thanks to his father's Newman Marvis credit card, she wouldn't be much longer.

While Jackie took the purchases off to be gift-wrapped, Jonathan decided that he wanted a new bespoke suit and took the escalator to the menswear department. He liked the word "bespoke" and hoped that his favorite salesman, Armando, would be there so that the two of them could gainfully employ the word.

Three thousand dollars' worth of men's designer goods later, he was back at the apartment, hiding the day's purchases in his closet. He congratulated himself on the booty, having once again been rewarded by the fact that salespeople were such easy targets. All he had to do was flash a smile and dangle a fat commission in front of them. They'd overlook all manner of details, especially at Christmas time when they were too busy to argue about names and signatures.

His smug self-satisfaction was evanescent. On Christmas Day, Anna gave him a new set of professional kitchen knives. In return, he had given her so much that it made her uncomfortable. She felt undeserving of such opulence and was so overwhelmed by the blizzard of gifts that she insisted he return most of them, keeping only the perfume basket and one evening gown with matching heels to wear on their honeymoon.

Jonathan was demonstrably disappointed, but he said he understood. He returned the purchases the very next day to a very disappointed Jackie, lessening the blow of lost commissions with a bouquet of flowers and convincing her to refund him the price of the clothes in cash.

* * *

Six days and a short, non-stop flight to the Mexican Riviera later, the newlyweds arrived in Cancún for their honeymoon. After collecting their luggage, they passed through customs and immigration without delay and were met by a driver with a white SUV and whisked through the sultry Mexican night to The Royal Tarlton Hotel. The car windows were open, inviting in the tropical breeze and the exotic scent of night-blooming jasmine. Jungle insects buzzed and whirred in the distance while tropical birds trilled greetings to the rising full moon.

They arrived at the most luxurious hotel in the Yucatán Peninsula, where a doorman in a crisp white jacket ushered them into its plush, welcoming embrace. They checked into a junior suite on the hotel's Club Floor, the spacious room boasting a bathroom big enough to live in and a patio overlooking glistening white sands and the turquoise Caribbean Sea.

Jonathan took Anna by the hand and led her through the French doors and out to the patio railing. Twirling her around to face the ocean, he stood behind her and slipped off her of her lacy white underwear, his touch making her gasp in anticipation. Pulling her close to him, he put his hands around her waist and whispered in her ear, his breath hot with desire. "We can unpack later."

They didn't get around to unpacking until late the next morning, and the rest of honeymoon passed in a languid blur. They spent their days under blue cabanas, drinking margaritas to cool their sunburns and reading for hours. They enjoyed romantic dinners on the beach every night, dining on freshly-caught sea bass and sipping chilled champagne while the waves crashed rhythmically, and the stars wheeled above them like cosmic carousel horses.

They greeted the new year in the hotel's Pub Grill, both of them dressing up for the occasion. Anna wore the silver evening gown she had kept from Jonathan's gift extravaganza on Christmas. Bias cut and full length, it hugged her curves like a Ferrari hugs the roads along the Amalfi Coast, the back of the dress plunging like a car that had missed a curve outside Positano. Jonathan looked distinguished in a black double-breasted blazer and a gold Hermès tie, his winter white wool pants breaking perfectly on his black Gucci shoes.

A five-piece band serenaded them as waiters scurried back and forth under gold and silver balloons that bobbled above them. Sparkling Christmas lights dotted the room, and Anna saw every colorful twinkle as a good omen, as if each blink of light were a wish for good fortune in the coming year and for happiness ever after.

* * *

Favorable portents and fairy tales aside, the new year signaled the end of the honeymoon. Back in Dallas again, Anna was in her loft office the night before her inevitable return to the office, catching up on emails on her Blackberry and paying bills on her home computer.

Her office was right across the hall from Jonathan's dressing room, and when she finished her tasks and started downstairs, she couldn't help noticing that one of his suitcases was open. In it were at least twenty elaborate Christmas ornaments from the lavishly decorated trees that had been displayed about The Royal Tarlton, the fabric loops used to hang them having been neatly cut.

Curious, she asked Jonathan about the ornaments later that night. He waved it off, scoffing at her. "Oh, lighten up, sweetheart. They build the cost of stuff like that into the price of the room, just like the shampoos and the soaps. They expect people to take them."

Anna didn't want to argue with him, but she didn't think he was right about that.

PART II

Chapter 8

The newly-wed DeLucas had their first serious argument when Jonathan gave Anna his January paycheck. As both a lawyer and a divorcée, Anna knew that comingling bank accounts was ill-advised, but Jonathan was adamant, asking that she deposit the check in her existing bank account. When she balked at his suggestion, his jaw clenched and his teeth started grinding like gristmills, signaling that he was angry with her.

"Don't you trust me?" he accused, his green eyes darkening like the Texas sky before a tornado. "You're my *wife*. Why did you marry me if you don't trust me?"

Anna hated conflict of any kind, having grown up in a household where her parents spent a great deal of the time fighting, her father cursing at high volume and her mother crying and slamming doors. Terrified of losing her husband after less than a month of marriage, she assented without further protest, adding him to the checking account and ordering a debit card in his name.

A week later she was in New York on business, so Jonathan took advantage of her absence and got started on his goals for the year. He opened the box marked "Documents" that was tucked away in his closet. Riffling through the old papers, he came across a file folder marked "Ostrich Farm." He leafed through it and put it back in the box. *Small potatoes.*

He found what he was looking for and stuffed a few folders into his briefcase. After going into Anna's office and turning on her computer, he successfully activated the special wedding present the mailman had delivered that morning—his new debit card.

For all of Anna's smarts, she didn't pay a lot of attention to her bank transactions because she could keep all the numbers in her head. Even better, what little banking and bill paying she did online, she did at home. A technophobe to the point of near-paranoia, Anna knew that anything she put into her computer at work could be—and probably was—monitored by someone somewhere. For an idiosyncratic variety of reasons, she managed her financial matters on her home computer using a personal email address and still opted to receive paper copies of bank and credit card statements as backup.

The icing on Jonathan's new-found financial layer cake was Anna's open hatred of her Blackberry. She steadfastly refused to get a personal smart phone, swearing that she would never subject herself to the electronic whims of a second box of circuits that would just make more demands on her time. Her technical intransigence meant that he only had to monitor the mail and check the home computer regularly to ensure that she never saw the alerts the bank would send her every time he used his new debit card. Simplifying his life was the notebook containing all her online passwords that he had found while snooping through her desk while she was at work.

After activating his card, he read all the messages in her email inbox, becoming angry when he saw several from Cindy and Nicky. Cursing under his breath, he deleted all of them, then emptied the computer's trash folder—a procedure he would follow routinely in the future. After ensuring he had left no duplicitous stone unturned, he picked up the phone by the computer and made a telephone call.

"Yellow Rose Secretarial Services," drawled the woman who answered. "This is Samantha. How can I help you?"

"Hi there, Samantha," Jonathan said. "Could you please tell me how much you charge for word processing, printing, and binding?"

"Well, it depends on the job," Samantha said, explaining the array of services provided by Yellow Rose and how much they cost.

"Do you take checks or credit cards?"

"No, sorry. Not for first time customers. We only take cash and require a ten percent deposit up front."

After Jonathan told her what he needed, she gave him an estimate. "Thanks, I'll be in touch," he said hanging up and hatching a plan.

* * *

Jonathan breezed through the door of Yellow Rose Secretarial Services a week later, his smile broad and gleaming. He walked to the lobby desk where a plain, middle-aged woman with salt and pepper hair was sitting. Handing her a bouquet of white roses, he grinned suggestively and cooed, "How is the most beautiful office manager in Dallas today? Remember me?"

Samantha immediately recognized the aristocratic man who had come in a few days earlier to put down a deposit on his project. He was the best dressed client she had ever seen, and she dealt with suit-wearing businessmen all the time. He had flirted with her too, something that hadn't happened to her in a very long while. When he handed her the flowers and gave her a peck on the cheek, she was so flustered that she plunked the roses in her coffee mug by mistake.

"Are my documents ready, gorgeous?" he asked.

"Yes, thanks, um, here they are, um . . ." Samantha stammered, pointing to a box on the floor.

Jonathan pulled out his wallet and peeled off thirteen one-hundred-dollar bills and handed them to her. "Thanks," he said, giving her a wink. "You're one in a million."

He picked the box up with a grunt and went back to the apartment to organize his new documents before dropping off a large manila envelope at the local Federal Express office.

* * *

Anna was in her home office one quiet Saturday afternoon, painstakingly logging billable charges into her expense report form. She noticed a two-thousand-dollar charge on her law firm credit card at a store called "Wheels and Deals" in Plano, a sprawling suburb north of Dallas. Having never done any kind of business with the store, she had no idea what the charge could be. She called American CreditCorp, and they agreed to delete the charge, but her curiosity was aroused.

She looked up the phone number for the store online and called it. A pleasant man named Steve answered. The owner of the store, he explained that someone claiming to be a Dr. Andrew Thornbury had called to purchase an expensive racing bike. Because the good doctor was a very busy surgeon, he had requested that the bike be delivered directly to the parking lot of a local pancake house, where he was having a surprise birthday party for his son.

The doctor had all the pertinent credit card information—including the card's security code. The charge had gone readily through, and the bike was delivered and spirited away. The ultimate loser in the shell game was poor Steve, who would have to take a big loss on the fraudulent transaction.

When she got home from work that night she told Jonathan about the bicycle incident. He looked at her sternly when she finished the story. "It was stupid to call the store after the charge was taken off the account," he warned. "You don't ever want to dig too deeply into things like that. You could run into some bad people."

She took his scowl to represent concern for her well-being, and it made her feel loved.

* * *

Anna's old car finally gave up the automotive ghost. She was driving back to Dallas during rush hour after a meeting in Fort Worth when a late winter thunderstorm rolled in off the plains like a tsunami made of rain. It was a real toad strangler—as they say in Texas—swamping the stretch of highway that connects the two cities. Unimpressed by the gale force winds, the eighteen wheelers on the road kept their speed at sixty miles an hour or more, and every time one of the lunatic truckers passed Anna's old Toyota, a wall of water bashed it like it was off the rails in a car wash.

The windshield washers were unable to keep up, and she could barely see the road in front of her. She pulled off the highway onto the shoulder, praying that none of the speeding trucks would rear-end her tiny car. While she nervously waited out the storm, the mat underneath her feet started to get wet. Peeking under it, she saw streams of water rushing by below her, the undercarriage having completely rusted through.

She tried to restart the car when the onslaught of rain finally abated, but it made sounds like a cat caught in a ceiling fan. The alternator light blinked on and off, taunting her with an ominous "click-click-click." Her only option was to call Jonathan, who gallantly drove to her rescue with a tow truck following behind him. While the tow truck driver hauled the dripping corpse of her car off to a mechanic, Jonathan took her back to the office. Not surprisingly, she later learned that the repairs needed would cost twice what the car was worth.

It was finally time for a new car, so the DeLucas started car shopping. Jonathan wanted her to have a Mercedes Benz. "You're a big city lawyer," he said, "You need to look the part."

Reminding him that it was imprudent to get a sixty-thousand-dollar car, even with their two paychecks, she reluctantly agreed that she'd at least look. So on one windy mid-winter morning, they bundled up and drove to Highland Park Motors, the go-to car dealership for local aficionados of German luxury cars.

They were perusing the shiny late-model machines on the showroom floor when a tastefully dressed, forty-something bottle blonde came over to greet them, introducing herself as Sue Worthing. Jonathan introduced himself, then put his arm around Anna and pulled her close to him. He beamed at Anna, then at Sue. "This is my wife, Anna," he said. "She's a high-powered attorney at Brown and Vincent."

Blushing at her husband's hyperbole, Anna shook Sue's hand and the shopping began. Sue graciously showed them the latest cars and answered Jonathan's many questions. When he had no more to ask, she gave him a stack of marketing brochures to take home. Goodbyes were said, and the DeLucas quibbled about cars all the way home.

* * *

After dinner that night, Anna washed the dishes while Jonathan covered the dining room table with spreadsheets and projections. Her domestic chores fulfilled, she walked over to him and gave him an affectionate kiss on the cheek. "What's all this?" she asked, sitting down at the table.

He pointed to the printout. "Those are the projected investment returns for a deal I've been putting together," he replied. "I'm going to show you why we can afford to get you a decent car."

Jonathan had been talking about putting a deal together ever since they had gotten engaged, but Anna didn't know that he was actively working on one. He handed her a second spreadsheet and said proudly, "And *these* are the projected commissions I'll make, depending on how many investors I can get into the pool."

Anna dealt with financial statements and projections every day in her work, but she had never seen anything like these numbers. The profits for investors were astronomical, and the commissions to Jonathan were extraordinary. Depending on how much money he brought into the pool, Jonathan could earn up to two million dollars per year.

She wanted to be supportive of her husband, but the attorney in her couldn't believe her eyes. Rather than risk bursting his bubble, she put on her lawyer hat and asked questions. "So how does it work? Why are the returns so enormous?"

Jonathan paced the small living room, his arms moving non-stop in animated gestures. "First, I put together a pool of investors," he said. "Then the pool invests in standby letters of credit issued by the world's largest banks—Deutsche Bank, Credit Suisse, or Barclay's Bank, for example. The massive returns are generated because the investment pool buys the letters of credit at a deep discount, then the banks sell them back into the secondary market at a big profit." He stopped his pacing and looked at Anna, a wide grin on his face. "And I get paid commissions on every penny of it."

Anna asked the obvious questions. "If it's such a great deal, why isn't the whole business world talking about it? More importantly, if it's such a great deal, why don't *we* invest in it?"

Jonathan was ready for this line of questioning and replied without missing a beat. "The program is highly confidential because the banks issuing the standby letters of credit want it that way. These deals are only done by the top ten financial institutions in the world. You have to know someone on the inside to get in the investment pool, and the banks require strict non-disclosure agreements."

"How did you get in on it?"

"Do you remember when I told you about my former business partner, Hamid Halabi?"

She didn't. "Who?"

"My old partner in the real estate development business. Anyway, we wanted to branch out and were just getting started on one of these bank investment deals when Hamid returned to Saudi Arabia." Jonathan saw recognition dawning in Anna's eyes as she started to remember the story. "Back at that time," he continued, "I knew an investment banker at Barclay's in London. He tracked me down at the dealership somehow and called me just last week." Jonathan pointed to the papers scattered around the table. "His team of analysts put these numbers together and sent them to me. He wants me to put together a new investment pool."

Jonathan got up from the table and went into the kitchen to refresh his cocktail. "Now, to answer your second question, *we* can't invest because I'm making commissions on the deal. As you know, counselor, that's a conflict of interest; besides, why risk our own money when we'll get rich on my commissions anyway?"

Anna had a dozen other questions, and Jonathan was getting frustrated with her, but he needed to practice his pitch so he forced himself to be patient. If he could satisfy her analytical curiosity, he could satisfy anyone's.

She finally started losing steam because the conversation was as boring as the ones she endured all day at work, and she was exhausted. Her closing comment on the subject was lawyerly advice. "You know that you have to be registered with the State of Texas as a broker-dealer to legally sell the kind of credit instruments you're talking about, don't you?"

"The lawyers at Barclay's have already considered that and concluded that I don't have to register because I'm not selling anything," Jonathan replied. He waved his hand dismissively. "I'm just making referrals to the banks, who *are* registered as broker-dealers."

Anna was unconvinced. "I'm serious Jonathan. As a securities lawyer, I know what I'm talking about. You could get hit with big fines and jail time if you aren't properly registered."

Jonathan turned pale at the word "jail," but hastily recovered and scowled. "Can't you act like my wife for once instead of thinking like a goddam lawyer all the time? I'm your husband, and I would really appreciate it if you were more supportive of me."

He got up and crossed his arms, glaring at her. Shaking his head in disbelief at his spouse's failings, he went upstairs to his dressing room, shutting the door behind him and leaving her alone to ponder her many mistakes.

Anna went to bed alone for the first time since they had married, but she didn't sleep.

* * *

Anna didn't share Jonathan's financial optimism and wouldn't budge on a new Benz. He was tired of listening to her complain about how much her rental car was costing, so he walked over to GEM's used car lot across the street from the main dealership. He found the swarthy manager, Buddy Boudreaux, smoking a cigarette out in the parking lot. The recently divorced used car salesman helped Jonathan locate a gunmetal gray SL320 convertible with ten years on the clock but only five thousand miles on the odometer. Jonathan negotiated a deal for his wife and took the documents home for her to sign later that night.

After she left for work the next morning, he made copies of the signed papers on her old ink-jet printer, then went back to the used car lot. He gave Buddy the originals and asked for his referral fee on the sale in cash. "You know how it is, Buddy," he said. "My ex finds out about every check I get. Then she calls her lawyer, and then he calls me, and on and on. Bitch must be psychic or something. She's bleeding me dry, man."

Buddy nodded knowingly and sympathetically. In the interest of brotherhood and for the pleasure of screwing over an ex-wife, even if it wasn't *his* ex-wife, he opened the safe and paid Jonathan's fee in cash.

Chapter 9

Anna's work schedule went from barely bearable to outright brutal. In addition to the Nerd Merger, she was working on an IPO for one of Harry Vincent's clients. The company had developed a highly efficient wind turbine and needed capital to help build the towering structures. The project was in the very early stages, when utmost secrecy was required by federal law. In furtherance of the cabal of silence, one of the lawyers had given the IPO the code name "Project Blowhard," which led to a lot of off-color jokes around the conference table.

While eating lunch at her desk and cleaning out her inbox between conference calls one day, she came across the B&V monthly deal summary. An electronic newsletter, it relayed requests from clients of the firm who were looking for something—a company to buy or sell, a chief executive officer to hire, a programmer to design software, and so on. The information was strictly confidential and subject to the attorney-client privilege.

One of the entries caught Anna's eye. Larry Frederickson, a partner in the real estate section, had a client who was looking for investors to help fund the construction of a resort on a private island off St. Bart's in the Caribbean Sea. The island was named Hibiscus Cay, and the development would cover most of it, consisting of single family homes, condominiums, a five-star hotel, and a world-class golf course. Also in the plans was marina that would be built in the harbor at the island's southern end. Although suitable for the largest of private yachts, its waters were too shallow to permit entry to the leviathan cruise ships and the teeming tourist hordes they carried, thus ensuring the island's exclusivity and tranquility.

Remembering that Jonathan talked a lot about real estate projects, Anna called Larry. He was in the office and had time to talk, so they discussed the project for a few minutes, identifying what information could be disclosed without signed confidentiality agreements in hand.

Over dinner that night, she told Jonathan what she could about Hibiscus Cay. Because most of the information was privileged, she could only describe the project in broad and vague terms, omitting confidential details. The paucity of information aside, Jonathan was clearly excited about the island development. "This is a wonderful coincidence," he said, almost joyous. "Jack Garrison called me just the other day to touch base. You remember Jack. He represents Lamar Buchanan. Lamar is always looking for new projects, and Jack specifically asked me to let him know if I ever came across an interesting real estate opportunity in the thirty-five-million-dollar range." Jonathan was almost buzzing with nervous energy, striding animatedly back and forth across the small living room as he spoke. "Can you set up a meeting?" he asked eagerly.

Wholeheartedly wanting to help her husband succeed in his business endeavors, Anna said, "I'll call Larry in the morning. I'll try to get you a meeting, but I can't promise anything, and I can't promise when."

Jonathan was near giddy with delight, causing a look of concern to come over Anna's face. "Everything I just told you about the project is very confidential," she admonished. "Please don't mention it to anyone yet. I could get into a lot of trouble."

Jonathan took offense, his bright smile darkening into a scowl. "Of course, I won't tell anyone. Don't you trust me?"

Anna assured him that she did, not wanting to displease him again so soon after their last argument.

* * *

Jonathan ignored Anna's lecture on legal ethics completely. He couldn't wait to tell Marilyn Beauregard about the project. The voluptuous real estate icon was Jonathan's current extramarital entertainment and a major power player in the luxury high-rise condominium market. Although there were no condo towers planned for Hibiscus Cay, there was a big residential component to the project. Marilyn was well-connected to many wealthy international scions of business and was a natural fit for the project; besides, it was his birthday, Anna was traveling again, and he had no wish to spend the night alone.

The illicit lovers had first met at Levy's Grill a month earlier. Jonathan had been frequenting the establishment at lunch time and the occasional happy hour ever since Anna told him that all the big players in Dallas real estate congregated there for lunch meetings and post-closing cocktails. The decor was Swedish minimalist and the topic was real estate, Levy's being the gathering place for brokers, buyers, sellers, developers, mortgage bankers, appraisers, and title company executives. It mattered not if the property was commercial or residential, single-use or mixed-used, high-density or low-density, high-priced or bargain basement—deals were in the air at the popular establishment.

Jonathan had been there one cold January afternoon, sipping a scotch on the rocks and sniffing for opportunities while talking real estate with the other patrons in the bustling bar. He glanced idly out the glass front door of the restaurant and saw a gold Rolls-Royce Phantom Drophead Coupe pull to a stop at the entrance. He watched as the woman belonging to the half million-dollar car emerged and walked through the door.

She was short—five feet if an inch—and cozily wrapped in a full-length silver fox coat. Just about everyone in the room knew who Marilyn Beauregard was, and Jonathan recognized her immediately, watching intently as she entered the restaurant and located her lunch companion at a table in the back. She waggled her fingers at her friend in greeting, her gold Rolex Oyster with a sapphire face and a diamond bezel glinting in the restaurant's halogen lights. The Rolex was not alone. There were three tennis bracelets keeping it company—one with diamonds, one with rubies, and one with diamonds and rubies.

Marilyn's energy and determination were legendary, her business acumen having been the subject of many newspaper and magazine articles. A human dynamo, she was the Honey Badger and the Tasmanian Devil all wrapped up in one hot exterior. Well-known and highly respected for her straight-talking, take-no-prisoners negotiating style, she radiated sex and was obscenely rich. Rumor had it that she pulled down over five million dollars a year in commissions.

The provocative realtor sashayed seductively over to the table and shrugged off her furry refuge, unveiling a red St. John's knit suit that matched her rubies and showed off her enormous breasts to great advantage. She was heavily made up, and Jonathan could tell that she was no stranger to the plastic surgeon's knife, but the package was stunning. He was already bored with Anna in bed, rarely bothering to sleep with her after he got access to her bank account and credit. He still had many appetites to sate, and Marilyn Beauregard was an overflowing cornucopia of potential satisfaction.

He watched the two women chat and sip wine until the waiter left to place their orders, then put down his drink and sauntered over to the table. "I am so sorry to interrupt," he said, bowing elegantly, "but I just had to come over to tell you that you are the most beautiful woman I have ever seen."

Demurely polite and oozing Southern charm, the "Condo Queen"—as Marilyn was known in real estate circles—invited him to join them until their lunches arrived. After a brief conversation and the exchange of business cards, Jonathan left when the waiter returned. He immediately called the florist because Marilyn truly did stand out in a crowd.

They had kept in touch since then, often lunching or meeting for coffee at an intimate out-of-the way café. His marital status mattered not to her because she had no interest in any type of commitment with anyone other than her one true flame—a six-foot six-inch oil wildcatter turned fraudster and multiple felon.

Her larcenous lover was presently cooling his heels in a low-security federal prison in Beaumont, Texas, having been convicted of selling worthless interests in imaginary oil wells. Marilyn made no secret of the fact that she was standing by her wayward man. But she was a woman with needs after all, and Jonathan was enthusiastically committed to satisfying them.

The night of Jonathan's birthday, they enjoyed a three-course gourmet meal delivered to Marilyn's penthouse, then went straight to her luxuriously appointed bed. After Marilyn's multiple orgasms, and despite Anna's multiple warnings about confidentiality, Jonathan told the Condo Queen all about Hibiscus Cay. She was absolutely thrilled when he asked her to be the primary sales representative for the project.

* * *

It took a few days to arrange, but Anna put together a meeting for Jonathan with Larry Frederickson and his client Peter Grand, the real estate developer. Anna and Larry were standing outside one of B&V's conference rooms on the forty-fifth floor when they spotted Peter walking down the hall with a large cardboard tube under his arm. Larry was just introducing him to her when she saw Jonathan coming down the same hall with a short, expensively dressed woman by his side. She was wearing a perfectly tailored pink Chanel suit, the skirt quite short and her ample bosom nearly bursting free of her low-cut silk blouse.

Anna thought she looked familiar but couldn't place her until introductions were made all around. She immediately recognized the name Marilyn Beauregard because the well-known realtor was regularly featured in the society pages and business sections of the *Dallas Morning News* and *Dallas Magazine*. Regardless of who Jonathan's guest was, Anna was infuriated with him for breaching the lawyer-client privilege and bringing a stranger to the meeting. She was going to have to do some serious damage control with Larry and do it fast.

A nervous Jonathan, a puzzled Anna, and a nonchalant Marilyn settled into swiveling leather armchairs on one side of the table. Larry sat down on the other side, while Peter remained standing.

In his early fifties, of medium height, and amorphously shaped, Peter had tousled salt and pepper hair and wore a rumpled blue blazer, a yellow polo shirt, and khaki pants. He opened the cardboard tube and unrolled a sheaf of over-sized papers, including blueprints, artists' renderings, and spreadsheets. Using them to show the group where and how Hibiscus Cay would take shape, he discussed in detail the estimated development costs and explained the potential income streams.

When he finished his presentation, he sat down and said, "Now that you've seen the plans, let me explain why I'm here today. I currently own fifty percent of the island, and I have a partner who owns the other fifty percent. We're looking for one or more investors to put in a minimum of thirty-five million dollars to buy out my partner's interest and to fund development costs and operating expenses until the project starts paying for itself." He looked at Jonathan and nodded.

Jonathan stood up and addressed Peter. "Thank you for the opportunity to meet with you," he began. "I would like you to know that I have extensive experience in financing real estate developments. I have arranged funding for shopping centers, office buildings, condominiums, and warehouses from Pennsylvania to California." He went on to tell the Hamid Halabi story in self-aggrandizing detail, his narrative ripe with embellishments and puffery. Touting Hamid's unlimited wealth and worldwide financial contacts, he extolled the virtues of the successful projects the two of them had put together in the late 1990s. When his brief presentation was over, he turned to Marilyn and smiled.

Marilyn had been quietly taking notes in a pink leather portfolio with a gold Mont Blanc fountain pen. She took her cue and stood up, smiling at the men at the table and directing her comments to Peter. "I know you're wondering why I'm here. As you probably already know, I'm an expert in real estate sales, and although I usually specialize in high-rise condominium properties, real estate is real estate. I have a vast network of clients and moneyed contacts all over the world to draw on."

She leaned forward and pointed her ample cleavage directly at Peter, handing him a brochure that described her company and the prestigious properties it represented. Her voice breathy and suggestive, she said, "I know I could be a valuable asset to you."

Peter blinked nervously and took the brochure, never taking his eyes off Marilyn's décolletage. The meeting wrapped up, the parties having agreed that Jonathan would locate investors for Hibiscus Cay and be paid a fee of six percent of any money he raised. Marilyn would be the official and primary sales agent for the residential side of the project, also earning a six percent commission on every sale she made. Larry would continue to represent Peter and prepare the initial legal documentation, but Anna could not have anything to do with the project due to the conflicts of interest posed by her marriage to Jonathan. Having the same law firm represent both sides of a transaction was the most mortal of sins in the nebulous world of legal ethics.

After the others left, Anna asked Larry to stay behind, apologizing to him profusely for the breach of confidentiality that her husband had committed by involving a third party in the meeting without getting a waiver from Larry's client. Larry shrugged off the technical infraction with his usual equanimity, and she was immensely relieved. Now she would have to impress upon Jonathan the severity of his transgression. In turn, he was going to have to explain how he knew Marilyn Beauregard and why he hadn't told her that he was bringing her to the meeting.

* * *

It was early May, and the azalea bushes bordering the sidewalks and paths along Turtle Creek were still in full, vibrant bloom, the leafy bushes bursting with spring's colorful bounty. Crepe paper blossoms in pink, purple, orange and fuchsia fluttered like butterflies in the gentle spring breeze, their flowery wings blazing gloriously in the warming sun.

Anna finally had a Saturday afternoon off, so she and Cindy took advantage of the balmy weather to have lunch on the patio at a popular restaurant in Highland Park Village. During late spring and early summer, the locals preferred to eat al fresco, relaxing in the cool shade of mature trees and watching luxury cars disgorge the affluent clientele that swarmed the patio like high society bees.

Anna and Cindy hadn't seen each other in months, and their phone calls had been few and far between. Anna didn't have the heart to tell Cindy—who was dressed today in a prim vintage yellow

Christian Dior day suit—that one of the reasons was Jonathan. He genuinely disliked Cindy, claiming that she was too loud and bohemian for his tastes. The DeLucas recently had a nasty argument when Jonathan went so far as to tell Anna that he didn't want Cindy around. Anna had no idea what Cindy could possibly have done to engender such rabid opprobrium from Jonathan, but rather than argue with him, she only made plans with Cindy when he was working.

The two friends munched on caprese salads and steamed mussels while observing the Saturday lunch crowd. They were debating the wisdom of ordering dessert when Cindy, who had always been a devout bachelorette, said, "I can't believe you've been married almost six months." She looked at Anna inquisitively. "Is it everything you had hoped it would be?"

Anna stumbled over her words. "Uh, most of the time. Well, um, some of the time. I mean . . ."

Cindy's brow furrowed out of concern. "What is it? What's wrong?"

"Nothing in particular," Anna replied. "Just little things."

"Such as?"

"Well, for starters, Jonathan absolutely despises Nicky. He got really upset when I spent time with him at our wedding reception, letting me know in uncertain terms that he doesn't want us even talking to each other."

Cindy tried to show encouragement. "Well, that's typical of men generally, don't you think? Besides, it's kind of romantic knowing that someone cares enough about you to get jealous."

"I thought so at first, but now I'm not so sure," Anna replied. "The other night he did something that really bothered me. I always take the phone into another room when I get a phone call because I think it's rude to talk on the phone in front of someone else. I got a work-related call the other night, so I took the phone into the bedroom. When I finished the call and came back out, Jonathan went ballistic, demanding to know who I was talking to and accusing me of hiding things from him. He was so mad . . ."

Anna's voice trailed off and her shoulders slumped. She was too embarrassed to tell Cindy about the big fight she and Jonathan had over Marilyn Beauregard, and she was unwilling to admit to anyone that something about Jonathan had changed since the honeymoon.

Cindy skewered a mussel with her fork, popping it into her mouth like a gumdrop. "Has he ever hit you?"

"Oh, god no, never," Anna protested. She started tallying and touting her husband's positive points, ticking them off one by one on her fingers, as if trying to convince herself that nothing was wrong. "He's very romantic and still sends me flowers every month. We have a lot in common. We like the same food, the same music, the same movies, and we share the same religious and political views. His parents have taken me into their family unquestioningly."

She looked at Cindy, searching for approval in her eyes. Cindy didn't approve, but she didn't want to get into an argument with her best friend on such a beautiful day. Instead of giving Anna her honest opinion, she chided her for not answering her emails. Anna didn't remember getting any emails from Cindy and chalked it up to a technology glitch, making a quickly forgotten mental note to check her home computer.

They concentrated quietly on their dessert menus for a few minutes, then Anna closed hers and said, "There's one more thing." She drained her wine glass and put it down. "I'm a little worried about how Jonathan handles money."

Cindy bit her tongue and forced herself not to say what her instincts were screaming at her to say. Her eyes sparking, she patted the corners of her mouth daintily with her linen napkin and raised one eyebrow. "How so?"

Anna heard herself say out loud the things that she had been trying to avoid thinking about for months. "He doesn't make nearly as much money as he told me and seems to spend it all before the next paycheck."

Not being the kind of friend who would say "I told you so," Cindy felt that she had to say something or she'd burst. "Do you think he might be a compulsive spender like your first husband?" she ventured.

Anna bristled at the comparison. "You know I love you, but you really don't know what you're talking about. You don't know Jonathan like I do."

85

That was true, so Cindy surrendered without a fight to defuse the situation. "Anna, honey, please don't be mad at me," she said. "You know me—always sticking my nose into other people's business when I shouldn't. Let's just forget the whole thing, enjoy this glorious weather, and order something deliciously decadent for dessert. In a few weeks, it'll feel like the inside of a hairdryer out here, and the spring flowers will look like extra-crispy bacon."

Just then, a mockingbird perched on a tree limb arching over their table squawked and made a deposit directly into Anna's wine glass. Cindy laughed so hard that chardonnay squirted out of her nose, effectively dissipating the tension between them. The friendship intact, they sat on the sun-dappled patio drinking wine, sharing juicy gossip, and polishing off a couple of pieces of chocolate cheesecake.

* * *

Cindy called Nicky as soon as she got back to the gallery. She summarized the lunchtime conversation, making no bones about her opinion of Anna's new husband. "I don't like Jonathan," she said point blank. "I think Anna rushed into the marriage, and she's either still so in love or so insecure about dying alone that she can't think straight. It also worries me that he's deliberately isolating her from her friends. I don't know what to do."

"I've had similar concerns," Nicky admitted. "But there's not much we can do about it. You know how hard-headed our soft-hearted Anna is."

"I know, but I'm afraid that if we meddle, we could wound her deeply and lose her friendship altogether. She was really upset when I suggested that Jonathan was like her ex-husband."

"If Anna is that blinded by love," Nicky pointed out, "she wouldn't listen to us anyway. All we can do is keep our opinions to ourselves and hope that he turns out to be a standup guy and not another empty suit. Only time will tell."

Cindy sighed. "You're absolutely right. I just wish there was something more we could do."

Nicky agreed.

Chapter 10

Jonathan couldn't believe his luck. Hibiscus Cay was manna from heaven, his ticket to the big time, and a legitimate deal for a change. He was finally going to be rich—not Bill Gates or Mark Zuckerberg rich—but definitely a multi-millionaire. Every gear in his brain was turning fast, the numbers and projections making him dizzy at the prospect of making a big score off Lamar Buchanan. It was a score so big that he could dump Anna and marry Marilyn if he wanted to. Big enough that he could get the hell out of Texas and go where the real money was—Palm Beach, Palm Springs, maybe even Europe. But he had a lot of work to do to get there, so he got busy.

The first thing he did after the meeting with Peter Grand was to call Jack Garrison. It took a few minutes to get past the vigilant receptionist, but Jack finally came on the line. Jonathan reintroduced himself and got straight to the point. "I've found a perfect investment for Lamar," he said. "It's a mixed-used real estate development with a minimum investment of thirty-five million."

"I'm listening," Jack said.

Jonathan made his pitch for Hibiscus Cay. He knew his skills had gotten rusty, like a baseball player who had been benched for too long, but he could feel himself getting back into his old groove as he presented the deal. He was skillful at selling things and ideas by appealing to the universal emotion shared, consciously or subconsciously, by just about everyone in the world—greed. As his speech was coming to an end, he tossed in the confidential revenue estimates that Peter had given him.

When Jonathan finished his pitch, Jack said, "It sure sounds like Lamar's kind of deal, but I've got to be honest with you. I asked around after we met at the polo match last year, and frankly, no one in the real estate business that I know has ever heard of you."

Jonathan's jaws clenched and his hands started to shake, forcing him to clutch the phone so tightly that his knuckles turned white. He willed himself not to get angry. "Oh, that's probably because I was the silent partner," he said with forced nonchalance. "I was always the behind-the-scenes strategic planning guy. Hamid Halabi was the face and financier of the organization."

Like other in-the-know real estate heavy hitters, Jack had heard of Hamid Halabi. Hamid had appeared on the commercial real estate scene suddenly and explosively, cutting a colorful swath across New Jersey, Colorado, and California. He threw millions around like chicken feed and built several successful developments before vanishing just as suddenly as he had appeared, blown back to Saudi Arabia in a sandstorm of unsavory circumstances after a string of highly publicized scandals. One of the tabloids printed photos of a bevy of blonde prostitutes helping him snort cocaine off the washboard-flat belly of a former Playboy centerfold. Shortly after that, an inebriated Hamid fled the scene of an accident after his Ferrari F12 Berlinetta careened off Beverly Hills Boulevard, taking out three parked cars and a stop sign before glancing off a tree and coming to its sudden and final rest as a pile of scrap metal. Hamid was unscathed, but his uncle was livid, summoning his wayward nephew home to his five homely wives as punishment.

Because of the horny Hamid's speedy return to his homeland, never to be seen in the United States again, it was impossible to verify Jonathan's claims of a business connection with him.

Jack didn't say anything for a few seconds. Jonathan sensed his hesitation and broke the brief silence. "If it makes you more comfortable," he said, "I have in-house counsel now, so to speak. I married Anna Thornbury. Of course, her name is Anna DeLuca now, but she's still a hotshot lawyer at B&V. You may remember her from the polo match."

"I remember her," Jack said. "B&V is a very reputable firm."

Sensing an opportunity, Jonathan went in for the close. "The developer of Hibiscus Cay and I would like to meet with you and Lamar at your earliest convenience to discuss the project. Which day of the week and time of day are best for you?"

He could hear papers rustling in the background and held his breath until Jack finally said, "Be at our offices on June 16th at 9:00 a.m. sharp. You'll have fifteen minutes to make your presentation."

Highly frustrated that the date was six weeks away, Jonathan nonetheless kept his composure. "That will be perfect," he said, cool as sweet iced tea in August. "I look forward to the meeting with you and Lamar."

"You'll only be meeting with me and my deal team," Jack said. "Lamar never attends preliminary meetings in person for anything under one hundred million."

Jonathan still wasn't ready to end the conversation and forged ahead. "What a coincidence," he said cheerfully. "It just so happens that I'm also putting together an international finance deal in that very range."

"One thing at a time," Jack said, curtly cutting him off. "Let's see how the first meeting goes." A female voice in the background called Jack's name. "I have to take another call," he said and hung up abruptly.

* * *

It was only the middle of June and already so hot that the highway shimmered under the sun's onslaught as Jonathan drove Peter to their meeting with Jack Garrison. Jonathan was missing the dealership's Monday morning sales meeting again. He knew he'd get in trouble for that, but he'd just lie and say his mother had a heart attack or something.

They arrived at the offices of Buchanan Enterprises, located in the eponymously named Buchanan Building. An imposing, polished granite building in downtown Fort Worth, it jutted from the flat Texas plains surrounding it like a Saturn rocket ready for liftoff from Cape Cowtown. They rode the elevator to the fiftieth floor and entered the plush reception area overlooking the city from three directions, the top floor offering a view so vast that the buildings of downtown Dallas could be seen off to the east. Texas-themed oil paintings bursting with bluebonnets, cattle drives, and oil rigs adorned the walls, and Frederic Remington bronzes dotted the lobby, the lifelike horses galloping in place atop black marble pedestals.

They sat in high-backed leather armchairs while they waited, sipping gourmet coffee that the cheerful receptionist had gotten for them. Jonathan's hands were trembling so hard that his coffee cup was rattling, the delicate porcelain cup chattering against the saucer "rat-tat-tat" like a set of gag gift wind-up dentures. He had to put the cup down to keep Peter from noticing and to keep himself from spilling hot coffee on his new suit.

A brisk tapping on the polished marble floors announced the arrival of Miss Jessica, Jack's executive assistant. A stunning model-tall blonde in a clingy red Diane von Furstenburg wrap dress and four-inch stiletto heels, she ushered them through double glass doors into a large conference room. Jack was seated at the far end of the biggest conference table Jonathan had ever seen. A slim oval shape, its finely grained wood was so dark and highly polished that it reflected the LED spotlights above it like an ebony mirror.

Five other men and two women sat around the impressive statement piece, all of them wearing expensive power suits and impatient looks. Miss Jessica indicated where Jonathan and Peter were to sit with a friendly gesture of her perfectly manicured hand, then left, closing the doors behind her with an almost imperceptible click.

Jack glanced down at his watch, then back up at Jonathan and Peter. "Good morning, gentlemen," he said. "You have exactly fifteen minutes."

* * *

Jack was in Lamar's office minutes a few minutes after Jonathan and Peter finished their Hibiscus Cay presentation. Unlike the down-home decor of the lobby, Lamar's penthouse work space was sleek and ultra-modern. Windows on three sides and an uncluttered glass desk allowed the Fort Worth skyline to blend into the space, as if the office occupants were floating on a cloud above the city's center.

He was staring out the floor-to-ceiling windows, his hands clasped behind his back. Dressed casually for the day, he was wearing crisply pressed blue jeans, a white oxford shirt, and black Tony Lama cowboy boots. A summer weight Ralph Lauren jacket hung on a coat rack that could have doubled for a Giacametti sculpture and might have been one.

A living Texas legend, Lamar was the youngest son of a millionaire oilman from Lubbock. Six feet tall and wiry, he had a full head of sandy hair framing a tanned, craggy face sculpted by the West Texas sun and wind. After working as a roughneck on his daddy's oil rigs for a few years after high school, he enrolled in Harvard, earning undergraduate and master's degrees in business. He ran the family oil enterprises for a few years before striking out on his own, and by age forty-five had amassed a net worth of six point two billion with a "B" dollars. Not resting on his petroleum laurels, he diversified his investment strategy, starting a private equity firm and hiring the country's most brilliant financial minds. Investing methodically in real estate, pharmaceuticals, technology, telecommunications, solar energy, and wind farming, he quadrupled his already impressive fortune. Known to be a ruthless negotiator, he was as deadly as a pissed off scorpion when it came to money and amassing huge quantities of it.

Despite his business reputation, Lamar was an old-school, Texas gentlemen, although six years of Ivy League education had diminished his West Texas drawl to near extinction, save the occasional "Y'all" among his closest friends. He was faultlessly polite around women, never failing to say "Yes, ma'am" and "No, ma'am" and "Thank you, ma'am" when talking to a lady, whether addressing his eighty-year-old sainted mother or his thirty-year-old trophy wife.

He was highly secretive, almost to the point of paranoia, and took great pains to stay out of the news. His charitable activities often frustrated his desire for privacy because he routinely gave away hundreds of millions of dollars, heaping mounds of cash on a myriad of worthy causes. But his public largesse belied his frugal nature. Though enormously wealthy, he never spent money frivolously or needlessly, eschewing public displays of wealth. Although he could easily afford his own fleet of jets, he flew commercial. He was frugal on the ground as well as in the air. So as not to draw undue attention from kidnappers and carjackers, he was chauffeured in a beige four-door sedan, and his driver was also his armed bodyguard. That was just common sense for a man in his financial position.

It was true, as Jack had told Jonathan, that Lamar didn't personally attend meetings unless the dollar amounts were large enough to capture his attention. Instead, he recorded every one of them using sophisticated technology. When time permitted, as it had today, he'd watch the meetings in real time.

"So," he said, walking to his desk and taking a seat in his Lucite desk chair. "What do you think? Are these guys for real?"

"Peter Grand is for real," Jack replied, idly scratching the bridge of his nose. "I've heard of him before, and it was easy to check him out." He flipped through his notes. "He's not a big player, but he's built some successful projects and has a reputation for honesty." He pulled another folder from the stack in his lap. "Jonathan DeLuca, on the other hand, is Mister Zero. We ran a preliminary background check and couldn't find anything on the guy. We were only able to confirm that he works at GEM Motorcars. That was easy, since we buy our vehicle fleet from Garrett Mason. As to DeLuca's real estate experience, we had the same problem. He said he did deals with Hamid Halabi, so unfortunately . . ."

Lamar knew the Hamid Halabi story and finished Jack's sentence for him. "There's no way to check him out."

"Exactly."

The two men bandied scenarios about for about ten minutes until Lamar said, "Who's up next?"

Jack glanced at his phone. "Texas Sun Technologies, a new solar power startup."

"Ok, get it going. I have charity golf game out at the Colonial Country Club with Bill Clinton and George Bush in an hour."

* * *

After waiting impatiently for a full ten days for a call from Jack, Jonathan was ecstatic when he finally got the news. Hibiscus Cay had made it past the first screening, and Lamar's people were ready to start their due diligence. A team of forensic business investigators, analysts, and accountants would delve deeply into everything pertaining to the island and its current owners. Copies of the blueprints, artists' renderings, forecasts, and projections were couriered to Lamar's team of corporate inquisitors, who would look for every detail relevant to an informed investment decision. The information would be sorted, scoured, analyzed, and questioned, then analyzed again before Lamar would even agree to agree to a deal.

In the meantime, Larry Frederickson and Lamar's team of lawyers had agreed that it was time to form a business entity to serve as the corporate vehicle through which the Hibiscus Cay project would be funded and operated, and through which profits would flow to its stakeholders. Jack and Lamar weren't comfortable with Jonathan heading the new company because they still hadn't been able to check his background in several critical ways. Jonathan had also admitted in their first meeting that his credit rating was abysmal, blaming it on his ex-wife's spending habits.

Not surprisingly, the lawyers warmed quickly to Jonathan's suggestion that his attorney wife be the sole stockholder, director, office, and secretary of the new company. Anna would wear those many hats in name only and would resign when operating funds were available to hire and pay a team personally chosen by Lamar to oversee his interests. Handling little more than minor administrative matters in the interim, she alone would control the corporate coffers. All parties would be required to sign documents waiving the various conflicts of interest.

Assuring the others that the proposed business arrangement would be acceptable to Anna, Jonathan was doomed to disappointment when he told her about it over dinner that night. Her arguments against the arrangement were legion, but Jonathan dispatched her complaints and protests with one master stroke.

"Are you really going to defy Lamar Buchanan *and* a senior partner at your law firm?" he asked, effectively ending the discussion.

Anna knew that refusing to act as head of the new company could interfere with the Hibiscus Cay project, thereby impeding the desires of a B&V client and possibly angering a powerful business tycoon in the bargain. Further forcing her hand was the fact that Larry Frederickson was on the firm's partnership committee and could end her legal career with a one sentence memo. Her job at risk if she didn't comply, she gave in to Jonathan's disturbing logic and a quartet of high-powered attorneys, agreeing to be the temporary head of the new enterprise.

Jonathan named the newly-formed company Frescobaldi Prime Investments. It needed a bank account, so he and Anna had lunch with Daniel "Please, call me Dan" Fairfield. A financial advisor in the wealth management division of Silverman Baggins, he managed Jonathan's 401(k) account—along with those of most of the employees at GEM. An affable optimist and old school southern gentlemen with an easy laugh and impeccable references, he opened a corporate account for the company and gave Anna a checkbook. She put it in her desk at home and forgot about it, given that there was no money in the account and none was on the near horizon.

Chapter 11

The air conditioner in Jonathan's new, ruby red STS demo car was barely keeping the inside temperature tolerable as one hundred and three unrelenting degrees beat down on the hood in paint-blistering waves. The heat was on him in a lot of ways. Prolonged absences from the dealership and long breaks spent sitting in his car making calls on his cell phone had drawn disapproving notice from the higher-ups. His immediate boss, Eric Adams, had already thoroughly berated him during his first quarter review, giving him ninety days to turn things around. Eighty-five of those days had passed with no improvement, and Eric made it unequivocally clear that if Jonathan wasn't working the phones or on the showroom floor eight hours a day, six days a week, he'd be fired and forced to repay his monthly draws going back to the first of the year.

Making matters worse, he was three months behind on his child support. His ex-wife was nagging him about it and threatening to turn him in and get him sent to jail. She knew he'd rather die than go to jail. On top of that, his current wife kept reminding him that his paychecks had steadily diminished to zero since they had gotten married, while his spending habits hadn't changed. Then his lawyer and former friend, David, dropped him as a client and he couldn't afford the retainer for a new attorney.

Trying to put a positive spin on things, he arrived at the dealership in better spirits. He knew he could at least count on the DuPrees, who were back in Dallas for their annual car purchase. He wasn't just selling Fred a car today, though. He was going to close him on the prime bank deal too. After that, he'd have enough money to quit his job, catch up on child support, and live off Anna until Lamar Buchanan and Hibiscus Cay vaulted him into the big time.

While the DuPrees were waiting for their new car to be washed and detailed, Jonathan invited them for coffee at a small restaurant across the street from the dealership. Mrs. DuPree's hair was pale pink this time, the tiny woman bearing a remarkable likeness to Texas State Fair cotton candy with eyes. Fred looked very much like a 1950s gas station attendant in a beige, short-sleeved, self-belted, polyester jumpsuit and beige tennis shoes.

Jonathan escorted them carefully across six lanes of traffic and into a small coffee shop in a bustling strip mall. He winked at the hostess upon entering, and they were immediately escorted to a booth near the back. After ten minutes of strong coffee and meaningless chitchat, he took advantage of a pause in Mrs. Dupree's ramblings about children and grandchildren. "So, Mr. DuPree," he interjected, "Did you have any more questions since we last spoke about the documents I sent you?"

"Yes, I do," Mr. DuPree replied. "And please call me Fred."

Jonathan leaned in closer and patted the large manila envelope he had brought with him and put on the table. "Just remember, sir," he whispered to Fred conspiratorially, "the opportunities I'm presenting are only available to sophisticated investors like you. Everything I'm about to tell you is highly, highly confidential." He glanced around the room in search of eavesdroppers, then leaned all the way across the table until he was almost nose-to-nose with Fred. "This deal can double your money in a year, maybe less," he said quietly. "But you must invest soon, and you have to invest a minimum of one hundred fifty thousand dollars."

"I saw your projections and they certainly got my attention, son," Fred whispered back. "But doubling my money in a year sounds too good to be true." The avarice in Fred's eyes betrayed his own words as he added, "I still have some doubts about this."

Frustrated to the point he thought his heart might burst, Jonathan kept himself from erupting in rage and screaming at the old man, *Write the check, you fucking redneck moron!* Instead, he took a few deep breaths and smiled patiently. He had tested his prime bank pitch on

Anna and had been rehearsing his speech like he used to in high school debate club, quizzing himself with flash cards when she wasn't around.

He leaned back in the booth and crossed his arms casually, a sanguine look painting his face. "Of course, Fred. Fire away." Ten minutes later, he had answered all of Fred's questions and summed up by reminding him that the investment would be insured by the FDIC, and the risk was therefore minimal.

Still, Fred hesitated. He shifted uncomfortably in the booth. "I don't know, Jonathan," he said. "A hundred fifty thousand dollars is a lot of money. I'm not sure I want to invest that much all at once."

Jonathan was prepared for such an eventuality. "Not to worry. You can invest in tranches—that means installments. What are you prepared to invest today?"

Fred thought for a moment. "Well, I suppose I could do fifty thousand now and the rest when my T-Bill comes due in December." He glanced at the missus, who was deeply absorbed in eating her blueberry cobbler. He looked back at Jonathan and shrugged. "Sure, why not?" he finally said.

Jonathan pulled a stack of documents out of the manila envelope and shoved them at Fred, helpfully handing him a pen. Colorful tags were attached to multiple pages of the documents, all of them instructing Fred to "Sign here." Jonathan pointed to the markers and explained, "You need to sign wherever there is a tag, and our corporate counsel will sign on behalf of the company later. I'll send you copies of the fully executed documents, along your receipt from First Trust Corporation, the fiduciary that will manage your investment."

Fred nodded and started signing. When he finished with the stack of small-print, single-spaced, doubled-sided legal papers, he took a checkbook from his back pocket and looked inquiringly at Jonathan. "Who do I make this out to?"

"Please make out it out to Frescobaldi Prime Investments LLC."

Fred gave Jonathan a blank look. "Who?"

Jonathan obligingly explained the origin of the unusual name and spelled out "Frescobaldi" for Fred. He paid the check and walked his new investors back to the dealership, giving Mrs. DuPree a box of chocolates and handing Fred an expensive cigar. "I'll give you a call in a couple of months regarding the rest of your investment," he said. "You'll receive your first interest check next March."

"I appreciate that," Fred said. "Thanks for thinking of us." He gave Jonathan a fatherly pat on the back and got in the car.

"Well, you're my best customers and I consider you to be friends," Jonathan said, closing the car door. "Drive safely, sir."

While Fred drove them back to New Orleans, Harriet recounted the events of the day, her head bobbing this way and that like a pink hydrangea in a West Texas windstorm. "I really like that Jonathan from the Cadillac place. So handsome and charming—and married to a lawyer, no less. I don't know why he's just a car salesman." Gazing absentmindedly out the window, she searched for answers in the summer storm clouds boiling off to the west.

Fred was used to the marathon talking sessions that accompanied him on these trips. He'd just nod and say "Yes, dear," from time to time. But he wasn't listening to his wife of forty-five years. He was thinking about international standby letters of credit and how much money he was going to make.

* * *

As soon as the DuPrees left, Jonathan told Eric he had a family emergency and would need to take the afternoon off. He drove home, went upstairs, and opened the box marked "Documents," locating the folder containing copies of the papers Anna had signed when she bought her used Mercedes. He took the folder into her office and rummaged through her desk until he found some blank paper and a pen. After practicing her signature a few times, he forged it on the investment documents that Fred had signed and dropped them in the mail on the way to his second stop.

An hour later, he was knocking on his parents' front door. Gina padded over and stood on her tiptoes to peek through the peephole, startled to see a giant distorted eye looking back at her as she heard a devilish chuckle on the other side of the door. "You almost scared me to death, Johnny," she chided halfheartedly as she opened the door. "You know I hate it when you do that."

"Sorry, Mom," Jonathan said, a sheepish grin on his face. He leaned over and gave her a loving peck on the cheek, producing a bouquet of seasonal flowers from behind his back.

"Oh, Johnny," Gina gushed as she took the bouquet and buried her nose in it, taking in the luscious scent. "You're so thoughtful. Come on in. We're about to have an early supper."

Jonathan entered the apartment to see his father rising feebly from the living room sofa. "What a pleasant surprise, son" Ricky said. "What brings you here in the middle of the afternoon?"

"I have the day off and wanted to see you. I could really use your sage advice about a business proposition," Jonathan replied.

Ricky's eyes turned sad. "I'm sorry, but I'm almost tapped out. I can't get involved in any more of your business ventures."

"No, no, not you, Pops. I just wanted to tell you about the Hibiscus Cay development I'm working on. It's legitimate, I swear." He told his parents all about Peter Grand, Lamar Buchanan, and the new company, Ricky listening with closed eyes. Jonathan thought he looked worn out and losing his fight.

Ricky opened his eyes again. "I think that sounds like a very promising venture, son," he said. "I wish you luck with it, and I hope it pans out."

"That's what I wanted to share with you and Mom," Jonathan said. "It already has." He took Fred's check from his jacket pocket and showed it to his father. "This is a check from our first investor."

Ricky took the check and drew it close to his coke bottle glasses. Peering through the haze of his deteriorating eyesight, he studied both sides of it. "That's wonderful news, Jonathan," he said, handing it back.

Jonathan asked the question he had come to ask. "Could you please cash this check for me? Our new company doesn't have a bank account yet. Anna is out of town for two weeks, and we can't open an account without her."

Ricky was dubious. He'd heard this all before. Jonathan knew the look on his father's face and kept selling. "I promise the check won't bounce," he said. "The investors are solid. You remember the DuPrees from New Orleans, don't you? We had coffee with them last year when they were having their car serviced."

"Yes, I remember," Ricky said, nodding. "Fred's a fine man. A veteran." A puzzled look crossed his wan face. "Can't you just put it in your personal account until Anna gets back?"

Jonathan shrugged helplessly. He felt like a little boy again, lying and pleading with his father the way he used to every time he had to worm his way out of some childhood kerfuffle. "You know 'Miss By-the-Book' Anna," Jonathan said. "She already told me unequivocally that she won't comingle investor funds with our personal funds. She's right you know."

Gina was washing the dishes in the galley kitchen a few feet from the living room, listening to her men talk. Exasperated by her husband, she chimed in. "Ricky DeLuca, your son needs a favor that is easy to do. Why do you put him through this? Just cash the check already." She looked lovingly at her son. "You know we're always here for you, baby boy. No matter what."

Ricky was too tired to argue with her. "Come to the bank with me in the morning," he said. "But after this, no more favors and no more money." He looked in the kitchen to see if his wife was still listening and saw that she wasn't. He turned back to his son and whispered, "I'm almost out of cash until our T-bill comes due."

"This deal is the big one, Pops" Jonathan said. "I can feel it. The family is going to be rich beyond our wildest dreams. I swear I won't ask you for money ever again. I promise."

"I sure hope so, Jonathan," Ricky said, helpless resignation permeating his voice. "I sure hope so."

Chapter 12

Jonathan was on the way to yet another one of his "monthly meetings." His hands were shaking almost uncontrollably, making it hard to hold the steering wheel steady. He had finally gone to the doctor when the tremors had gotten so bad that he couldn't hold on to a pen. Then he started breaking out in cold sweats without warning. The doctor told him that he was having panic attacks and prescribed an anti-anxiety drug, but the attacks were occurring more frequently. Even the much-touted palliative effects of the high-priced, highly-addictive capsules could not suppress the anxiety he felt in advance of these meetings.

He turned the radio up and tried to cheer himself by recounting the details of his latest glorious victory, basking in the near orgasmic pleasure of relieving Fred DuPree of fifty thousand dollars. He planned to use it to pay back some of the money he owed his father and pay his ex-wife just enough child support as necessary to stay out of jail. He'd keep some of the cash for business entertaining and keeping up appearances—at least until Lamar came through and all of Jonathan's financial problems were solved.

His thoughts turned darker as he drove. His doctor had warned him that the pills could make sexual relations difficult, but Jonathan had scoffed at the notion. Unfortunately, the doctor was right, and the problems started soon after he started taking the pills. Jonathan had long since lost interest in Anna physically, but from time to time he forced himself to have sex with her, just so she wouldn't become suspicious. Even when he did think it necessary to service her, he'd have a hard time getting an erection, then couldn't finish the job when he finally did. He could go at her for an hour, but nothing would happen. She obviously wasn't working hard enough to please him, but sexy little Marilyn couldn't satisfy him any more either. He ultimately resorted to using vibrators and had burned through a lot of batteries before he switched to the rechargeable kind. That kept his women happy when he needed them to be, but it didn't do one damn thing to help him. He was horny as hell half of the time, and there wasn't anything he could do about it.

He tried to get his mind off his physical frustrations and deal with the ugly task at hand. Pulling into the familiar strip mall, he parked the car and walked to an ATM that was conveniently located near his destination. After all, just because he had Fred's fifty thousand dollars, there was no need to stop using his wife's paycheck for sundries.

* * *

Officer Harry Wilson arrived at work at his usual time of 6:15 a.m. He switched on the lights in his little corner of the Collin County Supervision and Corrections Department and walked to his gray metal desk as the sickly green glow of fluorescent lights began to wash over the room. Grabbing his *World's Greatest Dad* coffee mug, he shuffled down the hall to the small break room, where someone had already brewed a pot of the day's sludge. He poured some into his mug, splashing a large drop onto his shirt. He swiped at the brown spot with a paper napkin, which did little to remove the stain, but left tiny white clumps of paper all over his shirt.

The cogs in the government's giant wheel began to turn as he walked back to his office, listening to the familiar sounds of a cumbersome bureaucracy waking up. Computers beeped to life, the copier hummed, and sleepy-eyed public servants gossiped while they settled into another day of working for the taxpayers. He got back to his office and squeezed around one of the battered metal office chairs that sat unevenly in front of his desk, turning his thoughts to the morning caseload with a bored detachment born of playing surrogate parent to non-violent criminals for over twenty years.

Harry had once worked for the Dallas County Parole Board, where he had become accustomed to dealing with all types of human detritus. He was not a man of the heroic, selfless servant-to-mankind variety, however. After an unpleasant incident in which a former "client" had gone into a drug-induced rage and attempted to stab him in the neck with a pencil from his own desk, he requested a transfer to a job that carried less physical risk.

He was honest and hardworking and labored diligently to keep track of the dozens of men and women who were under his supervision. Most of them were first-time offenders on probation for various crimes and sundry misdemeanors. Usually from impoverished families and almost always without fathers, his charges usually just needed an authority figure in their lives. Some were aspiring small-time hoods, others were errant adolescents who had chugged a few too many at a party and done something stupid and illegal, but not heinous. Harry always held the slim hope that the younger miscreants he monitored would show up in his part of the law enforcement system only once, then go on to lead productive, crime-free lives.

Then there were the ones who were full-grown adults from relatively stable backgrounds, but who were just plain lazy or wanted a life of ease they could never obtain through legally sanctioned means. Harry had tried over the years to remain impartial and non-judgmental in his dealings with the regularly scheduled flow of society's backwash that flooded his office. He strived to be sympathetic, but his best intentions faltered when he was assigned to monitor the rehabilitative progress of someone he just didn't like.

His first appointment of the day was a perfect example of the type. Good looking and highly intelligent, the man had grown up in a well-to-do family and had a college degree. It wasn't from a fancy East Coast university, but it was a college degree nonetheless. With that mix of nature and nurture going for him, the guy could have been a legitimate success in life, had he stayed inside the bounds of the law. Instead, he was just another smooth-talking phony who took advantage of anyone he could fool with his oily charm and fancy four syllable words. Harry always wanted to take a shower after his monthly appointments with Jonathan DeLuca.

Harry's distaste was enhanced by the fact that, in addition to squandering the natural gifts bestowed upon DeLuca as a member of the lucky sperm club, the feckless piece of shit was downright arrogant. That annoyed him immensely because DeLuca was on probation for conning an elderly couple out of their life savings. The well-dressed reprobate's father had paid over seventy-five thousand dollars to the aged victims, but that was only a portion of their losses. The judge had further justice to dispense, giving DeLuca ten years' probation and ordering him to pay restitution to the defrauded seniors in the amount of two hundred fifteen dollars per month.

Right on time, Jonathan DeLuca came into his office and took a seat. His schedule was tightly packed, so Officer Wilson wasted no time in working through the legally-required litany of questions. "Have you committed any criminal offense in the past month? Are you still employed with GEM Motorcars? Have you left the county in the past month without permission? Are you current in your child support?"

After all the questions were asked and answered to his satisfaction, Officer Wilson got up from his desk and walked to a metal file cabinet in the corner. Opening it, he pulled a specimen cup from a stack in the top drawer and handed it to Jonathan.

"You know the drill," he said. "Fill this in the restroom down the hall. Officer Adams will be observing to make sure you don't switch specimens. And don't forget to make your restitution payment with the clerk on your way out."

* * *

Anna was doing the weekly laundry and cleaning the apartment, an agreement she had with Jonathan since he did all the cooking. She went upstairs to his bathroom to get his towels and empty his trash and couldn't help noticing an ATM receipt and some folded pieces of paper in the waste basket. The discovery made her sigh heavily as she took them out of the trash. *What havoc has Jonathan wreaked on the checking account this time?*

Jonathan had a bad habit of forgetting to give her his debit card receipts. She discovered the record-keeping lapses after going to the

ATM one afternoon and checking the receipt to find that the account was almost two thousand dollars off. Anna had a facility for numbers and could keep the bank balance in her head. She was never off by more than a dollar or two, so she went through the accumulated debits and checked the account online. Most of the amounts were small—twenty-five dollars here, fifty dollars there—at the grocery store, the liquor store, the florist, and the dry cleaners. She had also discovered monthly cash withdrawals dating back to January, each in the amount of two hundred and fifteen dollars. The withdrawals had always been made on the same day of the month, and all of them had been made at the same ATM between 6:45 and 7:00 a.m.

When she had first brought up the subject of the bank account balance and the monthly mystery debits, to her surprise Jonathan didn't become defensive or angry. He explained—with some embarrassment—that the monthly debit was a payment to Bob Peterson, who had loaned him money after Mary cleaned out their bank account and he was temporarily strapped for cash. At the time, Anna had no reason not to believe him.

Having decided to let the latest debit card infractions go unremarked, Anna immediately overruled her own decision when she finished cleaning and sat down to look at papers she had found. The first was a notice from the Collin County Supervision and Corrections Department, reminding Jonathan to report in thirty days for his next court-ordered appointment at 7:00 a.m. Dated the day before, it was signed by Officer Harry Wilson, Jonathan's probation officer. Stapled to the notice was another piece of paper acknowledging the receipt of two hundred and fifteen dollars paid in restitution to "Jacob and Martha Leibowitz in the matter of Case No. 82334986."

The dollar amount jostled loose another memory. Anna hadn't thought much of it at the time, but after Jonathan moved in with her, she had noticed that every so often he was up, dressed, and out the door before at 6:15 a.m. After his third such pre-sunrise exit, she finally asked him about the early morning departures. He told her that he and some business acquaintances met for breakfast once a month to network and talk about deals. That sounded perfectly reasonable, and she had forgotten about it—until now. The amount of the court-ordered restitution was the same as the monthly payments to Bob, and the time stamps on the ATM receipts matched the days that Jonathan had his breakfast meetings. That couldn't be a coincidence.

She put together the pieces of the puzzle and the sordid picture made her heart drop like an elevator with a broken cable. Her husband had lied to her and had committed a crime. Pacing the apartment in a trance, she drank half a bottle of wine and rode an emotional rollercoaster in the next hours, rushing precipitously up mountains of rage and panic before dropping vertiginously into canyons of denial.

She couldn't stay married to a criminal, but the mere thought of divorcing Jonathan after only six months of marriage led her thoughts down dark pathways. Forty-five years old and out of time for finding love, she would most likely live the rest of her life—and die—alone. There were also practical considerations. What would her colleagues and the partnership committee think of her judgment and suitability as a potential law firm partner if she couldn't even hold her marriage together for a year?

Her normally rational nature was overridden by a host of unshakeable fears, and she decided not to jump to conclusions and to give her husband the benefit of the doubt. Jonathan might have his flaws, she rationalized, but he was not a criminal. Even so, she was still hopping mad that he had lied to her.

He arrived home that evening to find her waiting for him at the top of the stairs to the living room, her face flushed with anger and her arms defiantly akimbo. He saw some papers in one of her hands.

"Would you care to explain these?" she asked, waving them at him as he walked into the room. Her eyes spitting flames of unconcealed rage, she threw the papers on the table and stalked into the kitchen to pour another glass of wine.

Jonathan looked at the crumpled papers and blanched, but quickly recovered. "It's nothing," he said, expertly hiding his emotions. He walked into the kitchen, brushing her aside and pouring a tall glass of scotch. "Just give me a chance to explain."

Anna looked at him icily and walked over to the couch, collapsing onto it. Stone-faced and as inscrutable as the Sphinx, Jonathan remained in the kitchen, still not explaining. She decided to help him along. "I figured it out. Those payments you make every month aren't payments to Bob, and those meetings aren't networking breakfasts. You lied to me. Worse, you're a criminal. Don't you think that's something you should have told me before we got married? We swore there would be no secrets between us." She started to cry.

"Anna, dearest, I am not a criminal," Jonathan said, putting his arm around her soothingly. "There was no trial, and I wasn't convicted of anything. Even though none of it was my fault, I didn't tell you about it because I was ashamed. I was afraid that you wouldn't understand and wouldn't marry me. I swear to you that I'm telling you the truth."

She shook off his arm and crossed hers. "You must be guilty of something," she insisted between sniffles. "Why else would you be on probation and paying restitution? Give me one reason why I should stay married to you, now that I know I can't trust you."

Jonathan kneeled in front of her, his eyes glistening with nascent tears. "You are my whole world," he said, "If you love me, you'll listen to what I have to say."

Anna sat back and said, "Fine. Talk."

Jonathan emotionlessly and methodically explained that he and his old real estate business partner, Hamid Halabi, had been putting together their first prime bank investment pool when Hamid learned of another investment vehicle that allowed retirees to invest their IRAs and pension funds in individual retirement accounts. The accounts would hold shares in ostrich farms all over the country. At the time, ostrich meat was the next big thing, and the completely legal IRAs were earning eight to ten percent. He and Hamid formed a partnership, and Jonathan's small percentage of the profits was his reward for bringing two friends of his parents into their first ostrich farm IRA. It was Hamid's deal all the way, but Jonathan's name was on all the partnership papers too.

A few months later, he discovered that Hamid had embezzled the money instead of investing it, fleeing the country under a variety of additional unsavory circumstances shortly after that. When the defrauded investors found out about the theft, they sued both men in civil court, and the local authorities filed criminal charges. Because

Hamid was well out of the range of any subpoena power, Jonathan had been left to take the blame alone.

The story sounded plausible to Anna because she was well versed in the laws of partnership liability, but there were still many pieces missing from the story. "How did you manage to get probation instead of jail?" she asked.

"I paid the investors a chunk of their money and agreed to the restitution payments, even though I didn't do anything wrong," Jonathan replied.

"If you didn't do anything wrong, why didn't you fight the charges?"

"Pops and I didn't want to run the risk that I could go to jail. You know I'd rather die than go to jail. Just call Pops, sweetheart. He'll confirm everything I just told you."

Anna did, and Ricky told her the same story. Her fury and doubts gradually abated as he explained in detail how Jonathan had indeed been just another of Hamid's innocent victims in the ostrich farm fraud. She ended up apologizing to Jonathan for having doubted him, and although deeply hurt that his wife had not believed in him, he generously forgave her and cooked them a delicious meal.

After dinner, he opened a second bottle of wine and slid a disc into the near obsolete DVD player that Anna insisted on keeping because it still worked. The movie she wanted to watch was called *Dirty Rotten Scoundrels* and was in the top five of her all-time favorites, even though it was over twenty years old. Jonathan had never seen it, but he liked both Steve Martin and Michael Caine, and if watching a lighthearted comedy about two con men stalking their common prey on a posh Mediterranean playground would help calm his wife down, so be it.

He rubbed her feet while they watched, and when she finally fell asleep on the couch, he slid to the floor to watch the rest of the movie. He thoroughly enjoyed it, laughing out loud several times and noticing that the lead actress, Glenne Headley, bore a striking resemblance to Anna.

The last scene of the movie flipped a switch in his busy brain. He turned off the television and searched the apartment until he found the

Robb Report he'd taken from the GEM Motorcars customer lounge over a year earlier. Instead of going to work the next morning, he called in sick and spent the day poring over the glossy magazine.

Chapter 13

Jonathan was conducting official company business over the phone a few weeks later. "That's excellent news," he said to the boat broker on the other end of the line. "I look forward to receiving your charter data on comparable yachts. Assuming we can make those numbers work and get the price down another ten percent, I think we have the basis to move forward. And please be sure to check the draw on her to confirm that she can make harbor where we discussed."

He hung up and leaned back in his chair, smug and self-impressed by how adept he was getting at yachting jargon. He leafed through the full-color marketing brochure that the boat broker in Fort Lauderdale had sent him, mentally salivating over photos of a one-hundred-eighty-foot Benetti mega-yacht christened Alpha Centauri. Orbiting primarily in the star-studded vicinity of Monte Carlo and Cannes, the majestic vessel usually made port in picturesque Monaco's main harbor, but was currently undergoing routine hull maintenance in nearby San Remo, Italy.

With a thirty-foot beam, she could accommodate ten guests in five suites, with crew quarters for twelve. Only ten years old, the yacht had been refitted with a new engine that would power a stately fifteen kilometer-per-hour cruising speed, more than enough to make quick dashes of twelve nautical miles—a distance that Jonathan might require from time to time.

The sellers of the yacht were a high-profile Hollywood couple, the wife a famous actress from Greece, the husband a famous actor from California. After twelve years of marriage, the wife hewed to her true nature and came out of the closet in a big and public way. Alpha Centauri was high-priced flotsam from the wreckage of the sinking marriage, and the embattled couple was highly motivated to sell the floating money pit to settle the messy marital dispute.

Jonathan made a list of additional questions about the yacht and went upstairs to Anna's office to email it to the boat broker. While he was at her computer, he researched the extradition laws in France, Monaco, Italy, and the Virgin Islands. When he finished his homework, he erased all the emails that Anna had received from Cindy, Nicky, Newman Marvis, and the bank.

* * *

Captain Barry Fogelson hung up the phone and considered his good fortune. He had been working the yacht market for years and had met a lot of interesting characters since he started brokering sales of the big boats. But Jonathan DeLuca was the smartest, he was in a big hurry, and he was itching to buy. They say that boats are holes in the water into which one pours money, and Captain Barry was anxious to find a big hole for the Texas millionaire. The commission on the sale of Alpha Centauri would be over half a million dollars—a life-changing sum.

Barry grew up in Islamorada in the Florida Keys. His father ran bone fishing tours up and down the archipelago, taking sport fishermen from Key Largo through Marathon and the lower keys, down south to Key West, and out to the Marquesas. Young Barry would fish with his father during school vacations, his father tutoring him in the art of angling for the slender, silvery fish: where to find them, which baits to use, how to play the fishing line and wear them out, how to reel them in.

Barry learned a lot about boats and loved life on the water so much that he joined the merchant marine right out of high school, spending his days and nights cruising the Atlantic coast and parts of the Caribbean. He was only in his third year of service when his father gambled away the family's life savings, along with the shabby old fishing boat. With no other way to make a living, the forlorn and now penniless fisherman drank himself to death within a year, leaving twenty-one-year-old Barry to take care of his chronically ill mother, who suffered from Parkinson's disease.

Barry took the meritorious path, quitting the merchant marine and casting about for work close to home. He eventually found his niche captaining boats for wealthy yacht owners who used their obscenely expensive vessels only once or twice a year and chartered the ocean-going hotels out to strangers the rest of the time.

Over the years, Barry took to calling himself Captain Barry, building an impressive list of clients and gaining a reputation as a skilled sailor and gregarious host. He earned enough to hire a part-time nurse to help ease his load at home so he could take on longer charters, but his mother's medical expenses continued to rise faster than his income. With his mother's health in continual decline, he finally quit the sailor's life altogether and moved them to Fort Lauderdale. He opened Fogelson Yacht Sales, working the phones from their small apartment when he wasn't showing yachts at the marina up the road.

He was finally making decent money, and if he could broker the sale of Alpha Centauri, he'd have enough to put his mother in the finest assisted living center in the area. She could get the professional care and attention she deserved, and he could get the rest he needed. A lifelong bachelor, his wandering sailor's life and his mother's chronic illness had intervened and interfered with his sporadic and generally tempestuous relationships. He hoped that he could finally find a good woman and settle down. Then he would buy his own boat and run bone fishing trips up and down the Keys again, just like he and his father used to do.

* * *

Captain Barry's assessment of Jonathan was on target in one respect. He really was in a big hurry because he was running out of time to execute his grand plan. He had already spent most of Fred's fifty thousand dollars, and he wouldn't have the additional one hundred thousand dollars until December. Jack and Lamar were taking their sweet time, and Jonathan could tell that Anna was starting to have her doubts about him. Fortunately for him, she was still paralyzed by her fear of abandonment, but he didn't know how much longer that would last.

Anna and her law firm were crucial to his schemes. Her professional status and law firm connections were necessary to give him credibility now, and to take the heat off him later when his creditors inevitably and inexorably looked to his wife for financial justice. Her birthday was coming up, so he planned to get her a gift so spectacular that she'd be thoroughly overwhelmed with gratitude and stop fighting him on everything.

With that goal firmly in mind, he and his mother were in the fur salon at the NorthPark Newman Marvis. Jackie in the ladies' wear department had referred Jonathan to a mousy woman named Martha, who was unctuously bestowing compliments on the obviously affluent customer.

"You have impeccable taste, Mr. DeLuca," she gushed, gesturing at the full-length, reddish-brown mink laid out on the floor of the salon to better display the design of the pelts. It weighed almost eight pounds and carried a price tag of eighteen thousand dollars.

"I wholeheartedly agree with you," Jonathan said, scratching his chin in contemplation of the furry floor covering that sprawled expensively and quite dead before them. "My wife deserves a beautiful coat like this one, don't you think Mom?" He looked at his mother, who nodded approvingly at his choice. He looked back at Martha and said, "I'll take it." He opened his wallet and got out a copy of Anna's Newman Marvis card, handing it to Martha and explaining that he had lost his card, and although his wife had the other one, she was in court all day.

Martha saw no point in making a fuss over the absence of a physical piece of plastic because she did this kind of thing all the time. Running the charge through without question, she scampered happily away, calculating her commission on the coat while hastening to deliver it to the store's embroiderer.

The ease with which Martha took and used Anna's account number stemmed from a Texas consumer law that Jonathan had learned about during his first marriage. In Texas—at least with respect to retail establishments like Newman Marvis—charges to one spouse's account by the other spouse were "presumed authorized." That meant that a copy of Anna's card—or just the account number and Jonathan's driver's license—made the account his to use, even though his name had never been added to it.

Jonathan had been mining this little legislative gold nugget for years and had been using Anna's account for months without her knowledge. After intercepting the mail and deleting her online statements, he'd make small payments from time to time to keep the billing department quiet or transfer the balance to his father's card before she found out. She was always buried in work and travelling so much that she still hadn't figured it out. He had hoped to use her law firm credit card too, but learned early on that the American CreditCorp account was the only one that she paid attention to. The bicycle scam made it clear that the law firm card was too risky to use—for now.

The birthday shopping made him late for his meeting with Marilyn and one of her top clients. He walked his mother hastily to her car, jumped into his, and roared down Northwest Highway. Turning left down Preston Road, he followed it down Turtle Creek Boulevard, screeching to a halt in front of La Bernaise Restaurant six minutes later. He bolted inside, scanned the crowded bar, and spotted Marilyn sitting in a booth in the back of restaurant. She was with one of her clients, a well-known insurance magnate and part-time race car driver named George Williams.

Jonathan knew that George would be bringing his in-house legal counsel along to the meeting, but he was pleasantly surprised to see that the attorney was not a stodgy, cigar-munching, pale guy with a paunch, but a tall, sexy brunette with sleek long hair and breasts so big that they gave Marilyn's pair some stiff competition.

He strode quickly to the table, anxious to meet the hot little lawyer and licking his proverbial chops at the thought of another investor putting money into Hibiscus Cay and perhaps joining his pool of prime bank patsies.

* * *

Anna and Jonathan were sitting on the couch the next morning, surrounded by empty boxes and piles of wrinkled wrapping paper. After breakfast at his parents' house and multiple mimosas at home, he had gone down to the garage half a dozen times, returning each trip with a load of packages in his arms. The boxes held clothing and accessories from every fashion designer currently in vogue, along with a five-piece set of designer luggage in which to put it all. The living room looked like a luxury boutique had blown up, the vulgar display putting Jonathan's Christmas splurge the prior year to shame.

Anna was protesting the uncontrolled consumerism when Jonathan presented her with the biggest box she had ever seen. She opened it and unfolded the tissue paper, revealing the beautiful coat within. She knew it must have cost a fortune and frowned at the pile of silky fur in her lap. "Jonathan," she said, weighing her words carefully, "you know I love you, but this is simply too much."

A cloud of disappointment scudded across Jonathan's face. "But you deserve all of this and more," he protested.

"But I don't need any of it. It's unseemly."

"Yes, you do. And it's not unseemly." His disappointment turned to anger. "I'm tired of you wearing second-hand suits and carrying luggage that looks like something chewed it up and spat it out again. We're going to be incredibly rich, and you need to get used to that. I will not have my wife looking like a peasant. It's embarrassing."

"But we're not incredibly rich. We couldn't see rich with the Hubble Space Telescope." She was getting upset, and Jonathan could tell that he had finally managed to light his wife's remarkably long fuse. She looked him firmly in the eye, repeating, "Where did you get the money for all of this?"

Feigning offense, he said, "I can't believe how ungrateful you are after everything I've done for you. I'm beginning to think that you don't really love me." He got up and cleared some empty boxes off a chair, sat down on it, and put his head in his hands.

"Jonathan, where did you get the money?" Anna repeated, not willing to let the matter pass.

He looked up at her, his emotional state opaque. "I was going to tell you my excellent news later," he said, "but I guess I'll just have to spoil the surprise. I landed some investors from New Orleans for the prime bank deal I told you about and took some of the money as an advance on my commission." As soon as he said it, he realized that he had let his mask down. It was a stupid error—almost as bad as leaving his probation papers in his waste basket.

Anna's stomach roiled as a wave of fear washed over her. "You took investor money and spent it on birthday presents for me?" She stared at him in shock. "Diverting investor money for personal use is a state and federal crime. It's fraud. Even worse, it's *securities* fraud." I could lose my law license. You—*we*—could go to jail." She trembled at the thought of the many adverse consequences that Jonathan's misappropriation of funds could unleash. "Take this all back," she demanded, nearly hysterical. "Take it all back first thing tomorrow."

Realizing he had pressed his luck too far, Jonathan climbed over the new luggage and enfolded her in his arms. He hugged her closely, like a python hugs a tasty antelope, holding her even tighter as she struggled to get away, kissing her softly on the neck where he knew she liked him to and groveling on. "I'm so stupid. Please forgive me. I was so excited about giving you the coat, I didn't think about the accounting issues and legal implications. I'll take everything back tomorrow." He tried to kiss her again, to make love to her like he always did after they argued.

This time she didn't succumb to his charms. She pushed herself wearily away from him. "I'm going for a walk—alone," she said. "Do me a favor and sleep upstairs tonight."

"But Anna, darling, I love you more than life itself," Jonathan cried out as she walked out the front door. Unanswered, he turned back to the piles of designer goods, packed everything neatly into the new luggage, and took it down to the garage. Scolding himself for having miscalculated so wildly with the gifts and accidentally spilling the DuPree beans, he went back upstairs and collapsed onto his grandmother's hideous green couch to take a nap. Always able to find a silver lining in any situation, he fell fast asleep a few minutes later, not a care in the world.

116

Chapter 14

October brought cool nights, cloudless skies, and a hostile takeover of one of B&V's top clients. Anna was the primary associate assigned to the account and would be working around the clock with five other attorneys to defend against the corporate aggression. Fortunately, it was one of Harry Vincent's clients and not the F-Man's, so she'd be temporarily free of the slings and arrows of his outrageous sexism for at least part of every day.

Meanwhile, the Nerd Merger had been concluded, and she had been summoned to New York for the celebratory dinner. The head of B&V's corporate section in Manhattan asked her to stay over another day to help the paralegals with the post-closing paperwork, so she took advantage of the extra night in the Big Apple to see Nicky.

They met for dinner at a posh uptown restaurant, and he hugged her hard while she cried from the happiness of seeing him. They caught each other up on the events of the past months, Anna letting Nicky do most of the talking because she was too embarrassed to tell him anything about her problems at home.

They were finishing their second bottle of Far Niente Chardonnay when he complained, "So why don't you ever answer my emails?"

"What emails?"

"I email you at your private address at least once a month, but you never answer."

"That's weird. Cindy said the same thing. I've been meaning to check the spam filter, but I keep forgetting."

The waiter returned with their desserts, and Anna was just about to tuck into some vanilla bean ice cream when her cell phone rang. She glanced at the caller I.D. on the screen and ignored the call, returning her attention to Nicky.

"Emergency?" he asked.

"It was just Jonathan," she replied distractedly. "I'll call him later."

The conversation wound down as they finished their desserts. Nicky paid the check and helped Anna into a taxi, kissing her goodbye on the cheek. She gazed wistfully at him out the taxi's back window until his silhouette vanished from view.

Nicky watched, downcast, as her cab disappeared around the corner. He knew her better than anyone, and he knew something was wrong. Even though it had started to drizzle, he decided to walk the ten blocks home. Wrapping his cashmere overcoat tightly around him, he flipped up the collar against the cold and wet, letting the frigid north wind numb his emotional pain.

When he got home to his Upper East Side apartment, he went straight to the wet bar and poured himself a drink, then sank into his leather sofa and thought about Anna. He had been in love with her since they were seven years old, but she had never viewed him as anything but a friend and surrogate brother. Heartbroken the first time she married, he claimed business as his reason to move to New York, but the real motive was to put distance between him and the fount of his unhappiness. He made an overt romantic play for her after her divorce from her first husband, only to receive the "You know I love you, but not that in that way" speech. She had even tried to fix him up with Cindy, and although the mismatched lovers became fast friends, the romance never really took.

Anna never knew it, but Nicky had tried unsuccessfully for years to purge his feelings for her with alcohol and cocaine, until a close brush with death by overdose shocked him into straightening up. He pulled his life together and became a Wall Street dynamo, but he still had an Anna-sized hole in his heart, and his latest heartache was self-inflicted. He cursed himself for having gotten the fateful romantic ball rolling when he walked over to Jonathan DeLuca that night in the bar, never expecting that his silly ploy to find his best friend a date would end with his being cast out of the picture yet again. He drained his drink in one draught and threw the empty Baccarat glass at the exposed brick wall, the delicate crystal shattering—like his heart—into jagged, pointed shards. *Stupid, stupid, stupid!*

* * *

Despite his extramarital dalliances, Jonathan was extremely jealous of any man who had contact with his wife. "I'm afraid you'll be dazzled by some flashy East Coast lawyer and leave me," he once lamented. Anna assured him that she'd never leave him—especially not for another lawyer—but he didn't believe her. He knew she saw Nicky Morgan when she went to New York. *Bitch was probably shacking up with him and lying about it.*

When she hadn't answered the phone the night before, the mere thought of the mere possibility that she and Nicky might have been together infuriated him, triggering an intense panic attack. Even though he had no intentions of staying with her any longer than was absolutely necessary, she was *his* wife. He was still in a foul mood when she called him back at work the next morning.

The GEM Motorcars showroom was bustling with activity, but after talking to her for a couple of minutes, he started screaming at the top of his lungs with complete disregard to his whereabouts. "I know you're cheating on me with Nicky Morgan," he shouted into the phone, not knowing that she had already hung up on him. "You stay away from that fucking back-alley loser."

Jonathan glanced up to see Eric Adams walking briskly across the showroom floor. When he arrived at Jonathan's desk, he leaned over and said, "Come with me." Once they were in his office, Eric closed the door and lowered the venetian blinds that covered the large glass window overlooking the showroom floor. He pointed to a chair in front of his desk and said, "Sit."

Jonathan remained standing.

Getting straight to the point, Eric said, "Your sales have been in the shitter since first quarter." He looked at Jonathan with inquisitive disappointment. "What in the hell happened to you? You used to be a superstar, but now you're our worst performer. You go missing from the showroom for extended periods of time, and you haven't shown up for the last three staff meetings."

Jonathan answered him with stony silence. Jonathan DeLuca the car salesman was history. Jonathan Frescobaldi DeLuca the international real estate and finance mogul shrugged his shoulders and glanced idly around the office, bored and indifferent to the consequences about to befall him. He no longer cared about his job at GEM Motorcars and had no reason to explain anything to a mere sales manager.

"You know, we might have kept you on little longer," Eric continued, "even with your bad first quarter review." He looked at Jonathan with bewilderment. "I even bent the rules for you and gave you ninety days to get your shit together. You were that good. But as if all that weren't enough, while you were out there having a temper tantrum on the phone, I got a call from Garrett Mason, who just got a call from one of our top customers, who said that *you* tried to get him to invest in some bank deal." He stood up and leaned over the desk, his eyes drilling into Jonathan's. "Are you fucking crazy, doing something like that?" He waited for an answer, fuming, but none came. "You're fired, effective immediately," he said. "Clear out your desk and bring me your client files, business cards, and the keys to your demo car. Now."

Jonathan remained silent and impassive during Eric's tirade, immune to the situation. Once Lamar invested in Hibiscus Cay, Jonathan would bank over two million dollars in commissions. He no longer had to ingratiate himself to grotty little toads like Eric. "Are you quite finished?" he asked, flicking a piece of lint from one sleeve, as if to say that Eric was nothing more than an irritating speck of dust.

"No," Eric said, "I'm not. Don't ever show your face at a Garrett Mason property or come near one of our customers again. If you do, we'll take out a restraining order and sue you. Now get out."

"Fuck you and the horse you rode in on, Eric," Jonathan said quietly, walking imperiously out of the office and back to his desk.

Bob Peterson's desk was next to Jonathan's on the showroom floor. He looked at Jonathan and whispered, "What happened?"

"I just quit this shithole," Jonathan replied. "Can you give me a ride home, buddy?"

Bob took an early lunch and drove Jonathan home, stopping at a nearby micro-brewery for beers along the way. After Jonathan drank six of them, he told Bob all about Hibiscus Cay, Alpha Centauri, and how Frescobaldi Prime Investments would need an experienced, highly-paid operations manager in the very near future.

* * *

Jonathan drove Anna's car to the airport to pick her up when she returned from New York. He spotted her coming out of the automatic doors in front of the baggage claim area and leaped out of the car, running to help her with her luggage and kissing her passionately before she could object. He stowed her bags in the trunk and hopped cheerfully back into the drivers' seat.

His devil-may-care attitude wasn't working because she skipped the pleasantries. "Why are you driving my car?" she demanded.

"My demo car is having transmission problems, and there aren't any others available right now," Jonathan said. "I forgot to tell you when we talked yesterday morning."

"So how are you getting to work?"

"I thought we'd carpool since you're out of town so much. When you aren't traveling, you're in the office all the time anyway. It's only for a few days, until my car is fixed or a new one becomes available. We can make it work."

"I guess we'll just have to make do," Anna said, gazing desultorily out the window at the traffic on Northwest Highway while she contemplated the latest development.

Jonathan hoped she was buying the story, but she didn't look thoroughly convinced as she mulled through the implications of carpooling. He pressed on. "FYI—the deal with Peter and Lamar is really moving now," he said. "Peter said he'll pay for a company car for me until we get Lamar's investment money."

Anna looked at Jonathan but didn't react. He assessed her mood and found it unfavorable, deciding to tell yet another lie. "And by the way, darling, I have fantastic news. I talked with my contact at Barclay's over in London. He's been working on the bond rating for Lamar, and I might have to fly over as soon as the securities hit the screen."

Anna didn't know what "securities hitting the screen" meant, but she was too tired from the trip to ask for an explanation. "But what about work? You haven't sold a car in months."

Jonathan's face reddened with thinly repressed rage at the insult, but he managed to remain calm. "I have a week of vacation that I have to use before December, so this is the perfect time for me to pin down my deal with Lamar; besides darling, we're going to be so rich, I'll buy you your own car dealership if you want."

Anna said nothing during the rest of the ride home, finally breaking her silence when Jonathan pulled into the garage. Before they got out of the car, she turned to Jonathan and said, "You know how much I love you, but you have to be realistic." She reached over to take his hand, but he pulled it away. "I hope your deal works out, I truly do," she said, "But we have bills to pay now, and I don't get my bonus until December. There never seems to be enough money left at the end of the month anymore, and I don't know how you're going to make your child support payments."

Jonathan got out of the car and opened the door to the apartment. "You are so negative," he said. "Why can't you just believe in me?" Incensed, he stormed upstairs to the third floor, went into his dressing room, slamming the door and staying there until his wife went to bed alone—again.

* * *

Anna came home for lunch few days later to escape the stresses of the office for an hour. She arrived to find Jonathan asleep on the couch, the telephone in his inert left hand and a half-empty bottle of Crown Royal on the coffee table. He woke up when he heard the refrigerator door slam shut and sat up lethargically, his normally perfect hair in disarray and his cheeks flushed under a two-day growth of beard.

Anna called out from the kitchen. "Do you want a sandwich while you explain why you are drunk on the couch in the middle of the day?"

"I'm not drunk," Jonathan mumbled. He sounded like had marbles in his mouth. "I'm just tired. I was up all night long waiting for the call from London. The securities should show up on the screen any time now."

Anna's nose told her that Jonathan was lying—he reeked of alcohol. She put on a pot of coffee and put together a couple of turkey and cheddar cheese sandwiches, taking them to the dining room, along with a big mug of fresh, hot coffee. Jonathan joined her at the table.

"You keep saying the securities are going to show up on the screen," she said. "What does that mean?"

Jonathan guzzled half a cup of coffee and wiped his lips with his sleeve. "Lamar always leverages his investments using rated bonds as collateral. We've been waiting for Barclays to finish rating the bonds. When they do, the bonds will show up on the screen—which means they'll appear in Lamar's investment account. Then he can use them as collateral to borrow the thirty-five million dollars he's going to invest in Hibiscus Cay."

Anna worked in securities law, so most of what he said made sense, but some of the intricacies of this bank investment program still eluded her, making her subconscious itch. She poured more coffee in his mug. "It's already Friday," she reminded him, going into the kitchen for a glass of water. "You have to be back to work on Monday."

"So?"

"So, you can't go to London."

"Yes, I can. I quit my job."

Anna felt dizzy, her emotions swirling so fast that she had to lean against the kitchen counter for support. Her face turned as white as a three-day-old corpse as her water glass dropped to the floor, shattering into bits. "How could you just quit without discussing it with me?" she gasped.

"You make a decent salary," Jonathan said, rubbing his bloodshot eyes. "You have some savings. We can make it until the deal closes. We're partners in marriage and business too."

"I told you from the beginning that I wanted nothing to do with your business," Anna said. "I'm just a figurehead until Lamar invests

123

anyway. You don't tell me anything about what's going on, and you won't let me talk to Jack. I can't ask Peter or Larry about the project because of the legal conflicts of interest and because I know it would look really bad if your *wife* was questioning you behind your back."

Jonathan sneered at her. "Isn't my word alone enough for you, *wife*?"

Near tears, Anna stood up and prepared to go back to the office. Putting on her navy-blue blazer, she said, "I can't comply with my legal and fiduciary duties to the company if I don't know what you're doing. You've put me in a really bad position, Jonathan—legally and financially."

She headed down the stairs to the garage, Jonathan calling after her, "Always the lawyer, aren't you? If you really loved me, you would believe in me. I'm doing this for *us*." He was standing at the top of the stairs, his arms crossed and his face contorted with anger.

Anna stopped on the ground floor landing and looked up at him, her eyes darkening to gray. "If you loved *me*," she said, "you would never have put me in this position in the first place."

While his close-minded wife drove back to the office to face ten more hours of work, Jonathan went back to the couch and poured another large glass of scotch. He tossed back the last of his drink and thought about how close he was to pulling off his master plan. He decided to take another nap because he needed to rest up for his big meeting with Lamar and Jack the following morning.

* * *

Jonathan was flirting with the attractive receptionist in the penthouse foyer of the Buchanan Building when the conference room doors swooshed open and Miss Jessica motioned him to enter. The ebony conference table had been polished so diligently that it glistened like an oil slick. The big man himself, Lamar Buchanan, was sitting at the far end of the table, his long legs floating on top of it. His feet were comfortably caressed by cowboy boots made with leather of the baby-butt-soft variety, such casual cowboy chic generally costing around twenty-five hundred dollars a pair.

124

Jack made the introductions while Jonathan took a seat. A black speakerphone that that looked like a space-age catamaran hovered in front of Jack. Jonathan heard Peter's voice crackle from it. "Hey, Jonathan, Peter here."

Jonathan knew that Peter was in the Virgin Islands getting the title reports that Lamar's due diligence team had requested, but he found it disturbing that they had been talking before he had arrived. Giving no indication of concern, he accepted coffee and a cheese pastry from Miss Jessica, then the four men settled into negotiate.

About ten minutes into a detailed discussion of projections, real estate price comparisons, and marketing strategies, Jonathan chose an appropriate pause in the information exchange to interject his brilliant idea. Standing up and putting his palms on the conference table, he leaned forward to get closer to the speakerphone and said, "Gentleman, I am extremely pleased with our progress thus far and would like to present to you an idea that I have had regarding the marketing of Hibiscus Cay."

In a presentation worthy of P.T. Barnum, Jonathan explained his idea of buying a yacht to use as a floating sales office for the project. Plying the Caribbean and the Mediterranean Seas in search of Hibiscus Cay buyers, the yacht would generate enough in charter fees when it wasn't in use by the company to pay for its annual operation and maintenance.

"Imagine if you will," he began, "that you're thinking about buying a vacation home in the Virgin Islands. Imagine further, that you decide to investigate Hibiscus Cay and are told by the sales agent that, upon arrival at a nearby airport of your choice, you and your family will be whisked by helicopter to *this*." He presented the Alpha Centauri brochure to Lamar with a magician's flourish, lacking only a "TA DA!" to punctuate the moment.

He then gave both men a stack of papers showing the estimated expenses for the yacht and the projected income from charter fees. While Jack and Lamar reviewed the data, Jonathan began to pace the oriental carpet like a caged predator, gaining energy and enthusiasm with each step. He spoke again. "Once on board Alpha Centauri, you are taken on a grand tour around the island, delighting in all manner of

125

water sports: jet skiing, snorkeling, parasailing, and deep-sea fishing. You can hop aboard a boat tender and motor to the professionally designed eighteen-hole golf course, where your green fees and cart rentals will be complimentary. Meanwhile your wife is getting a deluxe spa treatment at the clubhouse while resort-provided babysitters entertain the kiddies in a secure play park close by."

Jonathan went in for the big finish, his vision becoming real through the act of speaking of it. "Imagine that, at the end of your long, luxurious day, you are back on board Alpha Centauri, where a professional chef prepares gourmet meals to order and champagne flows in rivers. A few hours later, you're relaxed and happy, your wife is relaxed and happy, and you've decided to buy your own piece of Hibiscus Cay." Spent from his exhortations, he sat down and concluded, "Just imagine."

Jack and Lamar exchanged the kind of look that longtime friends and business partners do. Jack cleared his throat. "Well, Jonathan, that was an impressive presentation," he said.

Peter's voice broke through the static coming from the speakerphone. "I like the idea Jonathan, but don't you think it's a little premature to be thinking about something like this?"

Jack chimed in. "Our thoughts exactly, Peter."

Jonathan was seething inside. *Can no one understand my genius? Am I surrounded by complete fools?* He was on the verge of another panic attack when Jack cleared his throat and continued. "Getting back to the business at hand," he said, "we're happy to tell you that Lamar has decided to invest in Hibiscus Cay. But not the full thirty-five million dollars at this time."

Jonathan felt his heart start to race. His vision was going blurry when Jack added, "But we can do one million dollars by the end of next month, four million dollars thirty days after that, and five million dollars per month for the following six months. We'll talk again after my team runs new numbers reflecting the multiple tranches."

Jonathan exhaled in relief and his vision cleared. He ran the math in his head. Five million dollars in the Frescobaldi Prime Investments account dollars by the end of the year meant he'd be paid three hundred thousand dollars in finder's fees in mere weeks and almost two million dollars more after that. He relaxed and spoke calmly into the speakerphone, no sign of stress in his deep voice. "Is that acceptable to you, Peter?"

"Yes. Definitely," Peter responded. "Let's proceed on that track. Meanwhile, I need to get off the call. The title reports are ready, and I have to get them before the government office closes for the day."

With that, the meeting ended and Jonathan left, near giddy with joy, but at the same time disappointed by the delay. He wanted the money right now—not later—*right now*. At least Lamar was on the hook, and though he might be dangling precariously from it, Jonathan knew he could reel him all the way in.

He drove back to Dallas daydreaming about his happy future and the fact that he would be a multi-millionaire in a matter of months. Taking the exit off I-30 onto North Central Expressway, he realized that the prospect of all that money was making him horny. He hit speed dial. "Darling," he greeted her when she answered. "How would you feel about dinner tonight? Somewhere in North Dallas—The Jupiter perhaps?"

* * *

After Jack and Lamar left the conference room, Lamar's bodyguard entered and walked over to where Jonathan had been sitting. A large, meaty obelisk without a neck, he had been aptly nicknamed "Beefy" by Lamar. Six feet three inches tall, he sported a military buzz cut and wore a gray suit too small to contain the muscles bulging beneath it.

Extracting a leather pouch from his left coat pocket, he took out a brush and a bottle of black powder, sprinkling the powder over the parts of the conference table where Jonathan had left finger and palm prints and photographing the results. He took two a roll of two-inch-wide masking tape from another pocket and placed several strips of tape over the powdery portions of the table. When he peeled it back, the sticky sides were blackened by dark whorls. He put the dusty tape in a plastic bag and put Jonathan's coffee cup in another.

His task complete, he lumbered down the hall to Jack's office, his wide bulk darkening the doorway. Jack waved him in, but he was too big to fit in any of the chairs, so he remained standing while Jack called the accounting department to request an expense advance.

When Jack hung up, he nodded at Beefy and said, "Standard procedure."

Beefy nodded knowingly. "Yes, boss," he grunted and shuffled off, leaving the doorway un-darkened once again.

Chapter 15

Anna was hanging up from a bi-coastal conference call when Becca called out, "There's a Bob Peterson on the phone for you." Anna had no idea why Jonathan's former co-worker would be calling her at the office, but she took the call.

"Sorry to bother you, but you need to come and get Jonathan," Bob said. "We're in the bar at La Bernaise. He's causing a commotion, and he's way too drunk to drive."

Anna glanced at the clock on her computer screen and groaned. It was only 3:00 p.m. "Could you please take him home?" she pleaded. "I'm really busy right now."

"He refuses to leave," Bob said. "I'm afraid he'll cause a scene if I try to force him. Maybe you can talk some sense into him. You need to get your car anyway." She heard Jonathan yelling in the background.

"You'd better get here soon before he does something stupid and gets arrested," Bob said.

"How long have you been there?"

"Just an hour."

"How can he be that drunk already?"

"He came here after lunch at Hotel LaLa. He was already drunk when I got here."

"Do you have his car keys?"

"The valet does."

Anna felt the burden of her spouse weighing heavily upon her. The vagaries of life with Jonathan were beginning to exhaust her, but she knew she had to go. "Give me a few minutes to get there," she said, hanging up and cursing out loud.

The popular gathering spot was only fifteen minutes away from the office, but she didn't have the car. She grabbed her purse and took the elevator down to the lobby, then took an escalator down into the tunnel system that connected the major downtown office building and protected pedestrians from the harsh Texas elements. Three minutes later she was on an escalator going up to the lobby of the Fairmont Hotel. Four minutes later she was in a cab.

Ten minutes later she walked into the bar at La Bernaise, and Jonathan was so surprised to see her that he fell off the barstool, cracking his head on the floor and generally making a fool of himself in front of several local movers and shakers. Jonathan's coordination was so banished to oblivion by an unknown quantity of alcohol that Bob had to help him out of the bar, holding him upright until the valet brought Anna's car back.

Bob poured him into the passenger seat while Anna rounded the front of the car, noticing that the entire right side of the heavy molded rubber front bumper had been scraped, and part of it was hanging off the car. There were onlookers to the sorry spectacle, so instead of causing another one, she checked to make sure that the bumper wouldn't fall completely off and drove her semi-conscious lump of a husband back to the apartment without saying a word.

When they arrived at the apartment and she pulled into the garage, Jonathan opened the door while the car was still moving and fell out onto the concrete floor. Anna waited patiently in the car, saying nothing while trying to keep herself under control. She took the apartment key off his keychain and handed it to him through the car window. He snatched the key with a boozy sneer, making three clumsy attempts to open the door before finally getting in. Anna heard him throw the deadbolt, completely locking her out of the apartment.

"GODDAMIT Jonathan!" she screamed, bolting from the car and storming to the cheap hollow door, unleashing her pent-up anger on it with her fists. "Let me in, asshole."

Cackling maniacally at having gotten the upper hand, Jonathan stumbled up the stairs to the living room while Anna continued to batter the door, cursing him with words he didn't know were in her vocabulary. As he cleared the first landing, he heard the car door slam and the engine grumble to life, the tires squealing in protest as Anna backed the car angrily out of the garage.

Jonathan didn't know where she was going and didn't really care. He teetered blindly into the bathroom and did his business, then tottered toward the living room sofa. He tripped over his own feet before he got there and fell face first onto the corner of the glass coffee table, cutting a deep gash into his scalp. As he began to pass out on the living room floor, he found himself hoping that his wife crashed the car and killed herself.

When his alcoholic fog cleared a few hours later, he discovered that he had left a big bloodstain on the carpet and had accidentally relieved himself in Anna's closet instead of in the toilet behind the adjacent door. His doctor had warned him not to drink alcohol while he was taking his anti-anxiety medication, but Jonathan had ignored the advice because the pills weren't working anyway. Angry that he hadn't been prescribed something stronger, Jonathan decided that the unfortunate episode was entirely the doctor's fault. *Stupid asshole probably got his medical degree in Guatemala.*

Whoever was to blame, Jonathan knew that he had screwed up again, and this was a particularly bad blunder in a lifelong parade of blunders. He began working on his apology while he cleaned up the bloodstains on the living room carpet and the smelly mistake he'd made in Anna's closet.

He was furiously scrubbing the closet carpet when he spotted a shopping bag tucked away in the back corner behind Anna's shoe rack. He opened the bag to discover a shiny Browning nine-millimeter handgun that his wife had never mentioned to him. Examining it closely, he checked the safety and popped the clip to check the load, then snapped the clip back into place with the heel of his hand and put the gun back exactly where he had found it.

* * *

Anna was still as mad as a hornet out for revenge after a fumigation. She hadn't spoken to Jonathan in almost four days, leaving early for work every morning and coming back late after he was already asleep upstairs. He took advantage of her prolonged absences to make phone calls. His first call on this particular morning was to Fort Lauderdale, Florida.

"That's wonderful news, Captain Barry," he said, his cell phone wedged between his ear and shoulder as he scribbled on a notepad with "Frescobaldi Prime Investments" embossed at the top in a fancy gold curlicue font. "I'll get back to you with your travel arrangements within the week," he added, ending the call and tucking his gold Mont Blanc pen into the pocket of his new Armani suit. He sat back in his regular seat at the coffee shop in Highland Park Village and considered his next move.

He could tell that Anna was getting harder to fool as time went on. He was hanging by a thread, and it would be highly inconvenient for him if it frayed completely and broke. It was essential to his plans that he worm his way back into her good graces. He had been obsequiously contrite after his drunken car-crashing, head-cracking, closet-peeing episode, but she remained steadfastly furious with him, chewing their latest bone of contention into dusty splinters. But he had formulated a plan, and he knew it would melt her frozen fortress of a heart, having lived quite successfully by the axiom that it was easier to ask forgiveness than permission.

Buoyed by the thought, he was looking sharp and in high spirits as he drove to Bennington Travel Services. Temporarily bereft of wheels after Anna had taken his car keys away, he had talked his father into temporarily paying for a nondescript rental car. He parked it out of view of the agency and entered the office with a bounce in his step, tossing the receptionist a flirtatious wave and walking straight into Helen Bennington's office unannounced.

Helen stood up when she saw him and leaned over her desk, offering her hand. "What a pleasure to see you again, Mr. DeLuca. Please sit down."

"Please, call me Jonathan." Walking to her desk and kissing her on the cheek, he presented her with a dozen yellow roses and said, "Something lovely for someone lovely."

Helen blushed. "How can I help you today, Jonathan?"

* * *

Jonathan heard the garage door open and turned the flame down under his home-made tomato basil sauce. He quickly poured a glass of Anna's favorite champagne, and when she came up the stairs to the living room, he walked to her and kneeled. Bowing his head, he proffered the glass with both hands as if giving it in tribute to a queen.

Anna put down her briefcase and took the glass, her sustained rancor finally giving way in the face of Jonathan's groveling. He was difficult to resist, especially after he stood up and wrapped her in his arms, whispering gently in her ear, "I'm so sorry, my love."

Thoroughly beaten down from the stresses of work and her problems at home, his touch still comforted her. Her steely resolve rusted away, and she broke her days-long silence. "What's the occasion?" she asked, shrugging off her coat and going into the kitchen to see what he was cooking. She peeked into a pot and savored the spicy aroma of the sauce that would soon cover a large helping of spinach fettuccini.

Jonathan turned off both burners and said, "I have a surprise for you." He wiped his hands on a dish towel and led her to the dining room table, pulling out her chair and pointing to a large manila envelope atop her dinner plate. "Do you remember when I told you about my idea for marketing Hibiscus Cay?" he asked.

"Yes, why?"

He nodded at the envelope. "Open it."

Anna undid the metal clasp on the back and took out a brochure for Alpha Centauri. She scanned it absentmindedly before looking curiously at her husband. "I don't understand."

"We're going to buy that yacht," Jonathan said. "I told Peter, Jack, and Lamar about my idea of using a yacht to market Hibiscus Cay some of the time and charter it out the rest of the time. They approved the idea, and you and I are going to Monte Carlo in ten days to tour the yacht and start negotiations to buy it."

Highly skeptical but undeniably intrigued, she looked more closely at the brochure. In its pages were dozens of full color photos of a floating palace that rose three stories high above the water line. With a hot tub big enough for eight people on the middle deck and a helicopter landing pad on the top, deck, the yacht carried an astronomical purchase price of thirteen million dollars—helicopter not included.

Jonathan continued talking while she studied the photos, not giving her a chance to interrupt him before he could cast his net around her and ensnare her with it. "I've already made arrangements for us to meet with the lawyers for the yacht owners," he said. "The boat broker will join us to assist with the negotiations. I also have plans to meet with United Bank of Switzerland and Credit Suisse on the prime bank deal I told you about. They're interested in getting involved in the deal along with Barclay's."

Anna had too many questions to count so she started with the basics. "Why do you need a buy a yacht when no one has invested in Hibiscus Cay yet? Even if you had investors, why would you need a thirteen-million-dollar yacht? And why does it have to be this one?"

Jonathan was expecting the third degree from his wife and was ready with the answers. "That price is a bargain for a yacht of this size," he explained. "The owners are divorcing and are highly motivated to sell, plus the captain and most of the crew have agreed to stay on after we buy her."

"But why do you have to go all the way to Monaco to buy a boat? Florida is a lot closer and would be a much cheaper trip."

"Anna, my angel," he said, masking his impatience. "Monte Carlo is where the people with the money are. That's why Lamar wants us to base our marketing efforts there."

It seemed like an impulsive way of doing things, but she wasn't going to second guess a business icon like Lamar Buchanan. Still, she was incredulous. "Where are you getting the money for this anyway?"

Jonathan strove mightily to contain his mounting frustration. "Lamar's going to front us the money for the down payment on Alpha Centauri," he said. "He's also paying for our plane tickets and is going to wire twenty-five thousand dollars to the company account to cover our other expenses."

Despite her trepidation and many cogent reasons not to take such a lavish trip, Anna had to think of her legal duties to Frescobaldi Prime Investments and her ethical duties to her law firm and Peter Grand. The point that Jonathan had made weeks earlier remained immutable—endangering the project would be career suicide. If her presence during the negotiations on Alpha Centauri was necessary to advance the Hibiscus Cay project, keep Lamar happy, and keep her job, she had no choice but to go.

"All right," she finally said, accepting defeat. "I suppose if Lamar is paying for everything . . ."

* * *

Jonathan congratulated himself on how well his Monte Carlo story had worked on Anna. The glamorous and enticing dream he had woven was such a success that she let him sleep in the bedroom again. The next morning, he promised to stop having bar meetings with Bob, and she gave him his car keys back.

Comfortably mobile once again, Jonathan was driving to a chic little French restaurant on McKinney Avenue to meet Marilyn's client, George Williams, who Jonathan had been working for both the Hibiscus Cay project and the prime bank deal. It was a beautiful November afternoon, the summer heat long gone and the winter winds and ice storms not yet on the horizon.

Along the picturesque way, Jonathan got his cell phone out of his jacket pocket with one hand and hit speed dial. When Miss Jessica answered, he asked to speak with Jack. He came on the line after a short wait and snapped, "Talk fast, Jonathan. I'm on my way out."

"I was just calling to check in on where we are with Hibiscus Cay."

"The due diligence team is still working."

"How much longer before they finish and we can get the first million?"

"I can't really say. Lamar is on vacation in Peru with his family. He can't be reached for at least ten days. We'll talk again when he gets back." What Jack didn't tell Jonathan was that Lamar was stalling until the private investigation they had ordered was completed. Jack could sense Jonathan's disappointment and brought some harsh reality to the discussion. "I'll be honest with you, Jonathan, this deal is not a priority for Lamar right now," he said.

"I understand," Jonathan said through clenched teeth. "I'll be in touch when Lamar returns. In the meantime, let me know if you and your team have any questions."

Jonathan hung up. "Shit! Fuck! Shit!" he screamed, pounding out his anger on the steering wheel. He was really cutting it close now. They were leaving for Monte Carlo the next day, and he had to nail something down before they got there or Anna might have to pay for the trip. Jonathan didn't want to contemplate the consequences of that eventuality. He turned onto a leafy side street, stopped the car, and made another phone call.

"Hello, Mr. DuPree. It's Jonathan DeLuca. How are you, sir?"

"Fine, just fine, Jonathan," Fred replied. "In fact, I'm glad that you called. I've been trying to reach you. I called the car dealership, but they said you didn't work there anymore."

"No sir, I don't. My other business endeavors were taking up a lot of time, so I left GEM to focus on them."

"Well that's certainly good news. I thought maybe you had been fired."

Jonathan knew that the dealership wouldn't tell anyone he was fired or say anything bad about him without risking a libel lawsuit. "Oh, no, sir. I resigned. It was all very amicable. Anyway, the reason I called is to remind you that it's almost time for the second tranche of your investment. I wanted to confirm that we're still on track."

"That's why I was trying to reach you," Fred said, clearing his throat before delivering the bad news. "I've decided to wait until March when we get our first interest payment before putting any more money in. This kind of investment is new to a simple old man like me, and I want to see how the first one plays out. I don't want to cash out my T-Bill until I'm sure about it."

Jonathan started sweating under his custom-made shirt. *What is it with old people and their fucking T-bills?* He felt a panic attack coming on and was unable to speak for a few seconds.

"Jonathan, are you still there," Fred asked, his voice muted and far away.

Shaking himself out of the fog that settled over his brain whenever he had an attack, Jonathan replied, "Yes, sir, I'm still here. I completely understand." Anxious to get off the phone, he said, "You have a great day, sir. We'll talk again in March."

"Now you and your wife have a nice Thanksgiving and a happy Christmas."

"Thank you, sir. We will."

Jonathan started coming out of the attack and steadied himself. He drove the short remaining distance to the restaurant, convincing himself that things could still work out. *Don't panic. Ok, so Fred is a frightened old fuddy duddy, and Lamar is dragging his feet. Maybe you can borrow more money from Marilyn. Worst case, Pops can help until Lamar comes through.*

* * *

"You got it, buddy. I'll see you in twenty minutes." Bob hung up the phone and called to his wife. "Mona!"

Mona came out of the kitchen, wiping her hands on her apron. A roly-poly woman with salt and pepper curls framing a round, happy face, Mona was active in the local church and supplemented their income by teaching piano lessons in their modest townhouse on Mockingbird Lane. "What is it, honey bun?" she asked

"I have to run out for a while," Bob replied. "I've got a meeting with Jonathan."

"Again?"

Mona had noticed that Bob's new job consisted of meeting Jonathan at a bar, where they'd drink and talk for hours about Bob's critical role as the vice president of operations of Jonathan's new company. One thing they never seemed to talk about was when Bob would get his first paycheck. She didn't mind that her husband wanted to do something new, as long as it kept him happy and out of her kitchen, but she didn't understand how Jonathan had convinced him to leave a steady job at GEM Motorcars and go to work for some company with a fancy foreign name that she couldn't even pronounce.

Bob had been a shift supervisor at the Dr. Pepper plant for almost thirty years, overseeing the day shift and two hundred workers. After a freak accident involving exploding soft drink bottles, he was left with a shattered right knee and deep scars all over his legs and chest. He threw in the factory towel and took early retirement with a comfortable pension and disability payments. He soon found retirement boring and decided to go back to work selling cars part time, eventually landing a full-time job with GEM motorcars. He was an above-average, though not stellar, car salesman, and he would never get rich doing it, but the job required very little physical exercise and provided substantial benefits.

Life was tranquil for the Petersons. Their kids were grown, their mortgage was almost paid off, and they didn't need a lot of money for anything else. Their big financial goal was to save enough money to take a Caribbean cruise for their fortieth anniversary. Mona was naturally surprised when her husband upped and quit his job to go off gallivanting about with Jonathan DeLuca, seemingly unperturbed by the fact that, so far, Fresco-whatsits had no operations and no money to pay the hefty salary that Jonathan had promised her husband. This perplexed her because Jonathan still hadn't paid back the money he had borrowed over a year earlier to buy that enormous diamond ring that his wife wore.

"I don't mean to be a scold, honey bun," she said, "But it seems like you boys do a lot of drinking and talking, but not much of anything else."

Hoping to alleviate his loving wife's unease, Bob walked over to her and kissed her gently on top of her head. "Now don't you worry about anything," he said. "Jonathan tells me that things are moving along nicely. In fact, he's getting ready to go to Monte Carlo and buy the yacht I told you about. Once he does that, I'll be so busy that you'll be complaining that I'm never here."

He took a wrinkled windbreaker off a hook by the front door and left, blowing her a kiss as he shut the door behind him. Mona sighed and went back into the kitchen to check on her pecan pie, shaking her head and hoping her husband hadn't hitched his wagon to the wrong star.

Chapter 16

The morning they were to leave for Monte Carlo, Anna woke up with the sun, rushed into the bathroom, and vomited twice. She was in a cold sweat, her body quivering uncontrollably. It felt like a fist was inside of her, squeezing her organs into mush. She called out to Jonathan. He walked into the bathroom, already dressed and ready to go to the airport, finding her crouched in front of the toilet. Her face was baby poop green, her eyes were watery, and the t-shirt she slept in was stained with something unidentifiable.

Anna brushed her hair from her face, beads of sweat pouring down her nose. She looked weakly up at him. "I can't go. I'm really sick," she said.

"You have to go."

"I can't. Look at me. I must have food poisoning or something." She turned away from him and threw up a third time. Wiping her lips with one hand, she said, "It must have been the fish I had for lunch yesterday."

"You absolutely have to go," Jonathan insisted, unmoved. "I need you to write checks for the deposit on Alpha Centauri and other business expenses while we're there."

Still hugging porcelain, Anna managed to ask, "Write a check with what? I've checked with Dan Fairfield at Silverman Baggins every day, and there's still no wire transfer from Lamar. How are you going to pay for everything?" She braced herself in the door jamb with her arms and struggled to stand up. Jonathan watched her, but made no attempt to help. She finally made it off the floor and over to the sink, splashing cold water on her face and looking questioningly at Jonathan's reflection in the mirror.

"Worst case, the securities will be on the screen by next Monday latest," the reflection said.

"That's cutting it awfully close. It's almost Thanksgiving. Businesses are shutting down early, and Monte Carlo is seven hours ahead of Texas. What if there's a delay in getting the money?" She dried her face and said, "You should cancel the whole trip. I think it's crazy to spend thousands of dollars to fly to Monaco to buy a thirteen-million-dollar boat for a hypothetical real estate project."

Taking great umbrage at the word "hypothetical" Jonathan bellowed, "I don't care if you understand or not. If we don't go now, we'll lose Alpha Centauri to another buyer. Need I remind you of the consequences to you and your career of blowing up the Hibiscus Cay deal?"

Anna didn't understand why the Hibiscus Cay deal would fall apart if they didn't purchase Alpha Centauri, but it was Lamar's money, and Jonathan was incontestably correct about the risk to her job if she refused to go. Now that he was unemployed, she had to consider their financial security first and her personal feelings last. Her head started pounding again as she staggered into the bedroom and collapsed onto the bed.

"Get up and get dressed," he ordered. "I'll run to the drugstore for some medicine. The car is picking us up in an hour, and you'd better be ready."

She took a hot shower while he went to the drugstore, letting the water beat down on her and hoping it would wash away her misgivings. Her instincts were imploring her to cancel the trip, but her fiduciary duties demanded that she go. The latter won the argument because Jonathan had skillfully boxed her into an uncomfortable corner when he volunteered her for the position as interim CEO of Frescobaldi Prime Investments. Sighing heavily, she dried off, got dressed, and finished packing.

* * *

They flew first-class to LaGuardia, then took a red-eye to Paris. After landing at Charles de Gaulle airport, they caught a connecting flight to Nice, arriving there an hour and a half later. Anna spent most of the trip sleeping or bolting to an airborne bathroom to throw up.

A team of uniformed airline personnel descended upon them as soon as they disembarked the plane, rushing them to one of the airport's helicopter terminals and escorting them out onto the tarmac to an eight-seat helicopter. Two more men jogged over and stowed the luggage while Jonathan helped Anna into the helicopter.

Everything had happened so fast that she was disoriented, her thoughts fuzzy and diffuse as she gazed out the window. They approached the public heliport serving Monte Carlo, the lights below them glittering like precious jewels strewn randomly on black velvet. In stark contrast, spotlights lit up the world-famous harbor like Times Square on New Year's Eve, and as the helicopter banked to the right in preparation for landing, she could see dozens of large, luxurious yachts docked in the calm waters below.

The sight was so otherworldly that it tempered her skepticism about Jonathan's business endeavors. Her doubts started to melt as she stared out the window with growing wonderment, thinking that she might have misjudged him. After all, Hibiscus Cay was a legitimate project in partnership with a famous billionaire and a client of her own law firm. The business relationship had been blessed by the firm's board of directors, and the benediction had been duly confirmed in writing by the firm's ethics committee.

If everything Jonathan said was true, she could quit her job and travel the world in luxury. Having worked like a machine since her high school graduation, she was only forty-six years old and already exhausted from everything she had overcome and all that she had achieved. Her work days sometimes felt like prison sentences, and her career prospects as a woman working in the male bastions of corporate law and corporate boardrooms were limited, if not nonexistent. The same could be said of her prospects of marrying again. The thought of a life free of the F-Man and his ilk was undeniably enticing, and the thought of a life lived alone was undeniably disheartening. Anna so wanted to believe her husband.

As if he sensed what she was thinking, Jonathan looked at her and took her hand, smiling inwardly at his latest victory over his wife. He had dangled the promise of future riches in front of her like a shiny bauble, and she had been mesmerized, just as he knew she would be. Everyone was. It never failed.

* * *

A driver with a dark blue Mercedes Benz sedan met them at the helicopter terminal in Monte Carlo and took them to the famed Hotel de Monaco. Anna still felt nauseated as Jonathan guided her gently by the elbow up the steps into the hotel. They crossed the spacious, elegantly decorated lobby, passing under an immense stained-glass skylight that hovered over them like a sapphire cloud.

He led her to a richly upholstered chair near the reception desk. He was supremely annoyed with her. After all, he hadn't put *that* much Xanax in her minestrone the night before. Maybe the second dose in her morning coffee wasn't such a great idea. He wanted her groggy and compliant, not throwing up everywhere. The trick had worked perfectly for him in the past, but apparently, Anna had a more sensitive stomach than the others.

After depositing her in the chair, he walked to the reception desk. Strategically placed to one side of the hallway leading to the elevator bank, its location ensured that guests had to pass by it every time they went to their rooms. Two sharply attired men were working behind the ornate mahogany desk, one of them a short man with a fleshy face, receding brown hair, and scornful brown eyes. He started babbling something in French, forcing Jonathan to ask him to speak English.

The man puffed up his chest, sniffed haughtily, and obliged. "Welcome to the Hotel de Monaco, Monsieur," he said in perfect English. "How may I help you?"

"I'm Jonathan DeLuca. My wife and I have a reservation."

The supercilious man tapped the keys of a reservations computer that sat behind the desk. "Yes, of course," he confirmed. "We have booked you into one of our junior suites." He handed Jonathan a form to fill in and took a stack of phone message from a cubbyhole in the wall behind the desk, handing those to him as well.

"Thank you, Mr. . . . ." Jonathan leaned in to read the gold nametag on the man's lapel, which declared him to be Gerard Elichery.

"Please, call me Gerard. Should you need anything during your stay, do not hesitate to let me know."

"Thank you, Gerard."

Jonathan leafed through the phone messages while Gerard worked busily at the computer. There were two messages from Captain Barry and one from the lawyers representing the owners of Alpha Centauri. Gerard looked up from his computer. "May I please have your credit card?" he asked.

Jonathan looked over at Anna. She had her head between her knees and appeared to be contemplating the oriental carpet. "Yes, of course. Here it is," he said. He handed Gerard the American CreditCorp card he had taken from her purse while she was throwing up in the airplane bathroom and finished checking them in.

A uniformed attendant led them to a suite on the third floor of the hotel with stunning views of the Mediterranean Sea and Port Hercule, Monaco's main harbor. Anna barely glanced at any of it, dropping her purse on the coffee table and going straight to the luxurious pink and brown marble bathroom to get ready for bed, too sick and exhausted to think about sightseeing or food.

A few minutes later, Jonathan heard her climb into one thousand thread-count Egyptian cotton sheets and pull the plush brocade duvet cover over her. He waited patiently in the sitting area of the suite until she was asleep, sipping a fifty-dollar glass of scotch from the very well-stocked mini-bar. Enjoying a Cuban cigar, he gazed out the heavily draped gabled windows at the yachts anchored below. On the hillside above, the imposing and brightly lit Prince's Palace overlooked the postage stamp-sized principality in all its Grimaldi glory. Row after row of luxurious high-rise condominium buildings lined the nearby hillsides, looking down on it all as if they were spectators in the Coliseum who had gathered to watch a staged Roman naval battle.

A sense of long-delayed gratification overtook him as he raised his glass in a toast to the opulent and breathtaking scene, whispering softly to the unseen occupants of the glamorous yachts below and the elite residences above, "I want this. I *deserve* this."

He finished his drink and put on his jacket, taking Anna's law firm card from the inside pocket. He tucked it back in her purse on his way down to the first floor and sauntered into The Lobby Bar in search of new possibilities.

* * *

Anna awoke to the smell of coffee. Jonathan was standing in the bedroom doorway, already showered, shaved, and dressed, looking like a young Thurston Howell III in a navy blue double-breasted blazer with gold buttons, ivory tropical wool pants, and brand-new topsiders.

"Rise and shine, sleepy head," he chirped, setting a breakfast tray on the bed beside her. "We have a meeting in the lobby in half an hour." Telling her that he had business with the front desk, he kissed her on the cheek and left.

Having barely eaten in two days, Anna was ravenously hungry and devoured the toast and scrambled eggs in minutes. After a quick shower, she dressed for the day in a navy-blue pantsuit, a crisp white cotton blouse, and a pair of white boat shoes. She went to the lobby, spotting Jonathan and a stranger in a corner seating area. She walked over, and Jonathan introduced her to Captain Barry Fogelson, the boat broker.

Short and barrel-chested, the corpulent captain was in his late fifties, his sandy hair thinning, and his florid face punctuated by rheumy eyes and a bulbous nose. He wore wrinkled khakis, a yellow polo shirt, a blue windbreaker, and scuffed boat shoes. His voice was deep and guttural from a lifetime of heavy smoking, and he sounded like a gravel crusher at a brick factory when he talked.

Captain Barry and Jonathan discussed the plans for the day while the three of them walked to a nearby parking lot and bundled into a rented Renault. The captain chain-smoked and talked non-stop while skillfully navigating the narrow, winding highway that connected Monte Carlo and San Remo, where Alpha Centauri was currently moored. The sinuous road provided stunning vistas at every curve, the sea on their right reflecting the morning sun like a piece of blue glass and throwing foamy whitecaps at the seaside cliffs. Arriving in the colorful hamlet on the coast of the Ligurian Sea in less than an hour, he drove them to the San Remo Sun Port and across the man-made seawall that separated the marina from raw ocean. He parked at the very end, and they all got out and walked to the gangway of a gleaming white leviathan that towered above them like a small office building.

Anna had spent a lot of time on boats, and she had seen quite a few private yachts in her travels. For a few stormy years when she was in her thirties, she dated a telecommunications magnate with a zest for life, sailboats, rum, and women. They had sailed much of the Caribbean aboard the bearded businessman's forty-two-foot sailboat. Her salacious sailor met his unfortunate and watery demise long after they had broken up, having done so in a manner befitting his larger-than-life personality and over-the-top bad habits. Although warned three times by the harbor master at Grand Exuma that the entrance to the harbor was jealously guarded by treacherous rocks and razor sharp coral heads, the ill-fated lothario ignored him. Blind drunk on rum and sky high on cocaine, he made a suicidal attempt to enter the harbor at night when no one was watching. The sailboat didn't make it and neither did he.

Gazing up now at Alpha Centauri, Anna didn't think anything could sink this giant beast of a boat.

Captain Barry's rusty foghorn voice interrupted her sail down memory lane. "Permission to come aboard, sir?" he barked at a man standing two decks above Alpha Centauri's water line.

Permission was granted, and the visitors climbed the gangway. They were greeted by Captain Salvatore Savino, a compact, fifty-two-year-old with salt and pepper hair and an aquiline nose like Jonathan's. He was meaty and tightly packed into neatly pressed gray pants and a combat green sweater with reinforced shoulder epaulets. He bobbed up and down like a buoy when he spoke in his halting English, his fleshy lips exposing a wide, obsequious grin. "*Benvenuto*. Welcome," he said in heavily-accented English, ushering them into the main salon with a grand sweep of his arm.

They all shook hands and introductions were made. "*Buongiorno*, Capitano Salvatore," Jonathan said in fluid Italian. "I am Jonathan Frescobaldi DeLuca, and this is my lovely bride Anna."

Anna looked at Jonathan as if he had sprouted horns. *When had he started calling himself that?*

Bowing deeply at the waist, Captain Salvatore kissed her hand and launched them on a tour of Alpha Centauri from stem to stern and top to bottom. After visiting every salon and cabin, their explorations quickly made clear that the photos of the yacht's interior had been taken in much better times. The paneled oak walls hadn't seen a coat of wax in years, and the oil paintings adorning them were faded and grimy. The linens on the queen size bed in the master suite were dusty, the chairs in the game salon were rickety, and the yellow and white striped cushions on the outside lounges were stained and dirty. Although the chicken cacciatore prepared for them by the ship's outgoing chef was excellent, the fuchsia silk upholstery covering the dining room chairs had faded to pale pink, and the table upon which they lunched was pitted and scratched, its once glossy finish now worn to a cloudy sheen.

After sorbet and espressos, Captain Salvatore took them below decks to see the engine room. The size of the DeLuca's apartment, its walls, floors, ceiling, and massive machinery were all painted a glistening hospital white. Eerily quiet because Alpha Centauri was docked, the room sounded like the inside of a jet engine when the yacht was underway.

The last stop and high point of the tour was the yacht's bridge. The navigational and other systems were state of the art. The five-foot-wide control panel was generously dotted with multi-colored lights and looked like a NASA control room. Anna could have stayed on the bridge for hours, but the crew had other duties to fulfill, and it was time for their American guests to leave.

Jonathan and Captain Barry spent the return drive to Monte Carlo talking about the events of the day, the shortcomings of Alpha Centauri, and the lower price that Captain Barry would try to negotiate due to the sorry state of the yacht's furnishings.

Anna listened quietly and gazed out the window, watching the setting sun dip into the sea and trying to absorb it all.

* * *

They arrived back at the Hotel de Monaco, and the men went into the bar for martinis while Anna went upstairs to take a bath. She started filling the cavernous marble bathtub and got undressed, dousing the hot water liberally with the expensive Hermès bubble bath that the hotel provided as one of its many body-pampering amenities. As the tub filled and foamed, she poured herself a generous glass of wine from the mini-bar and slid down into the luxurious water until it reached her chin.

She stayed there, daydreaming, until Jonathan returned and they dressed for dinner. Jonathan wore his new white bespoke dinner jacket while Anna was stylishly frugal in a consignment store, hunter green Escada evening suit that turned her eyes the same color.

They took Thanksgiving dinner at The Marie Antoinette, the hotel's world-famous, five-star restaurant. An immensely expensive and exclusive culinary temple devoted to overpriced, undersized *haute cuisine*, it was conveniently located off the hotel lobby, the entrance cleverly obscured behind mirrored doors. More mirrors covered the restaurant walls inside, an acre of glass reflecting the crystal stemware and table candles in a Rococo cotillion of lights.

Anna managed to embarrass her husband almost immediately when she set her evening bag on the blush ivory and gold carpet near her chair. A starchy, uniformed headwaiter with a scandalized look on his face scurried over, snapped the purse up, and placed it on a brocade footstool that sat on the floor next to her chair. She had noticed the stool when she sat down, but had no idea that there was such a thing as furniture for handbags.

As the night wore on, her embarrassment over her *faux pas* faded, and she was slowly and subtly seduced by the glamorous surroundings, the fawning waiters, and Jonathan's wondrous tales of riches and real estate. As she had during the helicopter flight, Anna found herself imagining a new future—a future in which everything Jonathan told her was true.

147

Chapter 17

The next day, Captain Barry was busy arranging for an independent survey and appraisal of the yacht, so the DeLucas had some time to kill. They wandered Monte Carlo's charming streets and strolled through the lush gardens near the hotel. Overflowing with colorful tropical plants, the rambling green spaces were home to peacocks that preened and strutted their colorful stuff for an audience of purple irises that swayed gently back and forth in appreciation.

A warm breeze wafted gently from the sea. They followed it past the hotel and behind the casino, crossing a lushly landscaped pedestrian plaza that covered the roof of a condominium complex nestled in the seaside cliffs. Tall concrete pilings encircled by ominously dark rocks supported the structure, with only a chest-high guard railing to impede a fall. Massive waves beat mercilessly against the rocks and pilings, the sound making Anna shudder as if a ghost had just passed through her.

She stepped quickly back from the unsettling sight, and they continued their wanderings, ambling along the road that bordered the harbor until they reached a set of steep stairs that led down to the Port Hercule marina. The children of Monaco learn to sail at an early age, and they saw a fleet of budding yachtsmen manning pint-sized sailboats scarcely larger than they were. Wobbling along like baby ducks behind a red rubber Zodiac watercraft piloted by an instructor, the tiny sailors inspired Anna to nickname them the "duckling princes."

Once the flock was out of the safety of the harbor and into the open sea, one of miniature mariners lost control of his tiny vessel and started bobbling off unsteadily in the opposite direction toward a passing freighter. The instructor bolted to his errant charge's rescue, coaxing him back to safe waters and saving the future heir to some great fortune from the consequences of his navigational mistake.

The duckling prince safe and sound, they continued past the impressive vessels docked in the marina. They crossed the street to a sidewalk café overlooking a segment of the famed Circuit de Monaco, home to the annual Grand Prix of international fame. Lunching in the sun, they listened to creaking hulls and straining guide ropes and imagined the sound of lightning-fast Formula One race cars zooming past.

Jonathan did most of the talking during lunch, and most of it was about yachts. Anna had no idea how he had become such an expert on the yachting styles of the rich and famous, thinking it a touch surreal that she was in Monte Carlo with her husband negotiating to buy a mega-yacht. Jonathan, on the other hand, acted as if he were born to the opulence that surrounded them, looking and acting every bit the Italian count, just as Cindy had once remarked.

They finished their lunch and walked back to the Hotel De Monaco. Anna checked the front desk for messages when they returned, but the one she was looking for wasn't there. Her lighthearted mood vanished, and when they got back to the suite, she demanded an explanation from Jonathan as to how they were going to pay the hotel bill if Lamar didn't come through with their expense money.

Jonathan ignored her and pulled a cigar from his coat pocket, lighting it with a silver cigarette lighter produced from his other pocket. He blew the first puff of smoke directly in her face. "Fuck you and your hillbilly attitude," he sneered. "We can't afford this, we can't afford that." Taking another puff, he exhaled loudly. "I'm beginning to think I made a mistake by marrying you."

Anna was beginning to feel the same way, but held back. "I didn't know you smoked cigars," was her only remark.

"There's a lot you don't know about me," Jonathan snarled. He looked at the Piaget watch that he had "borrowed" from his father without asking permission. "I have a meeting with Captain Barry and the boat surveyor," he said. "There is no need for you to come. I'll be dining in Le Club after our meeting, with or without you."

He brushed roughly past her and left, slamming the heavy oak door behind him so hard that a gilt-edged baroque mirror fell off the wall with a thud that shook the floor.

* * *

The next morning, Jonathan jostled Anna's shoulders until she woke up. She blinked sleepily at him. "What time is it?"

"It's already 9:15 a.m. and our first meeting is at 9:30 a.m.," he said, handing her a cup of coffee. "I'll meet you downstairs in the lobby. Hurry up."

Anna took the delicate china cup and hungrily inhaled the strong aroma. She hadn't bothered to go looking for Jonathan after he stormed out the night before and had no idea when he had returned to the suite, but he was up and dressed in his yachting outfit again. She pushed the button on the electric shades and watched as the blindingly blue waters of the Mediterranean came into view, the cerulean wavetops glittering like a billion diamonds dancing over the surface of the sea as the sun kissed the waters gently awake. Tearing herself reluctantly away from the majestic sight, she got dressed and went downstairs.

Jonathan and Captain Barry were sitting at a small table at the far end of the lobby with another man she didn't recognize. All three stood up as she arrived, and Jonathan introduced her to the boat surveyor from Miami. Anna didn't know why or when Jonathan had arranged for an appraisal of Alpha Centauri, considering that they hadn't even signed a letter of intent, but she listened attentively while the surveyor explained the yacht appraisal process.

The surveyor left just as Captain Salvatore arrived. He and Jonathan spent the next hour talking about the twelve-member crew and their current salaries, including Captain Salvatore's. Captain Barry had suggested salaries for each crew member, but the numbers that Jonathan tossed out like shark chum were at least three times higher than the going rate for general crew members and four times the customary amount for a captain—even one as experienced as Captain Salvatore. Anna did the math in her head and it boggled her mind. The crew salaries alone would be almost half a million dollars a year.

Captain Salvatore produced a well-worn catalog from his battered briefcase and the conversation turned to uniforms. He had helpfully dog-eared some pages with photographs of the uniforms he had in mind for the crew—both for everyday duties and for formal gatherings. Jonathan leafed through the catalog and then handed it to Captain Barry, telling Captain Salvatore that he had budgeted another six-figure sum for the uniforms. Not surprisingly, the stunned captain readily agreed when Jonathan invited him to join them for lunch.

The DeLucas and the bi-continental captains left the hotel and walked past the casino, arriving at the Café de Paris in less than a minute. The unlikely crew lunched on the patio, cozy and warm in the gentle early winter sun. Jonathan made idle chit chat with the other men while Anna watched the afternoon unfold in front of her. A seemingly endless stream of luxury cars and limousines passed by as she contemplated the strange twists and turns of life that had brought her here to the most glamorous place on the planet.

Three hours and two bottles of wine later, Captain Salvatore bade them goodbye and left for San Remo to prepare for the appraisal. Jonathan charged the lunch to the suite, and they returned to the hotel lobby for their afternoon meeting with legal counsel to the sellers of Alpha Centauri.

While they waited for the attorneys to arrive, Anna went to the reception desk to check again for messages. There was still no wire transfer from Lamar.

* * *

Captain Barry had already contacted the lawyers for the owners of Alpha Centauri via Skype and recognized them as soon as they entered the hotel lobby. He waved them over and introduced the DeLucas to Philip Bargeron and Nicole DuChene of the Bargeron Law Firm of Monte Carlo, with satellite offices in Paris, Nice and Florence.

Monsieur Bargeron was five feet four inches tall and almost as wide, with a shock of salt and pepper hair and horn rim half-glasses.

151

He wore a three-piece suit with a bow tie and spoke formally, his voice deep and his English flawless.

Mademoiselle DuChene was tall and thin, her brown hair tightly-wound into a small chignon on top of her head. Wearing a black Chanel suit, she sat primly and properly, taking an occasional note on a legal-sized pad. She pursed her lips when she spoke in her heavily-accented English, making one wonder if the mademoiselle had just sucked on a lemon.

She handed Anna the proposed letter of intent on the sale, and the three attorneys reviewed it together. Anna made some notes on the draft, Mademoiselle DuChene assuring her that the revised letter of intent would be ready the following day. Having finished her official duties to Frescobaldi Prime Investments, Anna excused herself and went upstairs to take a nap before dinner.

Captain Barry and the attorneys left, leaving Jonathan alone to congratulate himself on how well the negotiations were going. He sauntered across the elegant lobby to the concierge desk, encountering Gerard again.

Gerard looked up from his task. "*Bon jour*, Monsieur DeLuca," he said. "How may I assist you today?"

"Good afternoon, Gerard," Jonathan said. "My wife and I are so enchanted by your hotel that we would like to return for our wedding anniversary in late December. Might we book the same suite from December 13th through the end of the year?"

Gerard tapped some keys on his computer. "I regret sir, that the junior suite you request is not available for those dates. One of the larger suites is available at a rate of one thousand eight hundred seventy-five Euros per night, plus VAT."

"That will be fine." Jonathan said without blinking or balking at the cost of the suite.

"We require a deposit of five thousand Euros to reserve the room."

"Please add it to our bill," Jonathan said, discreetly handing Gerard one hundred Euros to seal the transaction.

"As you wish, sir," Gerard said, discreetly taking the cash.

Jonathan said "*Merci*," and returned to the room to put on his new tuxedo.

* * *

Captain Salvatore was on his way back to San Remo, thinking about his meeting with the potential buyers of Alpha Centauri. He wasn't quite sure what to make of Jonathan Frescobaldi DeLuca and couldn't get a solid read on the man, but his wife was a lawyer so the husband must be all right too. Not that there was anything he could do about it. It was no business of his who bought Alpha Centauri, but once she was sold, the captain, like the other crew members, would be subject to firing at will by the new owners, whoever they might be. Captain Salvatore had become an expert in anticipating and satisfying the whims and caprices of the *molto* wealthy. Because of his skills in such matters, he seldom lacked for work and had been sailing the Mediterranean for decades as an internationally certified mega-yacht captain. Captain Salvatore liked his job, and he wanted to keep it.

Born in Bologna, Italy, he lived the first twenty years of his life there. His father was a top executive and major stakeholder in the region's largest agricultural products business. Expected to follow in his father's landlocked footsteps, the dutiful son attended the University of Bologna to study agriculture and economics, but his heart belonged to the sea from the day he first saw it when he was only a boy.

His father would take him to visit his Uncle Gianni in Livorno on the northwest coast of Italy, where he eked out a subsistence living by fishing for John Dory and Turbot. Little Salvatore would bump along in his uncle's dilapidated scow, grinning with youthful glee at the feel of the wind in his hair, never noticing the boat's peeling paint. Enthralled by the wondrous delights in that small part of the Ligurian Sea, he dreamed of seeing more of them in the wider world on much bigger boats.

The sirens' song of the sea never released him from its spell. After two semesters immersed in studying macro-economics and the chemical composition of fertilizer, a recalcitrant Salvatore dropped out of school, enraging his father and breaking his mother's heart. Though summarily disinherited, he eventually reimbursed his father for the squandered tuition, but the chasm between them never closed.

Though banished by his family, Salvatore didn't set out to see the world on his own, having met the love of his life wife at university where she was studying Letters and Cultural History. Angelica Gabelli was the only child of two successful art dealers from Venice. Like Salvatore, she was expected to enter the family business, but her interests lay elsewhere. Deeply in love and wanting nothing more from life than to be with Salvatore and bear his children, the besotted Angelica left school to travel wherever her beloved chose to take her. Her parents told her never to return home.

The star-crossed lovers married in Livorno and lived for a time in Uncle Gianni's drafty attic. Salvatore worked odd jobs and fished with his uncle, while Angelica took in sewing and prayed she'd become pregnant. Her prayers were answered, but she miscarried, the complications requiring the removal of her uterus. Angelica was rendered infertile, leaving the Savinos forever childless.

Despite their heartbreak and financial struggles, they managed to save enough money through hard work and relentless parsimony to enable Salvatore to attend mariner's school nearby. Two difficult years later, he earned his captain's certificate and the right to be called *Capitano* Salvatore.

Although Angelica's youthful beauty faded over the years, her love for Salvatore never did. Not once in all their years together had she ever complained about the long stretches of loneliness she endured during her husband's extended absences. She always waited patiently for him to return from the sea, alone in a cheap rented flat in some obscure coastal town. She waited for him now, in a small cottage in the hills northwest of San Remo, not far from the port.

Anxious to get home safely to her, but still a little groggy from all the wine he drank at lunch, Captain Salvatore opened the window and let the cool sea breeze clear the clouds in his head while he focused on the treacherous road and thought about money.

His financial situation had improved vastly when he started working on mega-yachts. Now, with the princely sums the American was promising, he could retire in five years instead of fifteen. They would have enough money to buy the cottage with the vegetable garden that Angelica loved so much, and he could start his own charter business taking tourists and businessmen to Elba, Corsica, Sardinia and Monaco during the day, returning home to his sweet bride every night. At last, they could finally have the comfortable, settled life that that Angelica so richly deserved after his many years of wanderings.

The dream was irresistible. Putting his doubts aside, Captain Salvatore decided that he'd cover his stern and do anything necessary to ensure that Jonathan Frescobaldi DeLuca bought Alpha Centauri.

Chapter 18

Jonathan sat on a caramel-colored leather barstool in The Lobby Bar, perched uncomfortably on the horns of his current dilemma. Anna was still in the suite getting ready to go out for the evening as he sipped champagne and scanned the bar. She had been uncharacteristically quiet since they arrived in Monte Carlo, and that made him nervous. He still needed her cooperation because she was the only person authorized to sign on the company account, and the owners of Alpha Centauri were demanding a one hundred-fifty-thousand-dollar deposit. He couldn't put them off much longer, so he had to figure something out until Lamar came through with his investment.

As he gazed into his champagne searching for clues that might help resolve his quandary, a tall, sophisticated, blonde came in. Forty-something, buff, buxom, and dripping with diamonds, she gave him a cursory glance and sat down at the opposite end of the bar. She was unaccompanied, so he immediately left his barstool and went to stand next to the beguiling beauty.

Sensing his presence, she turned and looked him up and down disapprovingly, disdain in her icy blue eyes. Apparently unimpressed with what she saw, she looked away again, completely indifferent to the debonair man standing side her.

Not to be dissuaded, Jonathan put one hand on the back of her barstool and leaned in. "My god, you're beautiful," he whispered.

She turned to face him again and blushed. "*Danke*," she said.

Smartly clicking his heels and bowing genteelly at the waist, he took her Bulgari-bejeweled hand in his. He kissed it sensuously and introduced himself. "I am Jonathan Frescobaldi DeLuca, III."

"It's a pleasure to meet you, Herr DeLuca. I am the Baroness von Pfaffenhofen."

Jonathan sat down next to the Baroness and gazed deeply into her eyes. "How many times have you been in love?" he asked.

The Baroness blushed.

* * *

The Baroness Gisela von Pfaffenhofen *nee* Esterházy was indeed royalty, although being a royal in the 21st Century was not as prestigious, lucrative, or socially intimidating as it had been in past centuries. Unlike other vestigial royals, the Esterházys had not turned their castle near the border of Lichtenstein into a dusty museum, selling tickets to the unwashed masses who came to gawk at a dying way of life. Instead, Gisela's grandfather, the tenth Baron Esterházy, sold the castle and its adjacent hunting lands shortly before World War II and went into the chemicals business in Brazil. Gisela's father eventually inherited both the royal title and the mantle of leadership of Esterházy Enterprises. Under the younger Baron's dour stewardship, the family and the business moved back to Austria and the company branched out into the pharmaceuticals and cosmetics markets, quickly tripling its revenues.

Gisela had always been the bad girl of the family, quite frequently to her parents' very public embarrassment, but she eventually matured into an accomplished young woman. Having studied foreign languages at the Sorbonne, she was fluent in German, French, Italian and English, donning and shedding accents like she did her jewelry and lovers—depending on her mood.

When she was in her mid-twenties, her father declared it time for her to wed and pressured her into marrying a wealthy Viennese count who was forty-five years her senior. Five years after they married, the unfortunate—but satisfied—Baron von Pfaffenhoffen died in a gruesome accident. The royal couple was in a ski gondola coming down from the slopes in Gstaad when the unlucky Baron's boot became tangled in the gondola door. The horrified Baroness watched helplessly as her doomed husband literally reached the end of the line and was pulled underneath the carousel, the giant pulley squashing him like a cherry strudel.

The newly widowed Baroness was single again and stratospherically wealthy. Not content to rest on her riches, she was ambitious as well, convincing her father to let her run the family's cosmetics business. Having done so with great success for almost twenty years, she acquired even more riches and a long trail of discarded lovers. She was currently keeping a much younger man named Hugo as her companion. A museum quality specimen of pure Teutonic genetics as would have made the Hitler Youth proud, he was currently working out in the hotel gym, an obsession she heartily endorsed. But she wouldn't see him for hours, and the American stranger was rather intriguing.

"Your name is Italian, *ja?*" she asked, her Austrian accent heavy.

Enchanted by the Baroness's pulchritude and royal lineage, Jonathan leaned in to peek at her luscious pink breasts. "Yes, it is," he whispered in her ear, his breath on her ivory neck raising goose bumps almost as large as the diamonds encrusting the dazzling necklace that encircled it. "I'm descended from the Sicilian DeLucas on my father's side and Count Carlo Frescobaldi Bianchi of Florence on my mother's."

"What brings you to Monte Carlo, Mr. DeLuca?" she asked, her accent vanishing suddenly.

"My wife and I are here to conclude the purchase of a fifteen-million-dollar yacht," Jonathan replied, inflating the price for effect.

The Baroness failed to hide her irritation at the words "my wife," and Jonathan intercepted her train of thought before it derailed to his detriment. "We're divorcing," he quickly assured her. "Our relationship now is purely business because she is still involved in my company. Perhaps you have heard of Frescobaldi Prime Investments, the international real estate conglomerate?"

"No, I have not," the Baroness replied, tossing her hand and dismissing the subject. "Real estate is boring. Tell me more about your Sicilian and Florentine ancestors."

Jonathan told his tale and was nuzzling the Baroness' ear to get a closer look at the five-carat diamond drop earrings that graced them when he saw half of the bar patrons look simultaneously toward the entrance to the bar. His eyes followed the swiveling heads and landed on Anna. Dressed to kill in that slinky silver number he liked, she was glaring at him as if he were the intended target. He was impressed both by how beautiful she was and how angry she looked.

He broke away from the Baroness apologetically. "It is with great regret that I must leave you. My soon-to-be-ex-wife has just arrived and one must keep up appearances, even during a divorce."

"Indeed, one must," the Baroness said, turning away.

Jonathan hurried over and took Anna by the elbow, hustling her out of the bar before she could make a scene. As he did, he turned and winked at the abandoned Baroness, who was watching them leave, a bored and bemused look on her face. He made a mental note to have Gerard send her flowers and charge them to the room, wondering how to say, "You stand out in a crowd!" in German.

* * *

He didn't have much time to wonder because as soon as they were out of the bar, Anna threw off his arm and stormed off toward the elevator bank. She stabbed the "Up" button repeatedly, as if she were clubbing a freshly caught tarpon to death with a boat hook.

Jonathan caught up with her and grabbed her by the arm, whirling her around to face him. "What the hell is wrong with you?" he demanded.

She shrugged him off as if his touch were radioactive. "I'm going up to the room."

"I thought we were going to the casino."

"We're not going anywhere but home in the morning." She pushed past him and entered an empty elevator. They rode up to the room in silence, but as soon as they got in the door, she started shouting, her face scarlet with unrestrained rage. "Liar!" she screamed. "I just talked to Jack. You lied to me about everything."

Jonathan's face darkened, his body quivering with barely contained wrath. His hands started trembling as he clenched them tightly to his sides. "You did what?" he roared.

Anna lowered her voice a few decibels. "You heard me. Dan Fairfield called while you were downstairs nibbling on that woman. He told me there was still no wire transfer from Lamar, so I found Jack's number in your phone and called him. He told me they haven't finished their due diligence on Hibiscus Cay. You're not even close to a deal with Lamar yet, and you lied about his promise to pay for this trip. What else have you lied to me about?"

Jonathan approached her menacingly, his fists still clenched at his sides. "What the fuck were you thinking?" he shouted, livid. "I told you never to call Jack. If you screwed this deal up for me Anna, I swear you'll regret it, so help me god." He raised a fist but made no move to strike her as she ducked away. She ran into the sanctuary of the bathroom, locking the door behind her and infuriating him further.

"You're nothing but trailer trash with a law degree, you stupid bitch," he bellowed, pummeling fruitlessly on the bathroom door before punching the wall beside it. Rubbing his bruised knuckles, he went to the mini-bar, opened a two-hundred-dollar bottle of wine, and started swigging it straight from the bottle.

* * *

Anna waited in the bathroom and thought about ways to kill herself. Jonathan had brought her to the brink of a financial apocalypse and she could not for the life of her think of a way out. She thought briefly about defenestration out the suite's bay window, but with her luck, she'd probably just end up a penniless paraplegic. She listened quietly through the bathroom door until she was sure that Jonathan was asleep, then opened the door a crack and peeked through it. He was passed out on the small sitting room couch, snoring heavily.

She tiptoed out of the bathroom and let herself out of room, taking the elevator down to the first floor and leaving through the side entrance of the hotel. Consumed with dark and determined suicidal thoughts, she walked quickly to the pedestrian plaza they had visited earlier. Kicking off her shoes, she used her arms to hike herself up onto the six-inch-wide concrete guard railing until she was sitting on it. She stood up shakily and was about to leap into oblivion when a distant memory pierced the fog of her scrambled final thoughts. The intrusion of it caused her to pause as she remembered her first suicide attempt.

She was fourteen years old when a six-inch growth spurt wreaked havoc on her body. Suffering through excruciating growing pains in her knees and hips, she had to teach her taller, gangly body how to do things all over again. The toll it took was destructive. An over-stressed ligament stretched too far during a recital one night, and she collapsed to the stage in agony. Dance-weary and her body wracked by relentless pain, she begged her mother to let her quit ballet. Instead, her mother threatened to throw her out of house and sent her to a sports doctor for physical and psychological therapy.

Anna had been taking sleeping pills for years, insomnia being a frequent companion to high intelligence. She took fifteen of them one night when her mother was out, but they weren't enough to do the trick. She awoke eighteen hours later, her eyes bleary and her brain foggy. She watched a wavering shape materialize at the foot of the bed, hoping that she was dead and in heaven with her beloved grandmother.

But the hazy blob resolved into her mother instead, staring at her reproachfully from the foot of the bed. Her mother was clutching the brass bed rail so hard that her knuckles had turned white. As Anna regained consciousness, Caroline intoned in a voice as cold as an underground tomb in winter, "Don't you ever do that to me again." Turning on her heel, she slammed the bedroom door violently, leaving Anna completely alone.

Two days later Anna was back in school and back in dance class. Her mother gave her the silent treatment for almost two weeks, never mentioning the episode again. Her father never said a word about it because her mother never told him about the failed suicide attempt.

Flickering memories of her father snapped Anna back to the present. She sat back down on the icy cold railing, recalling the paternal nuggets of advice he used to give her after a bad dance class or performance, talking to her as if she were a son who'd lost a football game.

"When the going gets tough, the tough get going," he'd say. "It's not how many times you fall down, it's how many times you get up," was his frequent advice. His favorite was "Winners never quit and quitters never win."

Though trite and sometimes facile, Anna had learned those lessons well. They comforted her now, and her suicidal resolve wavered. Shivering from the frigid night air, she climbed carefully down, put her shoes back on, and walked unsteadily back to the welcoming womb of the Hotel de Monaco. She dreaded the drastically altered and uncertain future that awaited her, but she was determined to overcome whatever travails lay ahead.

Safely back from the watery abyss, she discovered that the door to the suite was locked, and she didn't have her key because she had not planned on needing it. She leaned against the wall and slowly slid down it until she was sitting on the thickly carpeted floor, reconsidering her decision not to jump off the nearby cliff.

She fell asleep until a few minutes later, a hotel security guard shook her awake, wary concern in his eyes. "Are you all right, Madame?" he asked.

It took her a few seconds to remember where she was and what had happened. The guard leaned down and offered her his hand. She took it and stood up on rubbery knees, smoothing the front of her dress and mustering her best nonplussed lawyer face. "I am so sorry," she said, her voice dry and cracking. "My husband has inadvertently locked me out of our room. I think he's fast asleep, and I didn't want to wake your other guests by pounding loudly on the door at this late hour. I sat down to wait and must have fallen asleep."

The guard said nothing, not mentioning that he and the hotel manager had been watching her on the hotel's closed-circuit camera system. He wordlessly took a plastic card from his jacket pocket and swiped it at the door's electronic lock. It blinked a green eye at them, and the door clicked quietly open.

Anna thanked the stern-faced sentinel and tiptoed into the suite, spotting an envelope on the floor. She opened it and gasped when she saw that it was the hotel bill, and the total was almost twelve thousand dollars.

Jonathan was still asleep in the sitting room, snoring like a diesel engine. Filled with regret, sorrow, and a new disdain for her husband, she snuck past him to the bedroom get a few hours' sleep. As she passed the bathroom, she noticed a fist-sized hole in the wall by the door where he had punched it and wondered how much that was going to cost her.

* * *

Anna paid the hotel bill when they checked out before dawn the following morning, using her law firm card in a blatant violation of B&V policy. She was so flustered by what she was doing that she couldn't even focus on the individual charges to verify the balance, praying that the charge wouldn't draw the attention of B&V's business department before she could get home and pay the bill. Jonathan stood silently behind her as she signed the charge slip, the time for his excuses and prevarications long over.

A black Mercedes sedan drove them at ninety miles per hour through the dimly-lit tunnel that connects Monte Carlo to France. Neither of them spoke during the ride to the Nice airport, and both were silent during the flights back to Dallas. Nothing was said during the ride home from the airport, and they slept in separate rooms again that night.

When she awoke the next morning, Jonathan was nowhere to be seen. She got dressed and went upstairs to her office to get her briefcase, noticing that Jonathan had piled his luggage at the top of the second-floor landing. The largest case was open and, just as it had once been filled with Christmas ornaments from The Royal Tarlton Hotel, now it was filled with Hermès soap from the Hotel de Monaco. At least thirty of the oversized bars in their signature orange wrappings were in the case. Looking closer, she saw one of the hotel's two-hundred-dollar terry cloth robes and a crystal ashtray from the suite wrapped within it. She shook her head at the incomprehensible petty theft. *Did Jonathan have no conscience at all?*

PART III

Chapter 19

Anna took her car to work the Monday after they returned from Monte Carlo, leaving Jonathan to his own devices. The first thing she did when she got to the office was wire money to American CreditCorp to pay the hotel bill. It wiped out her savings, but hopefully the firm would never find out about it and fire her over the misbegotten trip.

The second thing she did was call Jerry Goldblatt, the attorney who had handled her first divorce. The receptionist told her that he was still out of town on extended holiday, and since Anna was leaving the following morning for Boston and wouldn't be returning to Dallas until late Thursday, the divorce would have to wait. In the meantime, she'd keep her plans to herself and act as if nothing were amiss, so as not to alert Jonathan to her wedlock-ending intentions.

She was hanging up the phone when Becca buzzed her on the intercom. "Jonathan's on the line for you," she said. "He says it's urgent. I told him you were on another call, but he insisted on holding."

Anna was working on multiple deals that had to be completed by year-end and scrambling to return all the phone calls and emails that had piled up while she was in Monte Carlo. She picked up the phone and snapped, "What do you want? I'm really busy."

"You need to come down to the visitor parking garage right now," Jonathan said.

"Why?"

"Just get down here. If you don't, I'll come up there and get you."

The last thing she needed was Jonathan causing a scene at her office. "Fine," she said, slamming down the phone.

When she got to the garage, she saw him standing next to a Mercedes SL600 convertible in the same ruby red color as his last demo car. The top was down, and she recognized the saleswoman from Highland Park Motors sitting in the passenger seat. Irritated, she walked over to Jonathan, acknowledging Sue Worthing with a curt nod of her head.

"What do you want?" Anna demanded. "I don't have time for this."

"I want you to see something," Jonathan replied. He smiled and pointed to the shiny car that sparkled like Dorothy's magic slippers in the garage's fluorescent lights.

Anna glanced at the car and back at Jonathan. "What about it?"

Jonathan took her by the elbow and maneuvered her out of Sue's earshot. "Peter Grand agreed to buy me a car, and this is it."

Anna was unimpressed by Jonathan's overblown fantasies. "What does this have to do with me?"

"It's going to be the company car."

"I don't have time for this, and I really don't care what you do as long as I don't have to pay for it." She started walking away, but stopped and turned. "For your information, I will be resigning from the company as soon as I get back from Boston and have time to file the papers with the Secretary of State." She turned away again and went back to her office.

Jonathan put on a happy face and walked back to the car, cheerfully telling Sue, "Anna absolutely *loves* the car."

* * *

While Anna was giving a speech at a venture capital conference in Boston, Jonathan was sitting in Sue Worthing's cubicle at Highland Park Motors, wrapping up the details on the lease for the red convertible. At over three thousand dollars per month, the lease totaled over hundred thousand dollars over its three-year term—but that was a real bargain because it included OnStar.

Unknown to his wife, Jonathan had gone back to Highland Park Motors several times in the past few months, always dealing with Sue and always talking about how he had a big deal on the horizon. After his third such visit, Sue received a lovely flower arrangement and a card that said, "You're one in a million!"

While Sue did a final review of the paperwork, Jonathan told her all about his new yacht and how wealthy he was, promising her that his company would soon need an entire fleet of new Mercedes Benzes. With visions of Christmas commissions dancing in her head, she handed over the keys to the new convertible.

Jonathan slid into the luxurious leather seat, and even though it was December and turning cold, he pushed a button on a dashboard panel covered with almost as many blinking lights as the bridge controls for Alpha Centauri. With a quiet whirr, the supple top tucked itself gently away into a compartment above the trunk. He pointed the car toward Turtle Creek Boulevard and basked in the luxurious smell of his new Mercedes, delighting and rejoicing in it. It smelled like money.

* * *

Marilyn Beauregard was in the expansive kitchen of her expensive penthouse overlooking Turtle Creek and downtown Dallas. She was putting the finishing touches on a meal of southern specialties: shrimp gumbo, fried okra, and hush puppies. She was wearing nothing but flawless designer skin under a black lace apron that looked like it belonged in the bedroom instead of the kitchen. Jonathan would be arriving shortly, and because she wanted to keep the Hibiscus Cay business if she could, she was hoping that her down-home comfort food and her uptown sexual skills would blunt the blow of the bad news she was about to deliver. Her oil man lover had been released from white collar prison, and the time had come to end her little fling with Jonathan.

Marilyn suffered no guilt for the decision, because she had made it clear to Jonathan from the start that she had no interest in a serious relationship with anyone other than her wildcatter from Waco. She had other reasons to break it off. For one thing, Jonathan kept talking about divorcing his lawyer wife, and that was unacceptable. Although many wealthy men had tasted Marilyn's luscious fruits, and most of their wives knew about it, one simply didn't *talk* about it. Marilyn was regularly featured in the gossip columns and being labeled a home wrecker would be bad for business because it's almost always the wife who makes the final decision on home purchases. She didn't want the negative publicity that would engulf her if word of her having broken up a marriage got around town. She most definitely did not want to go up against a scorned lady lawyer from B&V.

Her unease justifiably grew after Jonathan's recent revelation that his wife had found out about them and cleaned out their bank account in a fit of jealous rage. Marilyn wondered why the two of them were still living together under such uncomfortable circumstances, but she loaned him ten thousand dollars anyway. In exchange, he promised to deflect Anna away from her.

Another motivating factor was that Jonathan had lost his ability to perform to her expectations in the bedroom and resorted to bringing battery-operated assistants to bed with them to do the work for him. He had become both inconvenient and impotent, so he had to go.

The doorbell chimed. Marilyn adjusted her apron to expose more cleavage and quickly checked her cherry red lipstick in the mirror beside the door. She opened the door to find Jonathan standing there with an enormous package under one arm. He dropped the package on an Eames chair in the living room and went to her, embracing her and kissing her passionately.

Breaking the kiss, she teased, "Well you're a frisky one tonight, sugar."

"It's because I have excellent news, my darling," he said. He opened the box, making a theatrical display of removing the fur coat that he had purchased for Anna's birthday but had never returned to the store.

Well-studied in the trappings of the ultra-rich and already possessing a closet full of fur, even the Condo Queen had never seen such a gorgeous assemblage of pricey pelts. She looked at Jonathan, her eyelashes fluttering like black butterflies "I swear this is just about the most beautiful coat I've ever seen," she gushed. "But why?"

"The occasion, my sweet," he said, "is that I have just closed a huge deal. Do you remember the prime bank investment program I told you about?"

"Of course. You've been talking to George Williams and his lawyer about it for a while." She licked a stray drop of champagne from her pouty lower lip. "Did Georgie invest?" she asked hopefully, estimating her finder's fee on the amount that "Georgie" had mentioned. Her heavily made up eyes sparkled at the thought.

"No, not 'Georgie,'" Jonathan said, "Although I think he will eventually. But I did find some investors from New Orleans who committed to put two million dollars in my prime bank investment pool. I made a huge commission, hence the coat."

He helped her shrug her tiny frame into the fur. Two of her could have fit within its sumptuous folds, and it hung on her like a badly pitched yurt. She looked questioningly up at him, her head poking above the collar like a turtle peeking out from its shell. "It's rather large, darlin'," she said.

"Not to worry, my love, we can have it altered," he soothingly assured her.

His words immediately rang hollow. As she climbed out from under the coat, Marilyn noticed the initials "ADT" embroidered in the black silk lining. It didn't take a rocket scientist to figure out what the initials stood for. She instantly abandoned her plan to let Jonathan down easily. She could live without the Hibiscus Cay commissions, but she had standards and would not tolerate an insult such as this.

Her customarily mellifluous voice turned surly as she struck like a bayou water moccasin, throwing the coat at him and hissing, "Just who in the hell do you think you are, giving me your wife's used fur coat?" Her rage was palpable, stirring the air between them, the force of her anger making her vibrate like one of the sex toys Jonathan had bought for their mutual entertainment. "What do you think I am?" she shrieked. "Some kind of hooker?"

Jonathan was momentarily speechless, having forgotten that embroidery was a service provided by all high-end fur salons, including the one at Newman Marvis. He cursed himself silently for the unforced error but recovered his composure and put on a hurt puppy face.

171

"Darling, I can explain," he said. "I'm divorcing Anna. I've already filed the papers."

He kneeled in front of Marilyn, catching a glimpse of the naked naughtiness barely covered by her filmy black apron. The view inspired him to grovel further. "It's true that I was *going* to give the coat to Anna," he cooed, "but when I made the decision to divorce her, I kept it for you instead. The furrier must have embroidered it without my knowledge as a courtesy." He stood up and held his arms out to her. "You are my one and only true love. I assure you that I will have a stern talk with the furrier. It's really his fault after all."

Not willing to let him off the hook, Marilyn glared at him, her eyes black as coal. "Get out," she said.

"But darling," he pleaded, "I love you more than life itself. I want you to be my wife. I want you to come to Monte Carlo and live on Alpha Centauri with me."

Marilyn would have none of it. She turned on the heels of her black satin slippers and stormed off to her bedroom, locking the door behind her and leaving Jonathan dejected and desperate in the living room. She picked up her gold-plated telephone and called the head of building security, asking him in her sexiest voice if he would please escort an unwanted visitor from her penthouse.

The removal of her immediate problem arranged, she made another call to her soulmate's halfway house in Lubbock, where she had bribed the night operator to put her calls through. As she waited for her beau to come on the line, she heard a scuffle in the living room when the security guards arrived and forced a loudly protesting Jonathan out the door, presumably dragging the fur coat behind him.

* * *

Anna walked out of the baggage claim area at DFW Airport late Thursday afternoon. She rolled her battered suitcase to the curb and scanned the passenger pickup lane, spotting Jonathan three cars back in the line of waiting vehicles. He was leaning against a car that wasn't hers—it was the ruby red Mercedes that he and Sue Worthing had brought to her office.

Despite the falling temperature, she felt her own rising as her face took on the same color as the car. Stomping over to it, the wheels of her luggage clattering angrily on the uneven sidewalk, she demanded, "Where's my car?"

Jonathan's staged welcome home smile disappeared. "This is our new car," he replied. "I told you that Peter was going to buy it for the company."

"Then you drive it," she said. "I'm sick of carpooling and I want my own car. Where is it?" Frowning, she folded herself into the car and sank into the butter soft, heated passenger seat.

Jonathan stowed her luggage in the sports car's tiny trunk. "Your old car is gone," he said, getting back in the car and pulling out from the curb. "I traded it in for this one."

Anna looked at him with unmitigated disbelief. "You traded in my car for a company car that Peter bought? How were you able to do that?"

"This car is so much better than your old piece of junk. I thought you'd be excited."

"But I liked my old car and *I* paid ten thousand dollars in cash for it. Explain to me how I'm going to get that money back."

"Peter will pay you back."

"When?"

"As soon as Lamar invests," Jonathan said. He paid the airport toll and merged the aerodynamic automobile smoothly into the traffic heading toward downtown.

Anna groaned and leaned her head on the cushiony headrest. She was running out of energy to deal with the cascade of half-truths and outright lies that Jonathan rained down on her. He acted as if the Hibiscus Cay deal had already closed and he had all money in the world. "You're delusional," she said. "I want my car back or I want my ten thousand dollars."

Jonathan looked at her and glared. "Don't worry, you'll get your money," he snarled. "And for your information, Lamar decided to increase the amount he's going to invest in Hibiscus Cay to fifty million dollars, and he's going to fund by year end. He gave me his ironclad promise."

Staring sullenly out the car window, Anna said nothing. *Wonderful. Another promise.*

* * *

Jonathan drove her to work early the following morning. She spent the ride lost in thought, having compartmentalized her feelings of sadness and loss for the moment. Her savings, her car, the money she had paid for it, and any faith she had in Jonathan was gone. She had to extricate herself from her morass of a marriage as soon as possible, but there wasn't much she could do about it just yet. As soon as she turned on her office lights, she was greeted by a desk covered in papers that had accumulated like a snowdrift while she was in Boston. There was so much work backed up that she'd be in the office all weekend just to get through half of it.

After a morning of returning phone calls, answering emails, and digging through the work piled up on her desk, she was eating a soggy sandwich at her desk and going through the mail from home. She was about to have a heart attack from the shock of seeing a nine-hundred-dollar balance on Jonathan's cell phone bill when Becca buzzed her on the intercom.

"Some lawyer from Monte Carlo is holding for you," Becca said. "He says it's urgent, but he can't reach Jonathan."

Anna took the call and spoke as amiably as she could with Philip Bargeron about the still un-funded deposit on Alpha Centauri, telling him that she'd pass the message on to Jonathan. She hung up and immediately called Jonathan on his cell phone. "Philip Bargeron from Monte Carlo called," she said when he answered, her voice lawyerly and completely devoid of interest. "He said that if you don't give them proof that you have the money for the deposit by the end of the day today, Dallas time, they will sell to another buyer."

"I'll handle it," Jonathan grumbled, hanging up without another word. He cut short his lunch meeting with Bob and hurried back to the apartment, bounding up the stairs to Anna's office and opening her desk drawer. He took out a stack of fax cover sheets with the B&V logo at the top and the firm's central telephone and fax numbers listed right below it. Anna's name and her direct extension were pre-printed on the "From" line. Taking the company checkbook from her desk, he expertly forged a check for one hundred fifty thousand dollars.

Not wanting to leave any evidence on the home computer, he took a photo of it with his new smart phone and emailed it to Philip Bargeron, informing him that the original was on its way. This seemed to appease the fussy foreign counselor, who grudgingly agreed to wait a few more days for the real check to arrive.

Jonathan experienced no remorse for having just committed wire fraud, exposing Anna to disbarment and arrest and exposing her law firm to litigation. He needed to buy time, and if it landed his wife in jail or her law firm got into trouble, so what? They were all just expendable pawns in his game, and he was getting ready to play with the big boys. If Anna was going to interfere with his plans by resigning from the company, she deserved what was coming.

* * *

Jonathan tossed his keys at the valet at Newman Marvis and strode inside whistling *Puttin' on the Ritz*. After spending some quality time with Armando in the menswear department, he went in search of Jackie in ladieswear, only to learn that she had been fired for having too many items returned to the store and for making refunds in cash. Jonathan felt not a scintilla of guilt about poor Jackie. She got greedy. It was her fault for selling him so much merchandise in the first place, and it was Anna's fault that he had to return everything. It wasn't his problem, but he was miffed at the inconvenience nonetheless.

He consoled himself with a trip to Chartrier's, where a coquettish salesgirl sold him twenty-five thousand dollars'-worth of precious metals and compressed carbon. For himself, he bought a Tag Heuer watch, several sets of gold and diamond cufflinks, and diamond studs for his custom-made tuxedo shirts. He also purchased a lovely sapphire and diamond tennis bracelet for his latest love interest.

The salesgirl hesitated when he presented a check from Frescobaldi Prime Investments as payment, but he easily charmed the unsuspecting girl into taking it. It was late Friday afternoon, and

Silverman Baggins would have already shut down its clearing procedures. It would be at least Monday before Chartrier's discovered that the check was worthless, and if the salesgirl was fired, it was her own fault for being stupid enough to take the check. He was probably doing the store a favor by exposing her ignorance.

Still unsated and wanting more clothes to fit his new continental image, he drove to Gerald's, the most expensive men's clothing store in The Crescent shopping complex. He had been building a relationship with the store's sales manager in anticipation of needing her assistance some day in circumstances such as these. After giving the petite redhead named Sally a kiss on the cheek, he handed her the brochure for Alpha Centauri. He gestured grandly to a picture of the yacht. "I want you to create a wardrobe for me to goes with *that*," he said, beaming with pride at his thirteen-million-dollar baby.

When Jonathan and Sally had selected thirty-thousand-dollars' worth of men's *haute couture*, he tried to pay for it with another company check. Unlike the other shop girls, Sally was no pushover. She placed a call to Silverman Baggins and was put through to Dan Fairfield's secretary. Dan wasn't in the office, so Sally told Jonathan that, without someone in an official capacity to verify funds for the check, his boatload of new clothes would have to wait.

Jonathan lost patience and screamed at her, "Don't you know how rich I am, you ignorant little cretin?" Shaking with anger, he pointed a finger at the startled woman and hissed, "You've just lost yourself a lifetime of commissions, you worthless brain stem."

He raved so long and so loudly that a well-dressed security officer came over and escorted him roughly from the premises, enraging him further. "Get your fucking hands off me, ape," he shrieked, flecks of spittle flying with every sibilant. "Your hairy ass is toast. Just wait until my wife sues. We'll own this place and I'll fire you first."

"Sir, you must leave now or I will call the police," the ape said quietly. "And you are never to enter this store again." He gave Jonathan a shove out the door where a group of onlookers had gathered to gawk at the public humiliation. Jonathan stumbled but didn't fall, storming off in a tantrum and snarling at the gaping crowd, "What the fuck do you think you're looking at?"

Undeterred by the ugly scene, Jonathan still had another ace in his pocket. He drove the short distance to the downtown Newman Marvis store, where he spent his imaginary dollars with an ever-so-helpful salesgirl who didn't think twice when he presented her with a copy of his wife's Newman Marvis charge card. After driving his new habiliments back to the apartment and stashing them in the upstairs closet, he freshened up, grabbed his travel kit, and went back out.

As he drove to University Park, he was in the mood to blow off some steam, so he unloaded a scathing and scatological rant into Dan Fairfield's voicemail, which made him feel much better.

Chapter 20

Anna looked at the clock on her computer and said "Shit, shit, SHIT!" out loud. It was already 7:00 p.m. An emergency meeting of the board of directors of Harry Vincent's top client had been called for the following morning, and corporate bigshots and business masterminds were flying in from all over the country to discuss the hostile takeover. That meant that Anna and half-a-dozen colleagues would be working through the weekend in the meeting's aftermath. Now she'd have to wait until Monday to find out how her car got traded in for the red convertible without her knowledge or consent.

Not wanting to walk through the dingy underground tunnel system after dark, but knowing that standing on the street at night to hail a cab or wait for Uber was near-suicidal, she reluctantly called Jonathan. The call went straight to voicemail. She finished some administrative work and called him again half an hour later. Still no answer. Giving up, she shut down her computer and grabbed her coat, heading into the creepy bowels of downtown Dallas after dark for the walk to the Fairmont Hotel's taxi stand.

Jonathan wasn't home when the cab dropped her off, and his new car wasn't in the garage. She called his cell phone again and heard it ring somewhere inside the apartment. The tinny, mechanical tones of *Puttin' on the Ritz* led her to his closet and his briefcase. His cell phone was inside of it, explaining why he hadn't answered it earlier. She scrolled through the call list. There must have been fifty calls from Captain Barry and dozens of calls to and from Florida, Monte Carlo, and various places in Italy and France in the phone's log. There were quite a few calls to Marilyn Beauregard, which Anna assumed were related to Hibiscus Cay. There were also multiple calls to and from someone named Sharon Hammond. Anna had no idea who that was.

Knowing that Jonathan didn't password protect his mailbox, she punched a few keys and listened to his messages. "Jonathan, Captain Barry here. Call me ASAP. We need to talk about the crew." Then, "Hi, Jonathan, it's Sharon. I guess you're busy. Call me back." Finally, "Hello Johnny, it's Mom. Just a reminder to pick up some cannoli shells on your way here."

The call from Gina came in at 5:30 p.m. and it was now 8:00 p.m. Apparently, Jonathan was having dinner with his parents, and she wasn't invited. Even though she was fed up with the DeLuca family and planning to divorce Jonathan, it irked her that he had disappeared with their only car. She went into her office and called the DeLucas' apartment. Gina answered.

"Hi, Mom," Anna said.

"Hello, dear. How lovely to hear from you."

Anna had no patience or time for vacuous small talk. "Is Jonathan there?"

"No, sweetheart. We haven't seen him since last Sunday. Is everything alright?"

"No, Mom, everything is not alright." First explaining that her husband was missing, she went on to tell her mother-in-law about things that had been bothering her for months.

When she finished venting, Gina said, "Well, sweetheart, the first thing you need to know about Johnny is that he lies."

Anna was shocked by the nonchalant and indifferent way that Gina made the statement, as if she had simply said that Johnny always forgot to brush his teeth before bedtime. "What do you mean 'He lies?'" she asked.

"Johnny has always had a little trouble telling the truth," Gina replied. He doesn't mean anything by it, and he doesn't lie about the important things. *Qué será será.*"

Anna was too befuddled by Gina's flippant attitude to talk further. "I have to go. If you talk to Jonathan, please remind him that I have to be at work early tomorrow morning, and I need the car."

She had an idea as she was hanging up the phone and turned to her home computer, conducting a quick search and making a call.

A man answered cheerfully, "You've reached OnStar. My name is Mike. How can I help you?"

"Good evening, Mike," Anna said as calmly as she could. "My name is Anna DeLuca. I'm afraid that this is a little embarrassing, but I can't find my husband, Jonathan. He isn't answering his cell phone, and no one knows where he is. We're all quite worried about him."

"I understand, Mrs. DeLuca. Could you please give me the password on the account?"

"What password?"

"All our clients have a password to protect their privacy. It's set up at the time the car is delivered. Don't you know the password?"

"No," Anna replied. "Apparently, my husband forgot to give it to me."

"I'm sorry Mrs. DeLuca, but I can't help you without the password. We have very strict rules about disclosing the whereabouts of our clients."

As a lawyer, Anna appreciated the liability issues that could result from a breach of customer privacy. She was highly annoyed, but it wasn't Mike's fault. He was just following the rules. "Thanks anyway," she said, hanging up.

Numbed by the latest distressing turn of events, Anna's ability to feel shock or surprise had been eroded by Jonathan's long, slimy trail of subterfuge and lies laid snail-like during the course of their short marriage. She was too weary to wonder or worry any longer, and as far she was concerned, he could stay away forever.

* * *

Gina came out of her cramped bedroom after the call, winking and whispering "Everything's O.K." to her baby boy on the way back into her small kitchen. She stuffed a cannoli shell and thought about poor Johnny's marital problems. It was such a shame that Anna had turned out to be such an awful woman. She was just bad as the others—maybe worse.

Thinking about it made her so angry that she forgot where she put her spatula. She stabbed one of the gooey pastries with a serving fork instead and dropped it with such force that the plate clattered on the countertop. She really wanted to let Anna know what she thought of her, but Johnny had asked them not to say anything about the failed marriage and to keep acting as if nothing untoward was happening until the ungrateful, lying *puttana* was served with divorce papers.

She skewered the last pasta shell so hard that it split in two, dumping the generously stuffed filling back into the baking pan and crumbling into a sticky mess. *Merda!* Salvaging what she could from the cannoli carnage, she took the serving plate into the cubbyhole dining room, smiling sweetly at the pretty brunette as she set it on the table. At least this new girl seems nice. Smart too—another lady lawyer.

The foursome had a pleasant chat over dessert, talking about how they were all going to have such a wonderful life together living on the beautiful yacht that Jonathan's business partners were going to buy for the Hibiscus Cay project. They were even going to celebrate Sharon's birthday on board Alpha Centauri—with fireworks!

Gina beamed adoringly at Jonathan. Despite his chronic misbehavior, she always knew that her handsome treasure would be a big success one day.

* * *

Anna awoke to voices coming from upstairs, immediately realizing that she had forgotten to set the alarm. She checked the clock. It was already 8:00 a.m., and she was supposed to be at work in an hour. Hearing the voices again, she threw on her robe and rushed upstairs.

Jonathan and his mother were in his dressing room, the furniture and the floor covered in empty shirt boxes and tissue paper. He was removing crisp new shirts from plastic wrapping and putting them in a designer suitcase that looked a lot like one from the set of luggage she had demanded that he return to the store. There were at least twenty new shirts inside. Meanwhile, his mother was packing new underwear and dozens of expensive ties in a matching duffel bag. Neither of them acknowledged Anna's presence in the doorway.

"What's going on?" Anna demanded. "Where were you last night, Jonathan?" She looked at Gina imploringly. Gina ignored her completely.

Jonathan closed the suitcase and looked up at Anna. "I don't have a lot of time to explain," he said. "I have to leave for Monte Carlo immediately." He went into the closet and came out with a stack of shoeboxes, emptying them and stuffing pair after pair of designer shoes into another suitcase.

Anna was flummoxed. "Today?"

"Yes, today."

The phone rang just as she was going to ask him why he hadn't told her about the trip. She went into her office to answer it. It was the F-Man. "Where the hell are you?" he screamed.

Suddenly remembering her job, she sputtered, "Sorry, my alarm didn't go off."

"And your dog ate your homework," the F-Man sneered. "I don't give a crap what happened, just get your sorry ass into the office. The board of directors will be here in less than an hour, and if you aren't here to greet them with the board books in hand, don't bother coming at all." Click.

She flew down the stairs, getting ready in ten minutes and coming out of the bedroom just as Jonathan was hauling two suitcases and the matching duffel bag down the stairs and out the front door. His new red convertible and his father's white Cadillac were parked side by side in front of the apartment. He was shoving the suitcases into the spacious trunk of the Cadillac as his mother came tottering unsteadily down the stairs with the rest of the bags. She brushed past Anna without a word and toddled down the front steps, handing them off to her son.

While Anna watched him stow the last of the smaller bags in the trunk of the convertible, she noticed the company checkbook sitting on the hood of the car. He closed the trunk and grabbed the checkbook, ducking into the car without looking at her.

She ran down the front steps as they were backing the two cars out of their parking spaces. "Jonathan!" she screamed. "How am I supposed to get to work? And what are you doing with the company checkbook?"

Jonathan ignored her and drove away, his mother trailing behind him in the Cadillac. Neither of them glanced at her even once, as if to do so would call down some foul curse upon them.

The realization that her husband had just driven off with her only means of transportation overrode the confusion she felt at what had just happened. She had to get to the office in a hurry, but she didn't have time to call for a car or a taxi. She ran back into the apartment, took off her high heels, and stuffed her feet into a pair of tennis shoes. Shoving her shoes into her briefcase, she bolted out the door and ran five blocks to the nearest DART train station, hoping to make it downtown in time save her job.

* * *

While Jonathan was abandoning his wife, Jack and Lamar were in Lamar's office reviewing the results of the exhaustive investigation that Beefy and his associates had conducted on Jonathan. The two businessmen were stunned to learn that their worst thoughts about him were rosy compared to his smarmy real-life story. Although their preliminary investigation had yielded little information of value, the second, in-depth investigation uncovered—among other things—that Jonathan DeLuca had two different social security numbers. His sordid tale spanned three decades of petty and felonious financial crimes committed in half a dozen states. Jonathan DeLuca was snake-bit and there was no possible way Lamar was going to do business with him.

"Jesus, Lamar," Jack said when they both finished scanning the report. "You were right all along."

Lamar nodded. "Call Peter Grand and tell him we're going with Plan B. Then call the lawyers and get papers drawn up to buy off DeLuca without too much blowback. Don't go higher than ten grand. If he balks at the number, threaten him with a lawsuit and tell Beefy to have a personal chat with him for a few minutes."

Jack glanced at the file in front of him. "Even better, we can have him arrested if we want to. His probation papers say right here that he can't leave Dallas County—let alone the country—without permission. He said he honeymooned in Cancún, and we know he went to Monte Carlo a few weeks ago, so that's two violations that we know of. He also must remain employed and keep current with his child support payments. We know he quit his job, so that's three. The new report says that he's months behind in his child support, making it four probation violations. He'll take the bait."

Lamar thought for a moment, "Do you think the wife is in on some scheme with him?"

"I don't know," Jack replied, "but it's easy to find out."

Both Garrett Mason and Henry Vincent were friends of Lamar's. He fished and hunted with the former and golfed with the latter. "I'll make a couple of phone calls," Lamar said. "The wife will play ball. She has to."

Chapter 21

A silver Bentley sedan whispered to a stop in front of the Hotel de Monaco, disgorging an elated Jonathan. Gracefully unfolding himself out of the car that had been sent for him, he ran a hand over his slicked-back hair and entered the hotel as if he owned it.

Gerard was working the reception desk again and greeted him with an oleaginous smile and a stack of phone messages. "Welcome back, Monsieur DeLuca," he said. "I trust your trip was comfortable."

"Yes, very. Thank you, Gerard." Jonathan scanned the messages. Three were from Anna, two were from Captain Barry, and one was from Jack Garrison with news that Lamar had decided not to invest in Hibiscus Cay until after the first of the year. Jonathan went deathly pale but otherwise showed no outward emotion at the inconvenient news. His new land of opportunity was full of prosperous prospects, and his backup plan was already in the works. He'd find a way to buy Alpha Centauri—one way or another.

"Will your lovely wife be joining us this visit," Gerard asked.

"Yes, she will," Jonathan lied. "She's in court working on a very important case and will be joining me in a few days."

"Very good, sir. And how will you be paying for your stay?"

"With our American CreditCorp card, as before. You should already have the number on file."

"May I please have the card to run the impression?"

Jonathan made a show of searching through his wallet and pockets. Coming up empty-handed both times, he made himself blush, a trick he had mastered long ago. "Well this is awkward," he said. "It appears I don't have the card on my person." Snapping his fingers as if something had suddenly just dawned on him, he said, "How stupid of me. My wife has the card. She lost hers and took mine for her trip to New York for the trial. I forgot that she has it."

A look of mild annoyance crossed Gerard's face. Jonathan noticed his discomfiture and assured him, "My wife will bring the card with her. A few days' delay shouldn't be a problem for you or this fine establishment, considering that I have already paid a substantial deposit for the suite." He leaned over the desk and peered deep into Gerard's eyes, his own carrying unspoken threats.

Blinking under the withering gaze, Gerard said, "No, no of course not, Monsieur DeLuca. Your deposit covers three days' residency in the suite. As you are a valued guest, we can wait a few days for the card." He reached under the desk again, adding, "There is one more thing, sir. The Baroness von Pfaffenhofen asked me to deliver this to you personally."

He handed Jonathan a pale ivory envelope addressed to Jonathan Frescobaldi DeLuca, III in flowery feminine script. It was sealed with red wax, a royal crest nestling inside the melted paraffin. Jonathan handed Gerard an unsealed envelope in return and left for his suite. Gerard peeked into the envelope and tucked it into his breast pocket, smiling contentedly.

A smartly uniformed porter arrived with his luggage. Jonathan tipped him generously, spritzed himself with some complementary Hermès cologne, and went to the penthouse floor of the hotel to meet Gisela. She answered his knock at the door draped like a goddess in diaphanous white silk and chiffon lingerie that left little to the imagination, welcoming him with open arms and an open bottle of Veuve Clicquot.

* * *

Jonathan was thirsty for champagne and hungry for Gisela. He'd stopped taking his medication weeks earlier in preparation for this night, and he was ready to feel like a real man again. Gisela was happy to help him, having been denied her own sexual sweets for days due to unfortunate and unforeseen circumstances.

186

Jonathan strode into the room and took Gisela by the hand. "Come with me," he said, leading her to the bedroom and pushing her onto the canopied, king-size bed. He was on fire and there was no time for foreplay. He slid her negligee up to her chin while unbuckling his pants, stepping out of them and climbing on top of her.

Gisela was willing to overlook Jonathan's failure to engage in the niceties of seduction and made no protest when he flipped her over and entered her from behind. Hot and hungry, he ached with unleashed desire as he clasped her breasts with both hands. She arched her back to welcome him in deeper, then quivered uncontrollably and let out a sound that one would not ordinarily expect to hear coming from a baroness. Jonathan's body spasmed, and he unleashed a noise that sounded like something one would ordinarily expect to hear coming from a wild animal.

Near numb from the powerful, almost spiritual release, he rolled to his side, exhausted. They lay there motionless for a few moments until Gisela excused herself, telling Jonathan to get ready for more. He noticed that her initial compliance had given way to her customarily commanding demeanor. He was happy to obey her and relaxed back onto the bed, getting himself worked up again by picturing her in full Nazi bondage regalia. She spoke German after all.

He listened to the shower running while he recharged, deciding to use the new vibrator he had brought with him as backup, should his body betray him. He got out of bed and picked his jacket from the crumpled heap of clothing and lingerie on the floor. He was taking the vibrator out of the inside pocket when the shower stopped, and he heard the bathroom door open behind him. He turned around, hoping to see a hot dominatrix from Deutschland. Instead, he was greeted by a topless Gisela in gold pigtails and a mini-dirndl skirt that barely covered her dumpling-like derriere. It appeared that his lover was more Heidi or Maria von Trapp than Mata Hari or Marlene Dietrich.

A tinge disappointed, but never one to miss an opportunity for sex, he switched on the vibrator, its angry hum reminding him of one of his favorite movies. He brandished the gyrating gift proudly and channeled Al Pacino. "Say hello to my little friend, *liebchen*," he said, a lustful grin on his face.

187

Gisela was unimpressed. "Don't be ridiculous," she scoffed, swatting at it. "Get that thing away from me." She opened the top drawer of the gilded nightstand next to the bed and pulled out a masterpiece of masturbatory technology. Sleek, shiny, and boasting ten different settings for five different attachments, it put Jonathan's puny offering to shame.

She walked seductively to him, a wicked gleam in her ice blue eyes. He caught the scent of expensive body oil as she stepped past him and climbed into the bed again, her breasts and long legs glistening in the amber light of the crystal chandelier. She handed the pleasure-enhancing hardware to her newest subject and commanded, "Now you say hello to *my* little friend, *liebchen*. And set it to six."

Jonathan was happy to oblige, but he had never been good at obeying orders. To satisfy his rebel urges, he set it to eight without asking permission. It was a minor disobedience, and it took only seconds before the Baroness was too lost in a turmoil of non-stop ecstasy to notice it.

* * *

Gisela always took one of the largest suites in the Hotel de Monaco every winter to escape the harsh Austrian winters. They were in her dining room the next morning, snuggled comfortably into plush white robes and enjoying a leisurely late breakfast of scrambled eggs, caviar, and mimosas. The palatial suite's ceiling-high windows embraced a one hundred eighty-degree view of the harbor and the Mediterranean Sea. Jonathan could see the skittish little sailors in their tiny sailboats out for a morning lesson, remembering that his current wife had called them "duckling princes."

"So, darling, where is your lumpy boyfriend?" he asked between bites of breakfast.

Sensing jealousy, Gisela gave a casual flip of her hand as if swatting away an annoying insect. She felt no need to tell her current paramour that she had sent the buff Bavarian packing after finding him on top of the hotel's aerobics instructor, moaning and groaning while doing some very energetic push-ups. She made the discovery not in the hotel gym, but alas, on the Aubusson carpet that covered the floor of her suite's dressing room. She immediately dispatched both her Aryan Adonis and the carpet. "Don't worry about Hugo, *liebchen*," she replied. "He was just a pretty toy. I grew bored with him and now he is gone."

They heard a knock on the door. Gisela answered it and ushered Captain Barry in. Excusing herself, she went into her sullied dressing room to prepare for a charity event she was attending at the Japanese Gardens with her friends, the Grimaldi princesses. Jonathan wanted to escort her to the glittering event, but she had sagaciously pointed out that the paparazzi would be swarming all over them. Although the continentals accepted mistresses as par for the course, an American attorney like Anna DeLuca most likely would not appreciate seeing her husband on the cover of some tawdry tabloid. Jonathan accepted defeat and decided to use the free time to meet with Captain Barry.

The two men were standing at the tall bay windows perusing Port Hercule below them and smoking Dunhill cigarettes. Jonathan had taken up the habit again, now that he was in Europe where it was still acceptable. He hated the way the European brands tasted, but he had seen them in movies and thought they made him look mysteriously sophisticated. Captain Barry pointed out where Alpha Centauri would be anchored after the contract was signed and the down payment made. Jonathan ignored him. He was focused on a sleek modern yacht anchored two slips away, the enormous vessel making his mere mega-yacht look like a destitute relative in comparison.

Jonathan's lust for Alpha Centauri veered wildly off course as he pointed to the new object of his delusional desires—a superyacht. "What kind of boat is that?" he asked. "The one next to where Alpha Centauri will be berthed?"

Captain Barry got a pair of small binoculars out of his briefcase and peered through them. "It's a Feadship," he grunted. "I make her to be about two hundred fifty feet long."

"How much money for a boat like that?"

Captain Barry whistled. "Fifty million easy. Probably carries a crew of twenty. Operating costs would be . . . Shit, Jonathan. I don't know *what* they'd be."

"Find out if it's for sale," Jonathan said. "You wouldn't mind quintupling your commission, would you, Captain?" He walked to the Queen Anne dining room table and refilled his Limoges china cup from a sterling silver carafe. "In the meantime, where do we stand with Alpha Centauri?" he asked.

"Captain Salvatore tells me that the sellers are starting to get nervous because you haven't put down a deposit yet," Captain Barry replied. "As you know, it's customary for the broker to live on board during the appraisal, and I've been living on Alpha Centauri for weeks now. We can't stall much longer because the appraiser is on his way back to San Remo to finish his report."

Jonathan was unconcerned by the approaching deadline. "Anything else?"

"Yes. I need more money to pay for the rental car and to eat. The ship's chef has been ordered by the owners not to feed me until the deposit arrives."

Jonathan went into Gisela's bedroom while the querulous captain was still complaining. Returning a moment later, he handed his debit card to Captain Barry, along with a piece of paper with the PIN number written on it. "Use this for anything you need," he instructed.

The door to the dressing room opened and Gisela emerged. Dressed in a becoming royal blue Dolce and Gabbana suit, an ivory silk blouse, and Prada heels, she was adorned with the diamond and sapphire bracelet that Jonathan had gotten her at Chartrier's and the vintage diamond and sapphire earrings that her dead husband had gotten her at auction at Christie's. She kissed Jonathan goodbye and left, nodding regally at Captain Barry on her way out.

Captain Barry stared at her, mesmerized, as if he had just seen the ghost of Princess Grace. He watched the Baroness von Pfaffenhofen depart, and all he could say was "Yowza."

* * *

Jonathan and Gisela dined in a private room at The Marie Antoinette that night. Gisela knew exactly what the footstools on the floor were for, daintily setting her Swarovski crystal-encrusted Judith

Lieber bag on top of the one next to her chair without hesitation. The wine and conversation flowed freely as they feasted on escargot, Caesar salad, and chateaubriand. More than three hours later, Jonathan signed the check and they left for the casino.

He didn't want his intended meal ticket to know that he had no money with which to gamble, but he obediently followed her through a back door to the casino where the game was baccarat, and princes could become paupers in minutes. The scene was as glamorous as any in the many James Bond movies he had devoured growing up, lacking only a megalomaniacal arch-villain plotting world domination between spins of the roulette wheel.

A baccarat aficionado, Gisela always booked a private salon to avoid prying eyes and the paparazzi that plagued the casino like locusts. The salons were hidden behind wood-paneled walls that were decorated with serpentine scroll work in gold leaf. White-gloved attendants waiting patiently on either side of the door, ushering them solemnly into the richly appointed room.

They took seats at the baccarat table, and Gisela ordered twenty thousand Euros in chips. She turned to Jonathan. "Are you playing tonight, *liebchen*?" she asked.

"Not tonight darling," he replied. "I've had too much to drink. I prefer to gamble when I have my wits about me."

She shrugged and began to play. As she added to her stack of chips over the following hours, Jonathan filled the time observing and absorbing his lavish surroundings. The air was heavily laden with the scent of perfume, cigars, wealth, and power. He breathed in deeply, greedily inhaling the astronomically-priced atmosphere like an asthmatic in the Andes and found it exhilarating.

Jonathan Frescobaldi DeLuca, III was finally home.

* * *

Pleasing Gisela and satisfying her many voracious appetites took up a lot of Jonathan's time, but he didn't mind. He had a lot of catching up to do sex-wise. All in all, his new life was looking good so far.

Things were working in the bedroom again, the panic attacks hadn't yet returned, and Lamar would invest any day now.

They idled away a full day spending Gisela's casino winnings at the luxury storefronts conveniently located adjacent to the hotel. Chanel, Hermès, Louis Vuitton, Mont Blanc, Gucci and many others reigned in Monte Carlo. Jonathan shopped in the same stores back in Dallas, but they seemed posher somehow here in their native European habitat.

Gisela's gambling profits were spent by lunch time, so they retired to her suite for forty-eight hours of pleasant debauchery. Luxuriously encamped, they reveled in a drunken haze of sex and room service, subsisting on Norwegian lobster, Iranian caviar, French champagne, and Cuban cigars—some of which were used in ways and combinations for which they had not been originally intended.

The amorous pair finally emerged late one morning to re-enter the real world. Gisela had a full afternoon of appointments scheduled at the hotel spa and summarily dismissed Jonathan around noon. Less than an hour later, he was in the lobby of the hotel negotiating with Philippe Bargeron.

"The appraisal is finished, and Alpha Centauri is being readied to for her return to Monte Carlo," Monsieur Bargeron said curtly. "You must sign the letter of intent and make the down payment immediately if you wish to purchase her. There is another interested buyer, and the owners have grown weary of the constant delays. They instructed me to inform you that, unless they receive the funds by noon tomorrow, they will sell to the other buyer."

Jonathan brushed the threat off with an imperious wave of his hand. "Monsieur Bargeron, claiming to have an alternate buyer is one of the oldest tricks in the salesman's book. Nonetheless, I have the deposit check right here." He reached into his coat pocket and pulled out the original check bearing Anna's forged signature.

Monsieur Bargeron was unimpressed. "The owners have decided that they want a wire transfer and are not inclined to accept a non-certified check."

"My wife is in court," Jonathan replied. "She can't be reached and can't initiate a wire transfer until at least Monday. I am sorry, but if you must have the money by tomorrow, a check will have to do. Please tell your clients to take it or leave it. It matters not to me. I am already in negotiations to purchase a two-hundred-fifty-foot Feadship, and I will happily take my millions elsewhere."

He stood up abruptly, said "Good day," and stalked off in a well-acted huff, leaving the unhappy attorney with the fraudulent check. As he passed the front desk, Gerard called out, "Monsieur DeLuca, you have messages."

Too close to pretend that he hadn't heard, he walked nonchalantly over and took the stack of pink message slips, reading them on the way to the elevators. There were twelve messages starting Monday afternoon and scattered throughout the week, all of them from Anna. He tossed them in a gleaming brass trash receptacle and went up to his suite, arriving to a blinking red light on his phone informing him of yet another message. It was from the hotel manager, a man named Henri Baptiste.

Jonathan listened to the message, then picked up the phone and placed a call to the United States.

* * *

Captain Barry was in The Lobby Bar the following afternoon, drinking beer and reading the results of the yacht appraisal. He heard a commotion and looked up to see Jonathan stagger into the bar. He walked unsteadily over and heaved himself up onto the barstool next to Captain Barry, ordering drinks for the whole bar in a jumble of slurred words. When everyone had their cocktails in hand, he stood up shakily and toasted to the entire room at full volume, "To my new yacht, Alpha Centauri!"

The bar patrons clapped politely, Captain Barry chiming in with a robust "Hear, hear!" The talk turned to business and the survey results. Jonathan and Captain Barry had three more rounds of drinks while Jonathan regaled anyone who cared to listen—and even those who didn't—with tales of Hibiscus Cay and prime bank investment pools.

Ever more amazed by Jonathan's capacity for alcohol and hyperbole, Captain Barry noticed that the drunker Jonathan got, the shakier his grip on reality became. He took his chance before Jonathan lost it altogether. "When will the deposit money arrive?" he asked. "I don't know how much longer I can hold off the sellers."

Jonathan hiccupped. "Don' worry 'bout that. Tell 'em it's all wrapped up. No pro-blem-oh." He started wobbling back and forth on the barstool like a rowboat in a hurricane, Captain Barry catching him by the arm just as he started to topple off.

Jonathan was fading fast, so Captain Barry asked the bartender for the check and helped Jonathan sign it. He half-dragged the stumbling drunk to the elevator bank, punched the button for the elevator that served the Baroness' floor, and deposited him in it when it arrived, leaving him slumped in a corner.

The nervous boat broker walked to his car, convincing himself that everything was fine. He needed this sale and desperately hoped that Jonathan's drunken displays and ostentatious boasting were just the result of mixing too much alcohol with unbridled optimism. He had known a lot of successful men who could drink like fish and whore like pirates on shore leave but were savvy captains of industry too. He decided that Jonathan must be one of those. *After all, the guy hangs out with royalty, so he must be legitimate, right?*

Chapter 22

Lars and Ella Bjornberg arrived at the Nice airport the next morning on one-way economy class tickets from Miami. After collecting their meager belongings and taking a thirty-minute bus ride to Monaco, they arrived at the main bus station around 7:00 a.m. They had been instructed to meet Captain Barry, who would drive them to Alpha Centauri, their new home on the high seas. Lars had been hired to be the new head chef and purchasing manager, and Ella would be the new assistant chef and head of housekeeping. The comely couple was anxious to meet the yacht's other crew members, all of whom had sailed on her for years and would be instrumental in bringing the Bjornbergs up to speed on the vessel generally and her galley specifically.

Lars was six feet four inches of fine Swedish physiology, with deep blue eyes, a shock of sun-bleached surfer hair, and an impish grin. A strapping man in his early thirties, he was heavily tattooed, with bulging biceps and rippling abdominal muscles. Despite his imposing physique and intimidating body ink, he cooked like a professional and had a solid business sense.

His wife Ella was petite and perky, her white-blonde hair framing a tanned oval face graced by a button nose and dancing blue eyes that matched her husband's. Other than her eyes, she was her husband's polar opposite. Whereas Lars was taciturn at worst and laconic at best, she was vivacious and lively with a mischievous sense of humor. It was a pairing that worked somehow, and they considered themselves blessed.

Both descendants of seafaring folk from Stockholm, they were lovers of sailing and food, having met while studying at the Culinary

Academy of Sweden. They became inseparable almost instantly and married shortly after receiving their chef's certificates. They finally quit the oceangoing culinary life after five years of exhausting and unfulfilling work in the massive assembly line kitchens that lie deep in the bowels of the giant cruise ships departing Florida.

Settling in Fort Lauderdale, they earned their keep by crewing on private yachts as often as possible and offering catering services to vessels docked in the Bahia Mar marina when they were on shore. It was a tiring life, and they wanted to save up enough money so that Ella could take some time off and have a baby, so when Lars spotted Captain Barry's ad in *Yachting Magazine* offering an opportunity to make decent money for a change, he immediately called the number listed and liked what he heard. After résumé submissions, reference checks, and a personal interview with Captain Barry, the Nordic duo jumped at the offer to join the crew of Alpha Centauri at salaries that were double the amount of money they had made in any previous year.

Lars turned to his dozing wife in the seat next to him and shook her gently awake. "Ella, wake up," he whispered. "We're here." She squeezed his hand as she sat up sleepily and looked out the bus window, spotting Captain Barry waiting by a parked car next to the taxi stand.

They bundled into the cramped rental car, arriving at the San Remo Sun Port an hour later. Captain Barry drove them to the end of the pier, pointing to the yacht and beaming like a proud father. "There she is," he said. "Welcome to Alpha Centauri."

The Bjornbergs got out of the car and paused to gaze up at the stately vessel that soared above them like a Titanic-killing iceberg. The smooth white hull reflected the sun's early morning rays like a mirror as she lay anchored majestically in the calm waters of the harbor, bobbing gently up and down when the wake from another boat rocked her watery cradle.

Ella jumped up and down in sheer joy. "Oh, Lars, she's magnificent," she squealed.

Giving his pretty wife a bear hug, Lars ruffled the top of her head with his strong fingers, then went to get their bags from the car. Huffing a bag over each shoulder and picking up another in each brawny hand, he started bellowing an old Swedish sea shanty. Ella scampered joyfully behind him up the gangplank with Captain Barry far behind her, wheezing and struggling to keep up.

* * *

While the Bjornbergs were settling into their new quarters on Alpha Centauri, Jonathan was already awake and feeling miserable. His head was pounding from a brutal hangover, but before he could drink his first cup of coffee, Gisela blindsided him with unexpected and highly inconvenient news. She was jetting off to Paris for a week of shopping with her former roommate from the Sorbonne, leaving him on his own with a dwindling supply of cash.

"Why didn't you tell me you were leaving?" he asked, pouting like a little boy denied his ice cream. Gisela was his fallback plan. He'd been counting on talking her into letting him move into her suite and loaning him money for the deposit on Alpha Centauri or, better yet, the Feadship docked in the marina. He only needed a little more time to close Lamar on the Hibiscus Cay deal or locate a new mark to finance his plans.

"You will just have to manage without me for a few days," Gisela said. "Now go. I will see you next week."

Jonathan dressed quickly and left reluctantly. He and Gisela had been so busy making merry and making love that he hadn't gotten around to writing down her credit card numbers or learning how to forge her signature. Fortunately, the hotel had room service from three restaurants, plenty of amenities in the bathroom, and a shop where he could charge his cigars and cigarettes to the room. As soon as he got back to his suite, he called Gerard and asked him to have the mini-bar restocked right away.

Undressing again, he stepped into the spacious marble shower, turned all five showerheads to hot, and let the massaging streams of water work on his hangover while he let his mind work on his immediate quandary. He was toweling dry when he heard a knock on the door. He threw on a robe and opened the door to find a messenger holding a silver tray bearing an overnight mail envelope. He opened it while the messenger waited, taking out a single sheet of paper and skimming it quickly. Handing it back with instructions to deliver it directly to the hotel manager, he gave the young man a casino chip and sent him on his way.

Jonathan cogitated on his rapidly diminishing assets while he brushed his teeth. He only had a hundred Euros, a handful of stolen casino chips, and his increasingly frazzled wits to get him through until Gisela returned. The phone rang before he could settle on a solution to his conundrum, and he picked up the extension that hung on the bathroom wall.

It was Philip Bargeron, who had been up since 2:00 a.m., Monaco time, making calls to the United States to confirm that there were sufficient funds in the Frescobaldi Prime Investments account to cover the deposit check. The result of his investigation had displeased him, so the counselor dispensed with courtesy. "I made inquiries with your banking institution," he said. "I was informed that there are no funds in your account, making the check you wrote to us worthless, if not fraudulent. The owners of Alpha Centauri have instructed me to tell you that the sale is off. I will be delivering the bill for our services in this matter to you this afternoon. Good day."

Jonathan didn't particularly care about losing Alpha Centauri. He much preferred the Feadship anyway. He finished dressing and went downstairs to Le Club for lunch with a stuffy Swiss industrialist he had met in the bar the night before and was hoping to recruit into his fictional prime bank investment pool.

* * *

Jonathan awoke at 6:30 a.m. the next morning to the sound of someone pounding insistently on the door to his suite. The living and dining rooms were littered with dirty room service trays and empty liquor bottles. Butts of Dunhill cigarettes and Monte Cristo cigars filled every ashtray to overflowing, and it smelled like a Texas honky-tonk on a Sunday morning. Jonathan did too. He reeked of gin and cigar smoke. Pulling his robe around him, he stumbled to the door, his puffy eyelids hanging over his bloodshot eyes like rusty awnings.

Captain Barry was the source of the tempest. When Jonathan opened the door, he blew into the room like a toxic wind and started bellowing like a bull seal. "The Bjornbergs and I got kicked off Alpha Centauri last night. What the hell happened?"

"The deal fell apart," Jonathan said dispassionately.

"I know that. How? Why?"

"Anna is screwing me over," Jonathan said, closing the door. "She found out about Gisela and my plans to file for divorce. She stopped the wire transfer for the deposit and refuses to authorize a check on the company account."

Jonathan brewed a fresh pot of coffee in the suite's kitchen while Captain Barry paced the sitting area, shooting questions at him like harpoons. "What are we supposed to do? Where are we going to stay? How are we going to eat? How are the Bjornbergs going to get home?"

"Just calm down," Jonathan said, pouring two cups of freshly brewed coffee and dousing both generously with Courvoisier. He handed one to Captain Barry. "Stop worrying," he said. "I can fix everything."

He went into the bedroom and returned with his wallet, which was substantially thinner than when he had first arrived in Monte Carlo. He took out a slip of paper and handed it to Captain Barry. "Take this and check into the motel in Cap'd Áil, France," he said. "They should have this card number on file from your last stay. Have the hotel manager call me here at my suite. I'll authorize the charge."

Captain Barry grunted and shoved the paper in his briefcase, still fuming like a dirty smokestack. Jonathan could tell he was dubious, so he offered the skeptical skipper some encouraging words. "By the way," he said, "the Baroness and I are engaged. She'll be back in a few days and will loan me the money for the deposit until my main investor comes through. If Alpha Centauri is already sold, we'll buy the Feadship down in the harbor instead. Tell the Bjornbergs that I will triple the salaries we already offered them." He stood up. "Now if you'll excuse me," he said, "I must prepare for my meetings with two investors from Zurich who want to buy half of the interests in Hibiscus Cay."

"I hope I don't end up regretting this," Captain Barry grumbled. He left wearing a bad feeling like a foul weather slicker and drove to the motel just across the border in France, rationalizing along the way. Maybe if he gave Jonathan a little more time, they might salvage something from the wreckage of the cursed expedition they had embarked on together. He decided to keep an even keel and give Jonathan a little more time. He didn't really have any other choice.

* * *

Jonathan decided to work the bar at Café de Paris for a couple of hours, perhaps steal a purse if he had to. He had to do something to finance his needs until Gisela returned. He snuck down the emergency stairs, hoping to avoid the hotel manager. He knew he was risking an awkward encounter, having never met Henri Baptiste.

His fear was realized when Henri saw him sneaking behind a potted palm in the lobby. Recognizing Jonathan from his passport photo in the hotel files, he called out, "May I speak with you a moment, Monsieur DeLuca?"

Jonathan ignored him as if he hadn't heard and pretended to drop something. He was examining the marble floor as if looking for a lost contact lens when he saw his own face reflected in Henri's shiny black shoes and was forced to straighten up and deal with him.

Almost as tall as Jonathan, with jet black hair and dark brown eyes bookending his hawk-like nose, Henri looked every bit the no-nonsense, world-weary, bureaucrat. This corporate cog, however, was dressed as splendidly as Jonathan, wearing a bespoke suit from a tailor in Milan. "Please come to my office," Henri said, gesturing politely down the hall.

When they arrived, he closed the office door behind them and sat down at a tiny wooden desk. He motioned for Jonathan to sit, but Jonathan chose to stand. Henri got right to the point. "The hotel's lawyers reviewed Mrs. DeLuca's power of attorney. It is not in proper form under the laws of Monaco because it lacks an apostille."

Jonathan didn't let on that he had no idea what an apostille was. "I'm sure the hotel can wait until Monday to sort this all out," he said.

"Hotel policy requires me to run each guest's credit card weekly," Henri said. "I must have the original credit card or a proper power of attorney from Mrs. DeLuca no later than tomorrow."

"I can't possibly reach her right now," Jonathan explained. He glanced at his watch, highly annoyed. "She is currently in New York and will be leaving for Paris tomorrow afternoon, arriving here in Monaco on Monday."

"My apologies, sir," Henri said, "but my superiors have told me that you must provide what we need without further delay." He gave a shrug of resignation at his powerlessness in the faceless hierarchy, washing himself clean of the decision. "I'm sorry, but it is out of my hands."

Jonathan knew he was being worked for a bribe, and it tried his patience. "You are trying my patience, Henri," he said. He put his hands on the desk and leaned over it. "I'm sure the Baroness von Pfaffenhoffen would be most disappointed to hear that you have been uncooperative with me. I am her new financial advisor, and perhaps I will advise her to spend her winters and her Euros elsewhere." He paused for a few seconds for effect. "I just happen to have her number in Paris with me," he continued. "Shall we call her right now to discuss it?" He straightened up, crossing his arms and glaring menacingly at Henri.

Henri's face flushed, but he retained his continental composure. "That won't be necessary," he said. "I will speak with the billing department again and inform them that payment is forthcoming."

"Thank you," Jonathan said, reaching into his pocket and pulling out twenty Euros. "I appreciate your understanding and discretion." He pressed the money firmly into Henri's palm and left.

Henri snorted in derision at the paltry amount and picked up the phone.

* * *

Jonathan knew that his luck, his liquidity, and his bullshit were running out fast. He was out of cash and down to a handful of casino chips, so he lunched at Café de Paris, successfully snatching forty

Euros left as tips on unattended tables on his way out. Not wishing to press his luck further and risk another unpleasant interlude with Henri, he took the gentleman's way out and snuck back into in his suite to hide for the rest of the weekend. He hung out the tag that had "Do Not Disturb" printed on it in six different languages and took the suite's phone off the hook.

He used the time to think about his predicament. He only had to stall the hotel and the owners of Alpha Centauri until Lamar came through with the first tranche of his investment in Hibiscus Cay. After all, Lamar hadn't backed out of the deal altogether, but had only decided to delay funding until after the first of the year. That was only days away, but he needed funds right now. He wasn't sure if Gisela was sufficiently softened up to ask her for money, but he might have to test those waters sooner rather than later because he was running out of options. Bob was tapped out, Marilyn had dumped him, and Sharon didn't make nearly as much money as he had hoped. He didn't want to call Pops just yet, so he finally called Anna.

He immediately sensed that the woman who answered the phone was not the insecure, easy-to-manipulate Anna he had been exploiting for the past year. She had a high-pressure blowout, spewing profanities of such number and with such creativity as would have made her Marine father blush. She capped off the gusher of expletives by telling him that she was going to divorce him.

He begged and pleaded, then cried and threatened. He called her a dried up old hag and wished her a lonely, painful death and hung up on her. He probably shouldn't have said that last part, but he did wish she was dead or. . .

* * *

Jonathan came out of hiding on Monday afternoon, dressed in another new suit and new Bottega Veneta loafers. A firm believer in the adage that "clothes make the man," he considered himself a man among men as he sauntered across the hotel lobby and took a seat in a leather wingback chair. He ordered a double espresso from the roaming waitress and chain-smoked cigarettes while enjoying the female scenery arrayed about the lobby. Holding his cell phone to his ear, he pretended to engage in earnest conversation with a non-existent person until a French-accented voice suddenly called out, "Monsieur Jonathan Frescobaldi Deluca, III. Message for Monsieur Jonathan Frescobaldi DeLuca, III."

Jonathan snapped his fingers and waved the messenger over. It was the same young man who had delivered the fake power of attorney to his suite two days earlier. While the messenger waited fruitlessly for another large tip, Jonathan ignored him and read the message. The shock of its contents turned his face the color of volcanic ash. He jumped to his feet, knocking his cup of espresso onto the travertine marble floor, the delicate bone china shattering and spilling its contents on a nearby oriental rug. A waitress scurried over to clean up the mess as he rushed toward the elevators.

"No, no, NO! Not my precious Anna," he yowled in pure anguish, tears streaming down his face. His heart-wrenching banshee wails bounced and ricocheted off the highly acoustic marble floors and walls in mournful echoes, an audience of stunned hotel guests and concerned staff observing the entire scene. When he reached the elevators, he was sobbing and gasping for air. Frantically pushing the "Up" button and leaning against the wall on one hand, he wept into the other. "Not a coma, oh my god, not a coma . . ."

He collapsed into the first empty elevator to arrive and the doors swished closed. He stood up and checked his clothes for espresso spatter. Finding none, he smiled contentedly all the way up to the suite, mentally patting himself on the back for his award-winning performance. His brilliant theater piece was sure to buy him a few more days. He could make it for a few more days.

Chapter 23

While Jonathan was cavorting on the continent, Anna was struggling to keep her life together. She hadn't spoken to him since the day he bolted out the door and left the country. Despite her persistent and repeated efforts to reach him by phone, he wasn't answering his cell phone and wasn't answering the phone in his room either. She was forced to leave messages through the hotel receptionist as if it were still the 1950s. She made several calls to Jonathan's parents, but all of them remained unreturned.

In the meantime, she was buried with work, using it as a distraction while straining to keep up the appearance of business as usual, giving no hint to the outside world that her private world was fracturing around her. She worked late, drank herself to sleep, and rose early, repeating the routine every day, with no inkling as to her husband's whereabouts or activities. Like a mushroom in a dark cellar, she had been fed a lot of manure and left completely in the dark.

It was only natural that she unleashed all her pent-up fury when Jonathan finally called her more than a week after vanishing like a mirage and avoiding her like a pestilence. She was so enraged, she made the mistake of telling him that she was going to start divorce proceedings the very next morning. She hadn't wanted to show her divorce card so soon, in case Lamar Buchanan came through on Hibiscus Cay and she could ask for half of Jonathan's commissions in the divorce settlement. Instead, she had let her anger overwhelm her self-control, a mistake she vowed never to repeat.

She was contemplating how to put the divorce genie back in the bottle as she drove her rental car to the drugstore the next morning on the way to work. She needed aspirin for the splitting headache she had

204

from stress and a lack of sleep, but when she went to pay for her purchase, her debit card wouldn't work. The somnolent check-out clerk just shrugged, and the card reader at the checkout counter told her three times to "Please Contact Bank." Following the computer's orders, she went straight to her bank in the lobby of her office building. Although a part of her already suspected why a charge of only six dollars and thirty-nine cents had been declined, another part of her still held out a glimmer of hope that it was just a digital malfunction.

She located an available bank vice president named Mrs. Rogers, a polite, nondescript woman with graying hair. Mrs. Rogers led her to a cubicle on the perimeter of the bank lobby. Anna told her about the declined transaction at the drugstore, and Mrs. Rogers tapped some keys on her computer. "There's no money in the account," she said. "In fact, there were attempted debits of twelve hundred and sixty-seven dollars made after your cash balance reached zero."

Anna turned ghostly pale. "That's impossible," she stuttered. "There should be more than three thousand dollars in that account."

Mrs. Rogers looked at her sympathetically and turned back to her computer. A few keystrokes later, the printer in the corner whirred and she handed Anna a printout showing a long list of payments made to restaurants in France, Monaco, and Italy. Making matters worse, over two thousand dollars in cash had been withdrawn from ATMs in the same countries, chewing up the balance in the bank account and spitting the consequences back all over Anna.

She chastised herself for having been so naive and careless, too busy at work and too disoriented in her thinking to have thought to cancel Jonathan's debit card. Now, not only was her marriage a disastrous sham, she was also near penniless.

Forcing herself not to lose her composure and break down in front of a total stranger, she took a few deep breaths and said, "This is so embarrassing. My husband abandoned me and left the country without warning. Now it appears that he emptied the checking account too."

The kindly bank vice president saw through Anna's brave front and reached into her desk drawer, taking out a tissue and handing it to her. "We'll get it all sorted out," she said with a comforting smile. "You'd be surprised how often something like this happens."

Anna clasped the tissue tightly in her hand, not wanting to use it and, by so doing, succumb to her churning emotions. "Really?" she remarked, both surprised and saddened to hear that her dismal situation was not unique. She dabbed her eyes with the tissue and smiled wanly.

"Yes, really," Mrs. Rogers replied. "I've never heard of one running off to Monte Carlo, though. That's a new one."

"I imagine it is," Anna said, sniffling and blowing her nose.

"Don't worry, honey. Some of the attempted charges were made in Monaco just this morning, yet here you sit. Let me work on this. Come back later this afternoon and we'll talk again."

Anna left the bank and rode the elevator up to the hellish workday that awaited her, immensely gratified that Mrs. Rogers believed her bizarre story. Her heart warmed at having been the undeserving recipient of so much human kindness and empathy from a total stranger.

As she reached her floor and the elevator door swooshed open, she realized that she needed to apologize to Cindy and Nicky. They had been right about Jonathan all along.

* * *

Anna arrived at her office just as Becca was hanging up the phone and scribbling a message on a pad, her face awash with grave concern as she handed it over. It was from Roger Black, also known throughout the firm as the "Angel of Death." The pinch-faced, ill-tempered business manager was forty-two years old, of medium height, and had a head of ample coal black hair. A weight lifter and marathon runner, the inveterate bachelor was widely known for his razor-sharp intellect and copious amorous adventures.

The grim reaper of incompetent or unproductive associates, Roger handled the firm's financial matters, ruling the law firm coffers with an iron hand and a stack of pink slips. When Roger Black knocked on your door, you were a dead lawyer walking, just another corpse to be ejected summarily from B&V with a small amount of severance and very few job prospects. A mere visit by the Angel of Death to any of the law firm's seven floors would instantaneously set off the associate and secretarial email chain. Office doors shut hastily, and empty bathrooms filled to capacity at the mere mention of his name, everyone scrambling to avoid him as if his mere gaze, like Medusa's, would turn them to stone.

The color drained from Anna's face. Becca saw the panic in her eyes and tried to put a positive spin on the situation. "Oh, don't worry honey, I'm sure it's nothing serious," she said. "Maybe you're getting a big bonus or something like that."

Although Anna appreciated Becca's futile attempt to lift the shadow that was settling over her like a shroud, she doubted it was anything that benign. Her doubts were confirmed when, mere seconds later, a violet-visaged F-Man stormed into her office and slammed the door behind him. "American CreditCorp just called Roger Black to tell him that the unpaid balance on your account is over forty thousand dollars," he screamed, the veins in his neck visibly throbbing. "Then Roger called Harry Vincent, who called *me* and told me to find out how the balance got to be so high."

Convinced she saw steam coming from his ears, Anna suddenly heard rhythmic pounding in her own as her blood pressure skyrocketed. She was rendered near mute with astonishment at his words, her heart leaping into her throat. "What?" she croaked, her voice dry as dust.

"You heard me," the F-Man said. "Explain."

As Anna's emotions wrestled each other, she labored to find a rational explanation for Jonathan's irrational behavior. With measured words and stoic deliberation, she told the F-Man the same story she had told Mrs. Rogers at the bank, adding, "Jonathan must have figured out a way to use my American CreditCorp card too."

Flabbergasted by Anna's tale of woe and mega-yachts in Monte Carlo, the F-Man was skeptical. "Are you shitting me?"

"I shit you not," Anna replied. "I will swear on a stack of Baptist bibles that the excessive charges are wrong or fraudulent." She got her American CreditCorp card out of her briefcase and showed it to him.

"This is the only card that was ever issued on the account, and I'm the only person authorized to use it."

She held her breath and awaited her fate, but to her surprise, it didn't come. Instead, the F-Man looked hard into her eyes, and whatever he saw there caused his expression to change. He looked at the card and back at Anna. "I'll explain the situation to Harry," he said. "In the meantime, log onto your account and print out a list of all the charges." Getting up to leave, he added, "I'm going out on a long, narrow limb here for you, Anna. I know I'm a real asshole and that I make your life miserable most of the time. I'm hard on you because you're a talented lawyer. But despite that, and even though Harry really likes you, he told me to tell you that if you did anything unethical or illegal, he'll fire you himself. Come by my office in one hour. We'll go see Roger together and fix this if it's fixable." He left without another word, closing the door behind him—this time without slamming it.

As soon as the door clicked shut, Anna got up and locked it. She returned to her desk, crawled under it, and yielded to her emotions. She crouched there for five minutes with her hand cupped over her mouth so that no one could hear her cry. Then, having cried too many times because of Jonathan, she got back out from under her desk and logged onto her American CreditCorp account.

She was astonished by what she saw. It took her half an hour to interpret and absorb what she was reading and formulate an explanation for Roger Black. That wasn't going to be easy because the amounts of the unauthorized charges were staggering, some of them incomprehensible. Although Jonathan had insisted repeatedly that Lamar had paid for their plane tickets to Monte Carlo—along with Captain Barry's—Jonathan had clearly lied and charged the tickets to her law firm credit card. Then he had charged his first-class round-trip airfare back to Monte Carlo, along with another round-trip ticket for Captain Barry. There were also charges for two one-way tickets from Miami to Nice for two people Anna had never heard of.

In addition to the plane tickets, Jonathan's temper tantrum in Monte Carlo during their Thanksgiving visit had resulted in a charge of fifteen hundred dollars for repairs to the wall he had assaulted. Other charges included thirty-five hundred dollars as a deposit on a suite at the hotel for his second visit and charges from a motel in France—first for one room, then for two. Also listed were a French rental car company, restaurants in Dallas, Paris, and Monaco, and florists on two continents. The most baffling transaction was for ten thousand dollars, charged by a company in Lyonne, France, called Acme Pyrotechnie.

Anna's legitimate transactions only added up to two thousand dollars or so, all for law firm-related travel expenses and all billable to various clients. Jonathan's charges topped forty thousand dollars and all were billable to Anna. It had never occurred to her that he could use her law firm credit card without physical possession of it and without her knowledge. There was no time to investigate how he had managed the subterfuge, however, because it was time to face the Angel of Death. With righteous indignation, albeit great reluctance, she went to collect the F-Man and meet her professional doom at the hands of Roger Black.

To her great relief, the F-Man took the lead and ran interference for her, and when the meeting was over, her job was tenuously secure pending further investigation. She tried to thank the F-Man for his help in avoiding Roger's career decapitating scythe, but he would have none of it. "I never liked Jonathan anyway," he said, walking off to berate a second-year associate for a while.

Anna's next stop was Harry Vincent's office. She related her strange and ever-evolving story for the fourth time that day, promising to reimburse B&V for every penny of Jonathan's unapproved charges, should the firm ultimately be held liable for his fraud.

* * *

Her tour of humiliation finally over, it was pushing 3:00 p.m. and Anna had not yet done any billable work. She put it off a little longer and called Bennington Travel in search of answers and explanations.

Helen answered her private line on the first ring. "This is Helen. How can I help you?"

"This is Anna DeLuca."

209

The travel agent sounded as if she were in great distress, blurting out, "Oh my god, Anna. I'm so glad you called. Jonathan just called me from France in a panic. He said he needed to charge three more airfares to your law firm credit card, insisting that it was an absolute emergency. When I just tried to run the charges, I found out that the card was cancelled."

Anna lit into Helen like a pit bull on a junkyard trespasser. "It was cancelled due in great part to your malfeasance and incompetence," she said. She heard Helen gasp and powered on. "What in the world gave you the right to charge so many airfares to my credit card without my knowledge? I was almost fired this morning, thanks to you and Jonathan."

Like a deer caught in the headlights of Anna's accusations, Helen went into a panic, barely able to speak. "What?" she finally stammered breathlessly. "I don't understand. He told me that you knew about all of the flights."

"Why didn't you pick up the phone to call me and ask before running the charges through?" Anna said.

"You went along on the first trip, so I assumed you knew about the second one. When Jonathan called to book the tickets, he told me he had to get to Monaco right away or his business deal would blow up. Both times he told me that you would have authorized the charges personally but were in court all day and couldn't be reached."

"I'm never in court," Anna said. "I'm a corporate lawyer, not a litigator."

Unconcerned with the distinction, Helen started to choke up and break down. "He threatened to put me out of business if I interfered with his deal by refusing him," she blubbered. "He screamed at me and said that you and B&V would sue me for everything I've got if I didn't cooperate."

Helen's histrionics were convincing, and Anna's rage metamorphosed into understanding and sympathy. She herself had been fooled by Jonathan's charms, and the same could very well be true of Helen. Nonetheless, even if Helen was not knowingly involved in his widespread malfeasance, her negligent business practices had put Anna in a precarious financial position.

Adrift in a sea of scoundrels, Anna wasn't ready to trust anyone involved with Jonathan, including poor Helen. "I'm afraid your many assumptions were wildly wrong, and your trust in Jonathan was badly misplaced." she said. She heard Helen crying softly in the background but still needed some answers. "Who are the Bjornbergs?" she asked.

"Jonathan told me they were your two new crew members," Helen replied, surprised by the question.

"I've never heard of them," Anna said, stupefied.

"I swear he told me that you knew all about what he was doing."

"I don't know anything about two crew members," Anna said. "But I *do* know that Jonathan was never authorized to use my card and never had possession of it. I have no way to pay the huge amounts the two of you charged without my consent. Ordinarily, I would bring criminal charges and sue you personally for the price of the tickets, but I'm going to give you the benefit of the doubt. Jonathan can be very convincing, and he certainly fooled me. If, however, I learn that you were a knowing participant in his fraud, I will reassess my decision."

Anna hung up on a still-distraught Helen Bennington and immediately sent Roger Black an email explaining what had happened regarding the airfare charges. Within a week, B&V would have a new travel agent. Anna felt bad about Helen's losing the B&V account, but business was business, and her sympathies only stretched so far. At least Helen wasn't out any money. Anna, on the other hand, still had to find a way to deal with Jonathan's credit card charges.

* * *

As soon as she put down the phone, another line lit up. It was Dan Fairfield from Silverman Baggins, and he didn't have good news. Dan informed her that he had just returned from a week-long business trip to discover that Jonathan had tried to write hot checks on the Frescobaldi Prime Investments checking account to Gerald's, Chartrier's, and The Bargeron Law Firm in Monte Carlo.

Dan's revelations went from bad to worse when he explained that Jonathan had pitched his prime bank investment opportunity to him a few months earlier, hoping to present the deal to the bank's wealth managers as an investment option for their clients. Dan had forwarded the details of the plan to the department that analyzed such things, and they had just informed him that Jonathan's so-called "prime bank investment pool" was actually a scam. Thousands of such phony deals had cropped up in recent years, and the ploy was well-known in Department of Justice circles.

This last drop of information should have made Anna's cup of mind-bending surprises runneth over, but she had an ominous feeling that there were more to come. She authorized Dan to close the company account and asked him to let her know if and where Jonathan tried to pass more hot checks.

When she finally got home around midnight, she scoured the apartment like a crime scene investigator in search of trace evidence. She combed through drawers, rummaged through purses, and emptied the pockets of suit jackets and pants, both hers and the few that Jonathan had left behind in his closet. She totaled up her meager harvest and added it to the jar of loose change on top of the refrigerator. Together with the ten dollars left in the checking account after Mrs. Rogers credited her account for the fraudulent debits, Anna had exactly thirty dollars and twenty-nine cents to live on until payday, over a week away.

* * *

Anna was in her office early the next morning after a restless three hours of sleep. The insides of her eyelids felt like sandpaper, her stomach sour from the prior day's steady diet of caffeine, aspirin, and bad news. She couldn't afford to get fired, so her miasma of personal misery and indulgent self-pity would just have to wait while she focused on work. She asked Becca to put all non-urgent calls into her voicemail and didn't check her messages until almost noon.

The first voicemail was a collection call from Newman Marvis, demanding payment in full of the card's balance—over forty thousand dollars, just like the American CreditCorp card. She immediately returned the call and made an appointment with the credit manager of the downtown Newman Marvis store, then checked the rest of her messages.

The second message was from Sue Worthing. Anna had already planned to go to Highland Park Motors to unravel the mystery of her car, so when the phones quieted down during lunchtime, she drove to the dealership. Arriving in high dudgeon and determined to get her car or her ten thousand dollars back, she made a beeline for Sue, who quickly escorted her to an office tucked away in the back corner of the lobby.

Once inside, Sue introduced her to Neil McGrave, the dealership's business manager. Neil's long, narrow face was punctuated by closely-placed, beady brown eyes and encircled by neatly trimmed brown hair. His sharply tailored suit matched his sharply sculpted nose, and the overall effect reminded Anna of a well-dressed ferret. She sat down in a black leather and chrome chair in front of Neil's black leather and chrome desk. Before he could explain why they had called her, she demanded to know how Jonathan was able to sell her car without her knowledge.

Neil nodded at Sue, who uneasily explained how Jonathan had come in to lease the red Mercedes convertible for his company. "He said that you were in court," she began. "He paid the deposit in cash and took the papers away for you to sign. He came back a few hours later with your signature on a power of attorney and the new lease. I assumed it all was on the up and up because we had driven the car down to your office for your approval and all."

"I'm never in court because I'm not a litigator," Anna said with thinly veiled frustration.

Sue gave her a blank look.

Anna pressed on. "And I didn't approve anything," she said. "I had no idea why you and Jonathan brought that car to my office. He told me that his business partner was leasing it for him. I had nothing to do with the transaction."

Neil's beady eyes darted to and fro before landing on Sue. The two exchanged nervous glances, and droplets of sweat started to form on Neil's forehead as he handed Anna a file. "Before we talk about

213

your car," he said, "I assume that you knew nothing about these either."

Anna leafed through the papers. In addition to the forged power of attorney, there was the lease for the red convertible and purchase documents for two additional 600 SL convertibles. One of the cars was champagne gold and was to be titled in the name of Sharon Hammond. The other was black and was to be titled in the names of Ricky and Gina DeLuca. Jonathan had also arranged to have the new vehicles shipped to Monaco at an address to be determined and had dropped off his own convertible on the way to the airport so that it could join the other two in their overseas journey. Sue had called Anna because Neil had just discovered that Jonathan had given the dealership two hot checks for the deposits on the two new cars.

"These are forgeries," Anna said, dropping the file on the desk and taking a pen from Neil's pencil holder. She wrote her signature on the back of the folder and showed it to Neil and Sue. They easily saw the difference between Jonathan's spiky, jagged scrawl and her swooping hand.

Anna sat back in her chair and looked at Sue. "Who is Sharon Hammond?" she asked.

"Jonathan said that you were divorcing and that Sharon is his new girlfriend," Sue replied. She lowered her eyes, clearly uncomfortable with making the disclosure.

Anna didn't react visibly to the news, for fear it might compromise her negotiating position. Hastening to climb out of the rabbit hole into which she had fallen, she reminded Neil that her car had been illegally taken in trade for a car that was obtained fraudulently and was already back in the dealership's possession. The sale to Jonathan was therefore *ipso facto* null and void, and she was entitled to either get her car back or be paid compensation for it in the amount of ten thousand dollars.

Trying to weasel his way out of Anna's legal and logical traps, Neil pointed out that the dealership had spent almost two thousand dollars readying her car for re-sale and replacing the bumper that Jonathan had demolished. Not one to give up without a fight, Anna pointed out that both Neil and Sue were possible parties to Jonathan's frauds and forgeries, given that neither of them had bothered to speak with her directly to confirm that the multiple-vehicle transactions totaling over a quarter of a million dollars were legitimate.

Neil remained intransigent, but Anna remained determined. It took the threat of civil litigation, criminal prosecution, and a truckload of potential bad publicity to do it, but she finally got her car back from the ferret.

* * *

Despite the successful car quest, Anna's eyes and her mood were as leaden as the winter sky as she drove back to the office. It was obvious that Jonathan had been planning to move all three cars to where the repo man could never find them, leaving her on the hook for almost three hundred thousand dollars in payments. He must have hoped that the cars would be shipped before the checks bounced or the forgeries were exposed, but he had either wildly miscalculated the delivery date for the cars or was completely unhinged from reality. The latter seemed to be the most likely explanation.

She finally got home from work around 9:00 p.m., exhausted and weak from sleeplessness and sixteen-hour work days. Her emotions were as frayed as a three-hundred-year old Persian rug, and she didn't know how much longer her prodigious self-control could hold up. She feared that her defenses might collapse completely, and she would just melt into a shapeless puddle of existential protoplasm.

She still hadn't been able to reach Jonathan, although she wasn't sure what she'd say to him if she did. Trudging upstairs in search of clues to a variety of unpleasant mysteries, she found his old briefcase sitting on the floor. She looked inside and found his cell phone, along with dozens of debit and ATM receipts. Underneath them was a notice from the office of the Attorney General of the State of Texas demanding immediate payment of back child support and threatening criminal prosecution if Jonathan didn't pay what he owed his ex-wife. The date specified for his compliance had long passed.

Beaten down by the betrayals exposed during the past few days, Anna felt no emotion as she gathered the evidence of her husband's serial deceptions. She mentally catalogued his misdeeds, adding infidelity to the list and wondering how high the metaphorical body count would go before someone stopped the devastation.

In the meantime, she was going to find out who Sharon Hammond was and if she was another unwilling dupe that Jonathan had seduced with promises of riches or a willing accomplice to his plotting.

Chapter 24

Halfway across the world, Henri Baptiste was deliberating over a difficult decision. Hotel policy required that every guest's bill be paid on a weekly basis or a variety of consequences would ensue. He had grudgingly given Jonathan DeLuca a few more days to settle his burgeoning debt after hearing the news of Mrs. DeLuca's catastrophic car accident. The hotel operator had confirmed to Henri that the unidentified caller who delivered the long-distance blow had indeed used the word "coma."

Another important consideration was the reputation of the hotel and the sensibilities of its favored clients, such as the Baroness von Pfaffenhoffen. Henri was a discreet and patient man, and he wished to avoid an unpleasant scene with her current *objét de amor*. Further complicating his position was the fact that Jonathan DeLuca had lately been seen in the company of Miss Kathleen McGregor, a twenty-five-year-old heiress to an Irish whisky fortune. The redheaded ingénue was also a favored client of the hotel, so Henri found himself stuck firmly between a royal rock and a cash heavy hard place.

Business and public relations issues aside, Henri was rapidly losing patience with the obnoxious poseur. Every day since the Baroness had departed, and even after the news of his wife's car accident, DeLuca had been using the Hotel de Monaco as his personal playground. Henri could not understand why the man who claimed to be an international real estate magnate with royal blood had not rushed home to be by his wife's side. Instead, he spent each afternoon and evening deep in his cups, wandering the hotel and buying drinks and dinner for total strangers. Holding court in the hotel's bars and restaurants, he boasted of his new yacht, making uninvited business propositions to the men and scandalously suggestive propositions to the women.

When the hotel operator later informed Henri that Mrs. DeLuca had called several times in the days after her husband had claimed that she was in a coma, Henri's patience finally ran out, and he decided to act.

* * *

The Baroness von Pfaffenhofen was settling back into her suite on the day of the DeLucas' first wedding anniversary. She was on the phone with the head of security for her family's business enterprises when a tap on the door interrupted her conversation. Terminating the call, she opened the door to find Jonathan holding a bouquet of flowers that looked suspiciously like one of the arrangements adorning the hotel hallways.

He swept into the suite, whisking her off her feet and enfolding her in a crushing embrace before setting her down and kissing her passionately. "I have marvelous news, *liebchen*," he gushed. "I filed for divorce while you were away and will be free of my horrible wife in mere weeks."

He tried to kiss her again, but Gisela turned her back on him and walked toward the door.

Desperate and shameless, he ignored her sudden standoffishness and went in for the close. "In fact, my love, Anna is so angry about the divorce that she emptied our joint bank account and cancelled my credit cards. Considering that I'm divorcing her so that you and I can be together, I was hoping you might help me out until the divorce is final. I only need one hundred fifty thousand dollars and a guarantee of the hotel bill until I can recoup my millions."

The Baroness burst into haughty, derisive laughter. "You can't be serious."

"I'm very serious," Jonathan said. He got down on one knee and wrapped his arms around hers in supplication, as if begging for a pardon from the guillotine. "I love you more than life itself. Will you marry me?" he beseeched her.

218

Gisela pushed him away. "Surely you don't think that I could ever be in a serious relationship with an American commoner. I would never loan money to a shoddy charlatan like you." She strode regally to the door and opened it. "Inquiries have been made," she said, motioning for Jonathan to leave. "It has come to my attention that your royal connections are tenuous at best, and your real estate fortune is entirely fictional."

Jonathan stood up and started to speak, but she interrupted him. "I have heard all about your plebeian behavior during my absence. You are an uncouth clod, and I want nothing more to do with you. You must leave. Immediately."

Jonathan made no move toward the door. Not accustomed to having her orders disobeyed, the Baroness was incensed. "Go now before I call hotel security and have you physically escorted from Monaco," she said, walking to the desk and picking up the phone.

Jonathan's desperation turned to rage, contorting his face into a hideous mask. Bolting up from his knees, he stormed to the door, snatching two bottles of champagne from a Louis XIV sideboard along the way. When he reached the door, he pointed to Gisela's heavily adorned wrist. "You're not too superior to wear the bracelet I gave you, you Bavarian bitch," he hissed.

Gisela removed the trinket he had given her and hurled it violently at his head. "I'm Austrian, not German, you ignorant buffoon."

Jonathan ducked as the bracelet bounced off the wall and bent to retrieve it like an orphan scrabbling for coins in an eighteenth-century London sewer. He straightened back up to see the Baroness glowering at him contemptuously. Putting the bracelet in his pocket, he snarled, "What are you, some kind of psychopath?"

"It takes one to know one, *liebchen*," the Baroness von Pfaffenhoffen said, laughing derisively and pushing him unceremoniously out the door.

* * *

Jonathan was infuriated by Gisela's sudden rejection and panicking at the loss of his badly needed bankroll. The royal pain in the ass who had just dismissed him was his only source of funds to pay the hotel bill and the yacht deposit. He figured that he had maybe twenty-four hours before it all truly went to shit for him.

His brilliant master plan had been to live on his new yacht, marketing Hibiscus Cay and cruising extradition-free international waters while he worked his prime bank scheme up and down the Riviera and waited for the commissions on Lamar's investment to roll in. He really thought that he could close the DuPrees on their second tranche of money or that Lamar would come through in time to cover the deposit on Alpha Centauri. Things hadn't gone exactly as he had planned, but if he could just hold out until after the first of the year, when Lamar was ready to invest, it would be clear skies, balmy winds, and smooth sailing after that.

A call from Henri informing him that he would be turned over to the Monte Carlo authorities if his hotel bill was not paid within twenty-four hours temporarily doused cold water on his optimism and added urgency to the task at hand. Scavenging through his clothes, he came up with a handful of coins, a casino chip, and a few hundred Euros that he had stolen from the Irish heiress' purse when she had gone into his bathroom to throw up the expensive dinner and champagne with which he had plied her.

He opened the hidden wall safe and removed his gold and diamond cuff links, several gold tie clips, his father's Piaget watch, and the new Tag Heuer. Laying it all on the antique dining room table, he dropped the diamond and sapphire bracelet on top of the pile, then popped the cork on one of the bottles of champagne that he had lifted from the Baroness' suite. He sipped it while he added up his assets on hotel stationery and thought about time zones. An hour later, feeling more relaxed and even cautiously optimistic, he made another call to the United States.

* * *

While Henri was considering how to solve his Jonathan DeLuca dilemma, back in Dallas, Anna was rushing to stop the financial bleeding and cut her losses. She left the office on her lunch hour and drove to Chartrier's, hoping to exchange her engagement ring for cash.

She didn't have the receipt, and she knew she'd never get the diamond's full value, but she needed the money and didn't need the ring. Her marriage was effectively over, and the legal steps necessary to make it formal could be concluded in a matter of weeks—once her divorce attorney got back in town.

Already intensely embarrassed by having to return the diamond, her discomfort elevated to sheer mortification when the haughty sales clerk informed her that the three-carat flawless round cut diamond was a three-carat cubic zirconium, a high-tech imitation that an establishment such as Chartrier's would never deign to sell. The clerk handed the ring back to Anna, dangling it between two fingertips with distaste as if it carried some contagion.

The brilliant gem that once blinded Anna was, like her marriage, a fraud. The faux stone's facets mocked her with each light-catching sparkle, as if to say that she should have known better than to fall for Jonathan's trickery.

Demoralized by her latest discovery, she left the store dreading what was coming next. She drove back downtown and parked in the underground garage beneath the Newman Marvis mother ship. She took an elevator up to the floor that housed the central credit department and waited uncomfortably until the company's credit manager came out and guided her to his office.

They got straight down to business and went through the charges one by one. The account statement immediately dashed her slim hopes that a credit was in process for the fur coat and the luggage that Jonathan had promised to return. The present whereabouts of the costly items were unknown, but the debt they left behind was there in vivid black and white for all to see.

She showed no emotion as she explained that the coat and luggage were to have been returned, and that she knew nothing about any of the other charges. Realizing that she hadn't received a statement—paper or electronic—for months, it suddenly dawned on her that Jonathan must have been stealing the mail and deleting the online notices that would have alerted her to what he was doing.

She kept that tidbit to herself as she continued to review the bill, emphasizing the fact that her husband was never added to the account and had never been issued a card. Not once had she received a phone call to confirm that any of the charges were authorized.

The credit manager was unmoved and unmovable by her logic and entreaties. He curtly pointed out that, even if true, everything she had just said was completely irrelevant under current law. Unknown to her—and no doubt many others—in the great State of Texas, any charge made by the spouse of a credit card holder may be "presumed authorized" by retailers like Newman Marvis. Although the law seemed anachronistic to Anna, as an attorney she could understand its logic. Without such a law, married couples could defraud merchants all over Texas, one spouse making purchases only to have the other deny having authorized the charges. Her legal sympathies notwithstanding, she told the credit manager that she was insulted at his implications. She was a victim of the fraud, not its perpetrator.

The credit manager was unyielding. The best he could do was allow her to repay the bill over time in the amount of one thousand dollars per month. If she didn't, he would turn her over to a collection agency, and Newman Marvis would sue her for the full amount of the balance, plus interest and attorneys' fees.

Fearing the irreparable damage that failing to settle the account would do to her credit rating, she negotiated the payment down to seven hundred dollars per month, swallowing the rhetorical bitter pill and wishing she had a glass of real hemlock with which to wash it down.

* * *

Sharon Hammond finished tucking her ten-year-old twins into bed after a difficult and tiring day. They had been upset and fussy ever since she told them that she was taking a trip and that they'd be staying with Auntie Bess while she was gone. While the mother in her felt guilty about leaving her children so she could be with Jonathan in Monte Carlo, the woman in her wasn't about to pass up a free trip to Monaco. Although the children had not taken the news well, they were old enough to start learning about life's disappointments.

A thirty-eight-year-old single mother, Sharon was struggling to make ends meet and keep her family together. Although a lawyer and in-house counsel to George Williams' insurance conglomerate, she didn't make nearly the kind of money that attorneys working for the big law firms did. Her ex-husband was consistently late in paying the child support, and her property taxes kept going up. She was bone tired and desperately looking for a way out of the many ruts in which she found herself firmly stuck.

When Jonathan DeLuca had shown up at a business lunch one day and subsequently courted her with great style and dogged determination, she jumped at the chance to snare such a wealthy and worldly suitor. Knowing that he was probably the last man who would ever want her, she set out to make him hers. He had been easily won, and now she was going to be with him for a long overdue and hard-earned rest.

After they returned, they would marry. Sharon would be legal counsel to Jonathan's company, enabling her to keep her children's college fund afloat while making her own hours and yacht-schooling the twins aboard Alpha Centauri. She had already given her notice at work and had promised the twins that as soon as she returned, they'd all go live on a big boat and spend much more time together.

The phone rang as she was putting the last of the toys in a basket by the children's bedroom door. She rushed to the kitchen to answer it before the noise of it woke them and started the separation anxiety again. "Hammond residence," she said quietly.

"Hello. My name is Anna DeLuca, Jonathan DeLuca's wife," the woman on the other end of the line said. "Are you Sharon Hammond?"

"Yes, this is Sharon. And don't you mean *ex*-wife?"

"Not yet, unfortunately."

Sharon was taken aback, stuttering, "But Jonathan told me that you've been divorced since June."

"He lied."

Maintaining a lawyerly demeanor while assessing her adversary on the other end of the line Sharon said, "Jonathan's not here, if that's why you're calling."

"I know he's not there." Anna said, her voice flat and businesslike. "I'm calling because I've been informed that you are his girlfriend. I wanted to warn you that he is a fraud and a con man. He wiped me out financially and left me with his debts. I don't want that to happen to anyone else."

Sharon knew the real story and spat into the phone, "Spare me the fake concern. Jonathan already told me that you stole all *his* money and cancelled *his* credit card, just to get even with him for divorcing you. He even had to borrow money from me to get to Monte Carlo and close his big business deal."

"I hope you didn't loan him very much," Anna said. "In any event, I was fooled by Jonathan too, so I'm giving you the benefit of the doubt here. I'm going to assume that you're not a party to his various financial crimes against me and others. Nonetheless, it's obvious you're having an affair with him and were planning to run off with him shortly after he emptied our joint bank account and forged my signature on fraudulent checks from here to Monaco. I have many reasons to suspect that you are in on his schemes, and there's ample circumstantial evidence pointing in your adulterous direction."

"I don't believe you," Sharon protested. Swimming deep in the depths of denial, she was deaf to Anna's words, hating her for trying to unravel her dreams like treasured vintage lace caught on a rusty nail. "You're lying. Jonathan is flying me to Monte Carlo any day now. He's already bought fireworks to shoot off his new yacht for my birthday."

"Well bless your heart," Anna said in that way that polite Southerners do when confronted with abject idiocy. "I really don't care if you believe me or not, Sharon. I made this call as a courtesy. As far as I'm concerned, you and Jonathan can shove your birthday fireworks up your respective asses and fart flames all the way to the moon."

Sharon bristled at the insult. "You're just a bitter, crazy old bitch," she hissed, slamming the phone down in disgust. The noise of it woke the children. Sharon heard them call for her and rushed down the hall to tuck them in again. Once they settled down she went into her bedroom to finish packing so that she'd be ready to leave as soon as Jonathan summoned her. A new set of luggage from Newman Marvis was piled high against one wall and her gorgeous new mink coat was draped luxuriously over an armchair—clear and incontrovertible evidence that she had hooked herself a man, and a rich one at that.

Chapter 25

Jonathan marked the first anniversary of his marriage to Anna being summarily marooned by the Baroness and scrounging for money like a castaway searching for fallen coconuts. Meanwhile, Anna spent the day hard at work and working hard to keep her job. She had been summoned to a meeting with Doug Sherman, a licensed lawyer, a licensed psychologist, and head of B&V's human resources department. Assuming the worst, her already deflated spirit gave a last gasp like a punctured balloon.

She needn't have worried. Multiple meetings and conference calls among the firm's power players had taken place over a three-day period, and the firm ran an exhaustive background check on her. The primary purpose of the behind-the-scenes machinations was to determine whether she was involved in the fraudulent charges made on her law firm credit card. The firm's risk management committee needed to determine if she or Jonathan were looming liabilities and litigation magnets who could expose the firm or worse—its partners—to lawsuits.

Tilting things in Anna's favor was the fact that Roger Black had received written confirmation from the corporate counsel of American CreditCorp that B&V wasn't liable for any of Jonathan's charges. The terms of the firm's contract with the credit card company clearly specified that the individual attorney alone was responsible for payment of the bill in all circumstances, so no financial harm had been done to the firm and none was likely.

Helpfully pleading her case, Larry Frederickson pointed out to the executive committee that he, along with several other lawyers from the firm, had also been bamboozled by Jonathan DeLuca. The partners in the corporate section supported her too, telling the higher-ups that she continued to work like an unstoppable billing machine, keeping her hours and work quality up despite her ongoing personal drama. After a few days of deliberation by the executive committee, its members reached the conclusion that Anna had not been knowingly involved in the fraud. It was agreed that she could keep her job, but she'd have to deal with the credit card liability on her own.

Doug's office door was open when Anna arrived, and he waved her in. A large man in his early sixties, he had sparse white hair and a cherubic face. With his rosy cheeks and his fifty pounds too many, he could have easily moonlighted as the local mall's Santa Claus. Anna decided that he might have been the real thing after he told her about the executive committee's decision.

The job-resuscitating news delivered, Doug moved on to the primary reason for their meeting. "I know about what happened with your credit card," he said. "I also heard about your husband's bizarre trip to Monte Carlo. I'd like to know more about him and any other unusual things he's done recently."

Doug listened carefully as Anna told him about the hot checks, the cars, the fur coat, the girlfriend, and the forgeries. "Does Jonathan do drugs?" he asked after Anna recited her surfeit of sorrows.

"I've never known him to do drugs like marijuana or cocaine," she replied. "I did find a bottle of anti-anxiety medication after he disappeared. I didn't even know he was taking it."

"Does he drink?"

"Yes. Heavily."

"Has he ever been physically violent toward you?"

"He's been verbally abusive lately, but has never shown any hint of physical violence since I've known him."

"I'm glad to hear it, but you should still be cautious," Doug warned. "Do either of you own a gun?"

"I have a Browning nine-millimeter handgun," Anna replied. "I haven't been to the practice range in years, so I keep it in the back of my closet." Her brow furrowed in thought. She'd been so overwhelmed by the whirlwind Jonathan had reaped that she had completely forgotten about her gun. Now she couldn't remember if she had ever told him about it.

"Are you sure it's still there?"

"Not now."

"Find out"

"Yes, sir."

Doug handed her a stack of printed internet articles, urging her to read them. "In my professional opinion," he said, "your husband is a sociopath, possibly a psychopath."

Unable to marshal her thoughts or her words, Anna said nothing. She had never once entertained the idea that her husband was mentally deranged or could be physically violent toward her, even in his worst of tempers.

His face awash with concern, Doug concluded, "Jonathan's behavior is irrational, and the combination of alcohol and his medication can be volatile. Now with the missing gun . . ."

Doug didn't need to finish the sentence.

* * *

Five new messages were waiting for her when she returned to her office. Four of them were from Jonathan's parents—the first time she had heard from them since he left the country. The first message was from his father. Strident and accusatory, it excoriated her with now familiar lies: "Jonathan told us you cancelled the credit card." "Jonathan told us you stopped payment on the check for the yacht." "Jonathan told us that you emptied the bank account." "Jonathan told us that you sank his business deal."

Gina joined the blame game in the second message, her voice laden with disappointment. "Why would you do that to our poor Johnny? We thought you loved him."

The third message was from Jonathan's father again, this time a transparent attempt to pacify her with fake parental concern, the tone conciliatory. "Anna, honey, we really need to know what's going on with you. Please call us, dear. We have the money to fix this."

Jonathan's mother chimed in again in the fourth message, her voice desperate and supplicating. "Why won't you let us fix this, sweetheart? It's all just a big misunderstanding. You know Jonathan loves you more than life itself. *We* love you. Please call us."

Remembering how Gina had looked right past her as if she were invisible the day she drove off with Jonathan, she doubted that any of them cared one whit about her. They probably just wanted to enlist her help in cleaning up after their son's latest criminal escapade. Not knowing at this point if Gina and Ricky were in on Jonathan's intrigues, she had no intention of calling them back.

The final message was from her divorce attorney and was the best news she had received all day. He would be back in the office the following Monday and could see her first thing. The unhappy topic of divorce reminded her that today was the first anniversary of her brief and befouled marriage. She laughed out loud, fearing that not doing so and succumbing to her other impulses would propel her into a nervous breakdown.

Just then Becca popped in and handed her the recent arrivals to her in-box. Anna reviewed several letters addressed to her as the official shareholder contact for the hostile takeover of Harry Vincent's client. The shareholders opposing the takeover of the company were disgruntled by the low price per share being offered in the deal. Many were exercising their legal right to dissent from the proposed offer and seek a higher price in court.

She opened the final letter and read a brief and brutal missive berating the board of directors of the corporation and the attorneys representing said corporation, which included Anna. The closing words from the disaffected shareholder were quaintly archaic but succinct: "A pox on you all."

* * *

Anna looked for her gun as soon as she got home that night, but it was nowhere to be found. After emailing Doug to give him the unsettling update, she checked the doors and windows to the apartment to make sure they were secure. Too rattled to eat anything, she sat down and spent the night reading the materials from Wikipedia and The Mayo Clinic's website that Doug had printed for her.

Disturbed by what she read, she learned that sociopaths make up about four percent of the population, and there is no known cure for the mental disorder. Even incarceration fails to deter them because they are unable to learn from the adverse consequences of their actions. She compared her husband's behaviors to the traits and tendencies that were discussed in the research, and with the brutal clarity of 20/20 hindsight, she could see that Jonathan possessed almost every characteristic of the stereotypical sociopath: a disregard for right and wrong, a lack of remorse or empathy for others, superficial charm, glibness, and pathological lying combined with the ability to do it with a straight face.

Some of the traits hit very close to home, such as the use of others for personal gain, using wives and children for an aura of respectability, multiple and usually short marriages, promiscuity, and a history of childhood misbehavior enabled by the parents' social status. Jonathan's erratic behavior matched many other psychological afflictions that bedevil sociopaths, including a lack of realistic long-term goals, impulsive behaviors, risk taking, irresponsible work behavior, failure to honor financial obligations, and an unwillingness to accept responsibility for his own actions.

There was one more thing in the research that intrigued her. According to the psychologists who penned the paper, sociopaths use movies and television to learn how to mimic desired social behaviors and mask their antisocial ones, often becoming skilled actors, even using fake tears. She recalled that Jonathan had once told her that he had developed his sense of style and dress by copying his movie heroes. Was it possible that a movie had triggered his lunatic obsession of buying Alpha Centauri and using it to run con games in the Mediterranean? It seemed farfetched, but everything about him was turning out to be just that.

His twisted motivations and movie-induced madness aside, Anna could not but come to the inevitable and inescapable conclusion that Jonathan didn't marry her because he was in love with her. He married her because he needed her paycheck and credit to finance his schemes, and he needed her law firm as his beard of legitimacy. Adding marital insult to monetary injury, he had cheated on her too.

Now her gun was missing, and she was beginning to think that the pox wished upon her by the angry shareholder would have been preferable to her current sorry condition.

Chapter 26

Becca walked into Anna's office without knocking on the morning of December 24th and shoved a message at her. "It's urgent," she said.

The message instructed Anna to go immediately to Doug Sherman's office. When she arrived, Doug was with another man who stood when she entered. Doug introduced him as Ken Woods.

"Pleased to meet you, ma'am," Ken said, shaking her hand firmly. He was slightly shorter than Anna, but despite his small stature, she could tell that he was all muscle. His biceps bulged, his pectoral muscles rippled beneath his blue knit polo shirt, and his glutei maximi maximized the fit of his crisply pressed blue jeans. He wore his reddish-blonde hair in a military cut and radiated the capacity for sudden violence of action, leading Anna to suspect that he packed a lot of power in his compact packaging.

"Ken is a private investigator and bodyguard," Doug explained. "He assists B&V from time to time with certain delicate law firm matters. The firm has hired him to escort you to and from the office and anywhere else you need to go until your husband's whereabouts can be confirmed. Ken is highly experienced and armed. Please follow his instructions to the letter. Once we know where Jonathan is, Ken will do a threat assessment."

Anna found herself hoping that a "threat assessment" involved the breaking of arms and legs. "Thank you so much for your support," she said. "I promise the firm will not regret it."

Before they wrapped up the brief meeting, Doug picked up the phone and called the partners with whom Anna was currently working, explaining that she would need to be away from the office for the rest of the day.

* * *

Too busy grappling with the bizarre reality that she needed a bodyguard for protection from her own husband, Anna had no time to closely analyze how her circumstances had come to such an abysmal pass. She had to put a finger in the dyke of Jonathan's depredations and re-start her life before she could stop to mourn her many losses.

While Ken waited quietly in her office, she spent the morning combing internet real estate ads for apartments that she could afford, that were close to downtown, and that were available immediately. Not knowing when Jonathan was coming back from Europe, or even if he was coming back, she *did* know she didn't want to be at the old apartment when he did. After dropping her car off at home, she spent the afternoon in and out of Ken's black SUV in a blur of apartment tours, Ken ever-vigilant and close by her side.

By the end of the day, she had signed a lease for a studio apartment only five minutes from the office. Although not her first choice by far, the new apartment was available for occupancy in two days, clinching the decision. Having asked for and gotten an advance on her paycheck, she had just enough cash to make a deposit on the apartment, pay a moving company, and eat for a couple of weeks. Remembering that her refrigerator was empty, she asked Ken to stop at the grocery store on the way home.

Ken thought it was a bad idea to be out in such an open environment. "We don't want to invite an unpleasant incident," he cautioned.

After Anna pointed out that there was no point in having a bodyguard if she was just going to starve to death over the three-day weekend anyway, Ken relented and drove her to the store. He went in with her, watching her attentively as she maneuvered the bustling aisles, all crammed to capacity with last minute shoppers. His eyes were alert and darted back and forth like a tennis spectator as he searched for hidden dangers in the produce section and sudden threats lurking in the cereal aisle.

They cleared the checkout line without inviting an unpleasant incident, and Ken drove her back to her old apartment. He stood with his back to hers and scanned the parking lot for mobile menaces while she unlocked the door. He ordered her to stay in the entryway while he checked the garage and all three levels of the apartment, then double-checked the new high-security deadbolts that the apartment complex had installed that afternoon at Anna's request and the law firm's expense. Satisfied that she was alone and the doors and windows secure, he wished her a courteous "Merry Christmas" and reminded her to throw the deadbolts. Leaving without further word, he didn't mention that he and two associates would be taking turns monitoring her apartment until further notice from B&V.

Anna trudged sullenly up the stairs to the cold, empty living room and a hot, vengeful message from an inebriated, foul-mouthed Jonathan. His words slithered through the phone like poisonous vipers. "Happy Fucking Anniversary and Merry Fucking Christmas, you lying slut." Hate poured from his drunken lips, his next words hitting Anna like an intercontinental ballistic missile. "I know what happened with you and your so-called sports doctor," he hissed. "I never should have married you. You're damaged goods."

The warhead hit its target. Anna slumped to the floor in shock as long-suppressed memories washed over her in waves, cresting the barriers she had carefully erected over the years to keep them away.

* * *

Peter Grand packed up his project drawings for Hibiscus Cay and rushed out his office door. He and his family would be spending two weeks on the island while he tied up a few loose due diligence ends for Lamar. It was late on Christmas Eve day, and their flight connections were perilously tight. He was jogging to his car when his smart phone blooped, the screen displaying Jonathan DeLuca's new phone number. He let it go to voicemail and listened to the message on the way home.

Peter could tell immediately that Jonathan was drunk. His voice was slurred and his speech disjointed, but the gist of the message was that he wanted Peter to guarantee his hotel bill in Monte Carlo or he would be thrown in the Monegasque pokey. He had, with great difficulty, left the number for the hotel manager at the Hotel de Monaco.

Peter had no inkling that Jonathan was in Monte Carlo again and didn't know why he was there, so he called Henri Baptiste while he waited for his wife to finish packing. Henri told him a story that sounded like a plot from an old episode of *Dallas*, and Peter almost dropped the phone when Henri told him how much Jonathan owed the hotel.

It wasn't until he was waiting in line at the airport security checkpoint that he called Jonathan back, making it crystal clear that there was no possible way he would guarantee such a ridiculously high hotel bill. Just then, a burly TSA agent glared at him, motioning at him to hang up the phone, put it in the bin, and get ready to bend over for a body cavity search if he annoyed her. Peter complied without bothering to say anything more to the alcohol-soaked mess of a man in Monte Carlo.

* * *

Ricky DeLuca hung up the phone and shook his head at his wife. Gina had been listening to the upsetting conversation on the bedroom extension phone and was trembling in panic at her precious Johnny's foreign plight. She went to her husband and grabbed him by the shoulders.

"You have to do something," she begged, shaking him violently. "My baby boy can't go to jail. You know it will kill him." She broke into heaving sobs, her droopy body quivering like an underdone pudding.

"I know, I know, *mi amore*," Ricky said wearily. He gently removed her hands from his shoulders and clasped them tightly, kissing each one. "There's nothing we can do right now because we have to break our T-bill to get the money he needs. Only the bank can help us with that, and the banks are already closed for Christmas."

Cold hard facts did nothing to mollify his inconsolable wife. "But there must be something you can do," she pleaded, weeping uncontrollably until her fear suddenly turned to unrestrained anger. "It's that *puttana* Anna's fault," she spat. "Johnny wouldn't be in all this trouble if she hadn't cancelled his credit card."

Ricky hugged his hysterical wife and led her lovingly to the sofa. She continued to cry while he waited patiently for her to stop, thinking back on the decades he had spent cleaning up after his son and his seemingly ceaseless personal, financial, and legal imbroglios. Sometimes Jonathan kept his crimes inside the family by using his parents' credit cards or borrowing money that he never intended to pay back—and that they never really expected him to. More often, he bled away their resources by constantly getting into trouble that inevitably required money to fix—sometimes huge sums of it—and it was always Ricky's money.

Despite all their efforts to raise a normal child, Jonathan had spent half of his life doing things that would likely land him in jail and the other half trying to stay out of it. Ricky had spent over fifty thousand dollars on voluntary psychotherapy and twenty-five thousand dollars on court-ordered psychotherapy for their son over the years. None of it had worked, and now Jonathan's latest misadventures would probably wipe out the last of their life savings. Ricky had never told his wife—and he didn't have the heart to tell her now—that Jonathan had slowly brought them to financial ruin.

Gina snuffled and wiped her rheumy eyes on her apron. "It's our fault, too" she said. "If only we had . . ."

Ricky knew exactly what she would say next. When Jonathan was in his twenties, he was arrested for drunk driving at 3:00 a.m. on New Years' Day after racing through a red light at one hundred twenty miles per hour and blowing four times the legal blood alcohol limit on a breathalyzer. It was not Jonathan's first law enforcement rodeo, and the judge set the bail so high that Ricky hadn't been able to round up the cash to get him out of jail until the following day.

When he arrived the next morning to collect and castigate his wayward son, he learned that Jonathan was in a nearby hospital, having been severely beaten by his cell mate—a detoxing meth-head biker with sexual identity and anger issues. Ricky wanted to press charges against the beast for the brutal assault, but Jonathan wanted to forget the whole thing, refusing to talk about it. They never found out exactly what happened to him that night, but Gina and Ricky had suffered under the guilt of it ever since.

Gina whimpered and finished her plaintive wish. "If only we had bailed him out of jail sooner that time."

Ricky held his wife closer. *If only we had . . .*

* * *

It was 2:00 a.m. on Christmas Day in Monaco, and Jonathan was packing to run. Captain Salvatore had finally come through with the cash, and he was about to say *au revoir* and *arrivederci* to the Mediterranean—for now.

It had been sinfully easy to talk the Italian sailor into cashing a check from Frescobaldi Prime Investments in the amount of twenty-five thousand dollars. All it took was the promise of an even bigger salary as captain of the Feadship that he had decided to buy instead of Alpha Centauri. He tossed the diamond and sapphire bracelet in as a sweetener, suggesting that Captain Salvatore give it to his wife for Christmas. Grinning with self-satisfaction, he watched the gullible captain snatch the shiny bait like a hungry barracuda, swallowing the lies hook, line, and sinker. Nothing could be done with the check until Monday, when Jonathan would already be on his way back to the United States.

He had no intention of using Captain Salvatore's money to pay the Hotel de Monaco. *Fuck Henri and the Hotel de Monaco. They can handle the loss. Assholes.* He certainly wasn't going to give it to Captain Barry or the Bjornbergs either. *It's not my fault if they were stupid enough to uproot their lives and travel all the way to Europe before the deal was even done. Idiots.* He didn't plan to pay Captain Salvatore back either. *Screw him. If he's too stupid to fall for such a simple scam, he shouldn't be captain of anything anyway.*

Knowing he had to travel light, he was frantically stuffing his best shirts, ties, suits, shoes, and whatever else he could fit into his duffel bag. He resented having to leave so many beautiful things behind. It seemed as if every abandoned item was whispering to him, *"This is all Anna's fault. This is all Anna's fault."* It was all Anna's fault—and it was her loss too. There were still millions to be made, and Jonathan Frescobaldi DeLuca, III would be back on his feet in no time.

Meanwhile, he had to get back to Dallas somehow, but Anna had cancelled his first-class ticket home. Maybe he wouldn't even go straight back to Texas. He could stop off in Ireland on the way and pad his getaway cash with some of the cute redhead's fortune. Maybe he'd check out the action in Luxembourg and Lichtenstein along the way. He'd heard there was big money in those European mini-countries.

He finished packing and made one more round of the room, looking for anything of value. Convinced that there was nothing left worth stealing, he quietly opened the door to the suite a crack and peered down the hall. Finding it empty, he tiptoed out, silently closing the door behind him and padding catlike down the hall to the emergency stairway. Although he had learned where every exit door and stairway in the hotel was and where they led, he didn't know that they were monitored twenty-four hours a day by ingeniously hidden security cameras and silently alarmed from midnight to 6:00 a.m. His lack of reconnaissance came swiftly back to bite him as he let himself out of the stairwell door on the first floor and was greeted by Henri and two muscular police officers.

"Your time is up, Monsieur DeLuca," Henri said, a condescending grin on his face. He nodded at the two meaty columns that flanked him. They grabbed and handcuffed Jonathan before he could make a move to evade them. The tips of his highly-polished shoes left black, serpentine trails on the white marble floor as Monaco's finest dragged him out the front door and down the steps to a waiting police car, folding him into the backseat of the toy-sized cruiser. He could see Henri watching the humiliating spectacle from the top of the steps, laughing at him.

An uncontrollable rage welled up within Jonathan. "How dare you laugh at me?" he screamed. "I am Jonathan Frescobaldi DeLuca, III, and you will live to regret this."

Henri was unmoved by the empty threat. "*Joyeux Noel*, Mr. DeLuca," he said, smiling with scornful satisfaction as he watched the police drive off, taking the execrable imposter with them.

Ten minutes later, Jonathan was ushered into a holding cell in Monaco's main police station to await his fate. It was cold and dank, and he wasn't sure what time it was because the entirety of his possessions, including his shoes and watch, had been taken away. His two-hundred-dollar silk socks did nothing to keep away the winter chill that permeated the stone floors of the dingy cell and crept uninvited into his bones.

At first, he had tried to bribe the two policemen who arrested him, but that only insulted and angered them. Then he had offered to pay the hotel bill with Captain Salvatore's cash, but Henri informed the police that the Hotel de Monaco had a no-cash policy due to European Union money laundering laws, and that he was not inclined to negotiate with Mr. DeLuca in any event.

It was the first time in a very long time that Jonathan had been unable to talk himself out of a problem, and he began to panic, his hands trembling violently. It didn't take much imagination for him to realize how unsympathetic a jury of wealthy Monegasques would be toward him—if they even had juries in Monaco. If they did, he knew that the stuck-up citizens of the principality would brand him a cheap trickster and low-life American con artist. They'd gleefully sentence him to the maximum punishment possible, then gossip about him over cocktails on their mega-yachts while he languished in some medieval hell-hole.

Worst of all, he had been told by the officer who booked him into his holiday quarters that there was no possible way he could see a defense lawyer or a judge until the following Monday. Jonathan felt the panic attack taking control over him. He didn't have his medication with him and didn't know how he was going to survive three days in jail without going crazy. Shivering from the cold, he curled up tightly into the fetal position on the ice-cold cot to think.

* * *

While Jonathan was spending contemplative quality time with himself in a three by five-foot cell and planning his next move, Anna was surveying the old apartment and planning hers. Having given her old furniture away at Jonathan's behest when he moved in, she decided that she was going to take his to use as a bargaining chip in the divorce. Everything would somehow have to be stuffed into an apartment one-third the size of the current one—everything but the leprous green couch and some old clothes that Jonathan left in the closet.

She was making coffee and puzzling over his vile phone message from the night before when she heard Cindy's yellow Hummer H1 SUV rumble to a noisy stop in front of the apartment. Cindy had originally planned to spend Christmas with some artist friends whose works were frequently shown in her gallery, but she cancelled to help Anna move instead.

The doorbell rang and Anna went downstairs to let her in. Cindy breezed through the door, fresh as winter snow, wearing a bright red one-piece jumpsuit and thigh-high, black patent leather boots with stiletto heels. Her red curls peeked out from under a Santa hat with a jingling sleigh bell hanging from the end of it.

Cindy's effervescence dissipated instantly when she saw a mere shadow of her friend's former self standing in the doorway. A disheveled, puffy-eyed wraith, Anna's face was alarmingly pale, and she had lost at least ten pounds. Her well-worn S.M.U. law school sweatshirt and a pair of baggy sweat pants sagged around her like someone else's clothes.

Masking her shock at the uncharacteristic image, Cindy stretched out her arms to embrace her fragile best friend. "C'mere baby girl," she said, giving Anna a comforting hug. Releasing her and holding her at arms' length, she looked her up and down and said, "You look like shit."

"Thank you, I feel like shit too." Anna said. She tried to smile and motioned up the stairs like a game show spokesmodel. "Merry Christmas and welcome to the hell that is my current life."

They climbed the stairs together and sat for a while on the couch, drinking coffee and assessing the task at hand. Cindy listened dumbstruck to the sordid details of the saga of Jonathan DeLuca and his delusional quest for Alpha Centauri. "But why didn't you tell me or Nicky any of this?" she asked when Anna finished recounting the incredible story.

"I was too embarrassed," Anna admitted. "I didn't know what people would think if I divorced so soon after I married him. I guess I was so afraid of having another failed marriage and ending up alone that I either missed or ignored all the warning signs." She looked at Cindy with shame and sorrow in her eyes. "I'm so sorry I've been such a distant friend this past year."

Cindy patted her lovingly on the hand and went into the kitchen. While she poured the last of the coffee into her cup she said, "We've been friends for too long to let something as silly as a man mess with our relationship, sweetie darling." Returning to the living room, she pointed her coffee mug at Anna. "Truth be told, Nicky and I never liked Jonathan."

"Then why didn't you say something sooner?"

Cindy sat down beside Anna. "Because no one likes to be wrong," she said, "and no one ever wants to hear 'I told you so.' Nicky and I have been worried about you for a while now. We even talked about doing an intervention or something, but we decided to wait and see what happened instead of meddling and running the risk losing your friendship."

Anna sighed and put her head in her hands. "I'm such an idiot. I should have done a background check like you and Nicky suggested back at the beginning of the whole sordid affair."

"You're not an idiot," Cindy said lovingly. "One of the hardest things in the world for anyone to do is to admit being wrong, especially when it comes to love or politics; besides, what woman in love is going to run a background check on her new beau?"

"But I'm a lawyer," Anna said. "I'm supposed to know better. How could I have been so naïve."

"You're not naïve, honey," Cindy said. "It's just that you're like a rosebud in a bucket of turds. You never expect betrayal and dishonesty from others because you can't imagine engaging in that kind of behavior yourself." She took off her boots and stood up. "Now enough of this pity party. As we say in Texas, 'Some men just need killin,' and that Jonathan DeLuca is one of them. Now let's get you packed up. Then we'll call Nicky and tell him it's time to get the van."

* * *

Cindy spent the night at Anna's apartment, and they spent the next day moving. Cindy was more sensibly dressed for the day in jeans and a sweatshirt—both quite tight. She let Ken use her Hummer for the move to speed things along because it was perfect for hauling boxes and because she thought he was deliciously sexy. He insisted on monitoring their every movement until they were finished, and Cindy happily monitored his.

Four hours later, Anna paid the movers, and Ken did a sweep of the new apartment. Anna thanked him profusely and promised to throw the dead bolt behind her.

Cindy watched Ken's departing backside, wondering where he kept his gun. She had made a clandestine inspection and couldn't find room anywhere in those jeans for a toothpick, let alone a thirty-eight special. She gave Anna a hug, made an off-color quip about Ken's equipment, and left in poof of post-Christmas cheer.

Anna was sitting on her living room floor later that night, dressed in rumpled pajamas and surrounded by fast food wrappers. She was searching through files and boxes, looking for anything that might help her calculate the financial damages that Jonathan had caused her and for which she would mercilessly demand recompense in her imminent divorce filing. She finished toting up the fiscal tragedy and gasped when she saw six digits. Her husband had used up her cash and indebted her with her credit cards to the tune of almost one hundred fifty thousand dollars. It would take her years to pay back all the Jonathan-incurred debt.

In the course of her evidentiary excavation, she came across the box marked "Documents" that Jonathan had brought with him when he had first moved in. She crouched on her knees and looked through it, discovering paperwork and files that documented Jonathan's fraudulent deals and investment scams going back decades. She found private offering documents for ostrich farms and investment contracts for prime bank letters of credit. Some of the papers were dog-eared and yellowing with age, while others were recently and professionally produced on state-of-the-art word processing equipment.

When she reached the last file in the back of the box and discovered her personal journal hidden behind it, her heart nearly stopped. She hadn't written in the journal for years, and the last place she remembered putting it was in her office desk drawer. Cindy had packed up the desk contents, so Anna hadn't noticed that the journal was missing when the two of them tore through the apartment like dervishes in their mad rush to get her moved.

A blinding flash of truth hit her like a dinosaur-killing comet. She had always wondered how Jonathan seemed to read her mind and sense her feelings. Now she knew. Using the secrets hidden in her journal's pages, he had discovered all he needed to know about her from her own words. In the process of learning how to be the man of her dreams, he had also learned about the man of her old, but never forgotten, nightmares.

* * *

Anna was just a teenager when she grew six inches in one year, the changes to her body and bones wreaking havoc on her dance technique and her joints. She was in the middle of a dance recital one night when a ligament in her left knee stretched too far and tore completely. She collapsed to the stage and was carried off by two volunteer stagehands. When the thigh-high cast came off three months later, her knee was the size of a grapefruit and her atrophied calf and thigh muscles looked like sinewy toothpicks.

Her mother wanted her back in the practice studio as soon as possible because the advance scout for a national ballet academy was coming to Dallas to hold auditions. Hoping to speed the recovery, Anna's mother took her to a locally renowned sports doctor. Though not a practicing physician, he was a certified physical trainer and licensed psychologist who treated several well-known professional football and hockey players.

Even though Anna was fourteen years old, she had never gotten "the talk" from either one of her parents. Her prudish mother never told her about boys or sex, her father wouldn't allow her to date, and sex education hadn't yet made it into the Texas school curriculum.

Her first sexual experience was when her therapist climbed on top of her while he was running her through some mental relaxation exercises. She was lying on his office couch, breathing deeply, her eyes closed, when she felt a heavy weight on top of her and sour breath on her face. She opened her eyes to find him removing her sweat pants and unzipping his own, entering her quickly and, for Anna, painfully. He wriggled around, huffing and puffing and grunting like an animal until he made a funny face and shouted "Yes!" before slumping down on her like a beached whale.

Anna had been so sheltered that she thought the sweaty calisthenics were part of the physical therapy at first. Later she felt confused and ashamed, afraid to say anything to anyone. She hid her bloodstained panties under her bed until she could find a way to dispose of them when her mother wasn't looking.

Her "therapist"—who Anna eventually came to call "The Rapist"—sexually molested her three more times before she finally told her mother that her knee felt fine and she didn't need any more physical therapy. Her first suicide attempt was shortly after that.

Expensive psychotherapy had never been an option because she couldn't afford it, but she had once read in a magazine that journal writing could be a helpful tool in self-analysis. She started the journal after her first divorce, spending hours pouring her decades-old shame into its secret spaces. Although not the perfect remedy for her externally-caused mental issues, the writing helped her come to shaky terms with dozens of psychological demons.

But a new demon had snuck past her emotional gatekeepers, and a gaping hole opened in her soul as she fully comprehended Jonathan's Machiavellian perversion and the depths of his betrayal. He had used her journal to melt her battle-hardened defenses and win her heart, only to then turn her psychic horrors against her.

Calling once more upon the willpower she had assiduously cultivated over the years, she raised her protective psychological walls, encasing her embattled and embittered heart in an impenetrable shield, never to be breached again.

Chapter 27

Arriving at her office the next morning, Anna was greeted by a message from Peter Grand telling her that Jonathan was presently cooling his heels in the Monte Carlo jail. The news thrilled her to no end, because jail was where he belonged. She took great pleasure in picturing him in a cold, tiny cell, his facade and bluster blown. For reasons she never understood, he feared jail worse than he feared death, and she was happy to let him die and rot there.

Her vengeful fantasies notwithstanding, Peter Grand was a client of the firm and, much to her chagrin, she had been the person who got him involved with Jonathan in the first place. Collecting her many scattered thoughts, she called him back. They talked affably for a few minutes, Anna learning that neither Peter nor Lamar had ever offered to pay for anyone's trip to Monte Carlo—either time. In fact, none of them knew that Jonathan had gone back to Monaco until he called Peter asking for money to pay the hotel bill. Not surprisingly, Peter had never agreed to lease a new Mercedes Benz for the company, and no one—other than Jonathan—had ever entertained the idea of buying a thirteen-million-dollar yacht.

"We're not even close to a deal," Peter said. "What was he doing back in Monte Carlo a second time anyway?"

Wishing she knew, Anna told him about the problems that Jonathan had foisted upon her and others. Being neither angry nor litigiously inclined, Peter was understanding and unconcerned by the matter. They agreed that he and Frescobaldi Prime Investments would cease to have any business dealings, Peter saying, "No harm, no foul," before cheerfully wishing her luck and clicking off.

She called Doug Sherman to let him know that Jonathan was in a foreign jail and Ken's services were probably unnecessary, but Doug didn't want to take any chances and neither did Ken. He drove her to Jerry Goldblatt's office at lunchtime and waited in the SUV, watching the door to the small law office.

The meeting was brief. If Jonathan didn't protest the settlement that Jerry would propose in the filing, she'd be free of him roughly thirty days from the day he was served with the papers. That was the tricky part, given that he was still in Europe.

"Don't worry," Jerry assured her. "He has to come back here eventually. If he's anywhere in Texas, my guys will find him. We can even serve the papers on a family member if we know they're sharing the same residence." Anna gave him Ricky and Gina's address and threw in Sharon Hammond's phone number for good measure.

Later that night, Anna was assessing her cash flow situation and devising a plan to work her way out of the financial crevasse into which Jonathan had shoved her. She remembered his child support payments, looked up the number for his ex-wife in his old cell phone, and called her.

Mary answered on the second ring, and Anna got straight and brutally to the point. "Mary, this is Anna DeLuca—Jonathan's wife. The reason I'm calling is to let you know that you won't be getting a child support check this month."

"Well, *there's* a big surprise," Mary said, laughing sarcastically.

"The truth is," Anna said, "I've been paying your child support for months now so you wouldn't have Jonathan arrested. I couldn't make last month's payment because he wiped out the bank account and skipped the country." She briefly explained the sad scenario to an unsurprised Mary.

Anna heard the "click-click-swoosh" of a cigarette lighter and heard Mary draw smoke in deeply through her nose, exhaling it forcefully through her mouth. "So, he did it to you too."

"What do you mean?"

Mary elaborated. "Jonathan and I were married for ten years," she began. "We met at work and married soon after. I didn't make a lot of money, but I had a steady job and decent credit. He was always quitting his job to work on some deal, always promising this and that and talking about how rich he was going to be some day. All lies, of course. He was always getting sued for something too, and he spent a lot of time trying to stay one step ahead of the law. I thought about leaving him a couple of times, but then I got pregnant with my little Gina, so I decided to stick it out for a while longer."

"A few years back he rented us a big house and filled it with fancy furniture. It wasn't in my taste, but it was his money—or so I thought. I found out later that he had forged a check to buy the furniture. The victim sued him over it, and the store brought criminal charges. We got evicted from the house six months later, just a few weeks after he leased me a new Jaguar convertible. We moved into a room at the Bedford Suites in Richardson, and while I was looking out the window one day, some tough guys came and repossessed my Jag. That's when I left for good."

"You were living at the Bedford Suites too?" Anna asked.

"Yes," Mary replied.

Something unwelcome insinuated itself into Anna's thoughts. "But that's where Jonathan was living when we got engaged, so that means . . ." Her voice trailed off as she paused for a moment to absorb yet another lie. She sighed heavily and asked, "When did you divorce?"

"A year ago, in October."

"That means that he proposed to me while he was still married to you," Anna said, laughing at her own stupidity. "I am so sorry, Mary. Had I known he was married, I never would have gone out with him in the first place."

"Now don't you worry about that, honey," Mary said. "The marriage was already dead. It was the forgeries, hot checks, lies, and phony deals that killed it." She took another drag on her cigarette. "I suppose you know about the probation and all."

"Yes," Anna replied. "I found out by accident. When I confronted him about it, he told me it was all the fault of some man named Hamid Halabi."

"Jonathan was always blaming Hamid for his own screw-ups," Mary said. "Hamid was shady no doubt, but Jonathan was right alongside him, lying and thieving like a demon. Truth be told, if he wasn't my Gina's daddy, I wouldn't piss on him if he was on fire." She lit another cigarette and concluded her story. "So anyway, when I found out he was getting married again, I wanted to warn you, but I figured it probably wouldn't have made a difference. You wouldn't have listened, especially not to me."

"Based on the phone conversation I recently had with his current girlfriend, I have to agree." Anna admitted. "I called to warn her, but she refused to believe anything I said."

"Well don't worry about it. I didn't listen to his first wife either when she tried to warn me."

The breath of an angel could have knocked Anna over. She gasped and said, "Jonathan told me that you were his only ex-wife."

"Typical Jonathan," Mary snorted. "That man lies like he breathes. He was married for thirteen years before I met him and has two grown sons. He was always late paying their child support too. They've been estranged for years because of it."

A brief silence followed as Anna considered the latest revelations, Mary waiting patiently until she spoke again. "So how has he managed to stay out of jail all these years?"

"Simple," Mary replied. "His mommy and daddy have spent most of their lives cleaning up their baby boy's messes, rushing to save him every time he drops a load in his big boy designer pants."

Anna was not surprised by Mary's answer. "I really appreciate your honesty with me," she said, "and I'm sorry for everything he did to you and your daughter. Maybe his parents will help you out with the child support."

"Maybe, but I doubt it," Mary said. "They're no better than him. At least my new husband is a hard-working, god-fearing man and a wonderful daddy to my Gina. We'll be fine. I'll pray for you."

They wished each other luck and promised to keep each other up to date on Jonathan's whereabouts and activities, should either of them find anything out.

Completely drained but unable to sleep that night, Anna tossed and turned in her bed hour after hour. She counted Jonathan's lies instead of sheep, chastising herself for not having discovered the soulless monster behind the smiling face before marrying him and setting the course for her own destruction.

* * *

Peter Grand called her at the office again the next day to tell her that Bob Peterson had just called with news that Jonathan's parents paid his hotel bill in Monaco. Henri had dropped the charges, and Jonathan had been released from jail. He would be leaving Monte Carlo the following day.

Anna thanked Peter and hung up, a chill running through her as she calculated travel times. Taking into consideration the time difference and possible layovers at different airports, she estimated that it would be thirty-six to forty-eight hours before Jonathan was back in Dallas.

She called Doug Sherman and conferenced in Ken Woods, telling them that her emotionally unstable and possibly vengeful husband— who probably had her Browning nine-millimeter with a full clip in it— was on the move. They all agreed that it would be best for her to work remotely by computer from her new apartment until Ken could make special arrangements with the building's security team. She called her divorce lawyer with the update and briefly explained the situation to a flabbergasted Becca on her way out the door.

After two work days ensconced in her miniscule apartment attending to year-end business, she spent the New Year holiday unpacking the remnants of her old life and organizing them into some semblance of a new one. She insisted that Ken take the weekend off, even though it was possible that Jonathan was back in Dallas by now. Ken had vehemently refused at first, but she finally argued him into it after he extracted a promise that she would not leave the apartment or open the door for anyone until Monday morning when he would come back to escort her to work.

As she was sorting through a few remaining unpacked boxes containing odds and ends collected over the years, her meticulously maintained state of semi-denial gave way. Her thoughts were flooded by the memory of her honeymoon when she had been basking in sunshine and love in Cancún, safe and secure in her new husband's arms. A year later, the love of her life had been exposed as an impecunious imposter and amoral sociopath. Her marriage was moribund, her financial setbacks cataclysmic, and her future clouded by the ominous specter of endless lawsuits and onerous legal fees.

Rather than cry over spilled champagne she went into the cramped galley kitchen to heat up a frozen dinner—she no longer cared what kind it was. She ate it standing over the sink and washed it down with convenience store wine. When the bottle was empty, she looked deep into it, as if it were a crystal ball holding a glimpse of hope or a source of the strength to endure. She saw neither.

* * *

Back in the office the following Monday, Anna rang in the new year with a scathing message from Captain Barry. "Call me back immediately," the gravelly voice barked at her. "We've got a real emergency here." The bellowing boat broker went on to leave a rambling, profanity-laced diatribe in his unmistakable bullhorn voice, the message rife with salty language and sprinkled with scary acronyms like FBI, CIA, NSA and INTERPOL.

She understandably didn't want to talk to Captain Barry after the bowl of alphabet soup he had just served up, but if a fleet of calamities was steaming her way, she wanted to deal with it head on and get it over with. He went immediately into a rant as soon as she called him back, scarcely pausing for breath between invectives and curse words. She finally had to interrupt him. "I'm very busy, Captain Barry," she snapped. "Please slow down and tell me what you want."

The aggrieved mariner detailed his side of the sorry chain of events, explaining the hiring of the Bjornbergs and relating the promises Jonathan had made before they had all been blown so wildly off course. He concluded his depressing yarn by telling Anna that Jonathan had also stolen a significant part of Captain Salvatore's life savings before vanishing immediately upon having been let out of jail.

When Captain Barry finished his tale of maritime woe, Anna told hers. The captain's disenchantment worsened considerably as she addressed each of his complaints. "With respect to the debit card portion of your story, that card was for our personal checking account, not business. I was informed by the bank that Jonathan—or *someone* in fraudulent possession of the card—had been using it liberally and illegally in France, Italy, and Monaco, thereby emptying the account and leaving me penniless. I couldn't help you even if I wanted to."

"But Jonathan said it was fine for me to use the card," Captain Barry protested before clamming up, having realized too late that he just admitted having committed theft —to a lawyer no less.

"A simple phone call to me would have saved you a lot of trouble, Captain," Anna said after a brief silence.

"I wanted to call you to make sure it was all right if I used the card, but Jonathan told me you were in court and couldn't be reached."

"I'm never in court because I'm not a litigator, I'm a . . . Oh never mind," she said. "In any event, I would never deliberately strand two innocent people like the Bjornbergs."

"You mean three innocent people," Captain Barry corrected her.

She tried, but couldn't summon the same sympathy for Captain Barry as she had for Helen Bennington and even Sharon Hammond. She could feel his unease coming through the phone in whitecaps and pressed her advantage.

"I mean exactly what I said," she responded, correcting him back. "I have yet to form a conclusive opinion on your involvement in this matter, but since you just admitted that you are the culprit who emptied my checking account, I will probably sue you and bring you up on criminal charges for fraud, theft, and conspiracy." Captain Barry was grumbling something profane at her as she hung up on him.

Scarcely believing that Jonathan could have hired two total strangers to be crew members on a yacht he didn't own, she added them to the growing list of passengers on the ship of dreamers and hopeful hearts set adrift in the maelstrom of his wide and malicious wake. Fretting over the consequences of her husband's heartless perfidy, her stomach clenched when she thought of the many ways the growing hydra-headed agglomeration of potential plaintiffs might eventually come back to bite her.

She blamed herself. If only she had done a background check, she might have found out about Jonathan's criminal past and never married him in the first place. If only she had gotten to know him better before marrying him, instead of giving into her fears and rushing headlong into disaster. If only she had paid more attention to her personal finances online instead of doing it all in her head. *If only she had. . .*

* * *

The last thing Anna wanted to do was talk to Jonathan, but Doug, Ken, and Jerry all pointed out that it was in her best interest to determine his whereabouts for the purposes of serving him with divorce papers and ascertaining if he posed a threat. She didn't have his new phone number, but she did have the number for his topsider-licking toady Bob Peterson.

She called him while Ken listened in on the speaker phone, getting his voicemail and leaving a message telling him that it was urgent that they speak. He called her back almost immediately, brusquely telling her that Jonathan was out of town but refusing to tell her where. A minute after he rudely hung up on her, the office caller I.D. showed an incoming call from his cell phone.

Anna answered it, but it wasn't Bob. It was Jonathan, which meant that Bob had just lied to her. He too must have been mesmerized into joining the DeLuca cult and following Jonathan, lemming-like, off the cliff. Her righteous rage was fanned by the blatant insult to her intelligence, but she tamped it down hard.

"Bob said you were looking for me," Jonathan said, his voice devoid of inflection or emotion.

"Where are you?" she demanded.

"New York," he lied.

Chirping birds in the background sounded suspiciously like the ones Anna used to hear during Sunday suppers on his parents' patio. She heard none of the sounds of the big city, telling her that Jonathan's penchant for mendacity remained intact.

"Do you care to tell me what's going on?" she asked, as calmly as possible. "How am I supposed to pay American CreditCorp and Newman's? How and when are you going to pay me back the money you stole from me?"

Jonathan erupted, spewing a geyser of falsehoods and denial. "I didn't steal anything. You stole from *me*, you stupid fucking bitch. You took all my furniture." His acid voice burned through the phone. "It was Captain Barry who emptied the bank account after *he* stole the debit card out of *my* briefcase. Then *you* cancelled the credit card and landed me in jail."

"I didn't cancel the card; the law firm did."

"What difference does it make who cancelled it? And why wouldn't you talk to Pops? He's been trying to help. He has the money to fix this."

Anna was on the verge of tears, struggling to maintain control of her emotions. "There's not enough money in the world to fix this Jonathan," she said. "It's over. From now on, you can communicate with me through my divorce lawyer."

Jonathan's accusatory tone turned to feigned remorse as he turned on the tears. "Please don't leave me, darling," he sobbed. "I love you more than life itself. Just give me a chance. I'll have one hundred fifty thousand dollars for you within the week. I swear."

"Don't ever call me again," Anna said with disgust, slamming the phone down. She fell back in her chair, exhausted from the Herculean task of not letting the anger boil up inside of her until the pressure sought an escape and she ended up threatening to kill him, landing herself in jail.

She spoke with Ken for a few minutes before getting back to work, the two of them having decided that Becca would put all calls from Jonathan or his parents directly into her voicemail, where they'd be recorded for use in the divorce proceedings and, if necessary, to bring criminal charges.

* * *

The phone messages began later that afternoon and continued for days. At the end of each day, Ken and Anna would review them

252

together, then Becca would transcribe them and send a copy to Jerry Goldblatt.

The messages covered the full spectrum of emotions and a wide range of tones. At first there was undisguised hate: "I'm going to have you disbarred, you thieving bitch," Jonathan threatened. "I'm going to talk to the head of B&V and get you fired." He followed that up with "I hope you're happy, you ruined my children's lives," and "I know you're running around with different men every night, you filthy whore."

Briefly interrupting the hate-fest was a call from Ricky DeLuca. The elder DeLuca tried a new approach: "Hello, Anna darling," he said, syrupy sweet. "I have fantastic news! Jonathan told me he just met with the Senior Vice President of the Bank of New York up in Manhattan, and when the securities hit the screen in ten days, he'll send you a cashier's check for one hundred fifty thousand dollars."

Anna had regained some of her sense of humor in recent days and laughed aloud at the absurdity of the offer.

Jonathan called again after that. This time, it was Dr. Jekyll rather than Mr. Hyde who spoke: "It's Jonathan, darling. I called to let you know that I think of you every day." He sighed the sigh of the lovelorn. "You don't really want a divorce, do you? Who will walk with you in the park on Sundays?"

His plaintive tone changed in a schizophrenic second, and Mr. Hyde rejoined the party, touching on her deepest fears. "You don't want to die *alone*, do you?"

He faxed her a handwritten divorce settlement offer the following afternoon. In it, he generously offered to let her to keep his furniture and the gifts he had given her during the marriage, even though the former had been obtained illegally, and the latter had been returned to the store—other than the vagabond mink coat and the vanishing luggage. All she needed to do to act on this fantastic final offer was to write him a check for two hundred fifty thousand dollars. She was surprised that he hadn't also asked for shipping, handling, and processing too.

Caving at last to her anger, she broke the agreed-upon security protocols and called his parents' apartment. When he answered the phone, she suggested an anatomically impossible feat for him to perform with his settlement offer and hung up.

He called back thirty seconds later. "I was just bluffing, my love. Please don't leave me. I'm so sorry. I fucked up."

She couldn't believe her ears. *"I fucked up?"* His excuse for everything was a simple, *"I fucked up?"*

The final message came in at 10:00 a.m. the next morning. It was from Jonathan, and it was obvious that he was already drunk. "I hope you're happy, bitch," he slurred, "I just got served divorce papers by some asshole pretending to deliver a bouquet of flowers to my mother. You're going to be sorry for that someday. Just you wait."

Ken was alarmed by the menacing message and left Anna's office in a hurry. She got a call from Doug Sherman a few days later, informing her that Ken had conducted his threat assessment and had determined that she was in no danger from Jonathan. Anna didn't ask—and wasn't sure if she wanted to know—what that meant.

She never saw or heard from Jonathan again.

Chapter 28

Jonathan careened through Anna's life like a Texas twister in July, his brief but destructive whirlwind of deceit and white collar crime cutting a swath of devastation in a jigsaw pattern of broken lives and empty bank accounts. Caught dead center in the rampage, she hadn't heeded the warning sirens and spent an entire year digging herself out of the rubble that buried her in the wake of the storm's furious passage.

In January, she fended off The Bargeron Law firm, which was looking to her for payment of their legal fees related to the negotiations for Alpha Centauri. Unknown to her, Jonathan had promised to pay the fees as a deal sweetener, faxing the promise over her signature on B&V letterhead as proof. She explained everything to Philip Bargeron, who pointed out that he and his law firm would never have taken Jonathan seriously as a potential buyer of Alpha Centauri had it not been for Anna's status as a lawyer and the fact that so much correspondence had emanated from her law firm. Nonetheless, he graciously opted to drop the matter altogether, agreeing begrudgingly that they had all been had. Anna had gotten lucky, barely escaping the monetary liability and the possibility of criminal wire fraud charges for Jonathan's fax transmission of a bogus check.

A demand letter from the law firm that did the paperwork to incorporate Frescobaldi Prime Investments arrived in February. Although they understood that Anna had been thoroughly defrauded too, she had signed the law firm's engagement letter, and they had done legitimate work. She didn't fight them out of professional courtesy, and the parties agreed that she'd pay only half of the seventeen thousand-dollars owed, plus interest, over a period of twelve months.

At the beginning of March, her accountant informed her that Jonathan owed the IRS fifteen thousand dollars in back taxes pre-dating the marriage, which she could be forced to pay. With the help of one of B&V's top tax attorneys, she got an exemption from the joint tax liability, successfully dodging another expensive bullet.

Fred DuPree called in the middle of March looking for Jonathan and the interest check on his fifty-thousand-dollar investment. It took several weeks, two B&V litigators, and an affidavit from Harry Vincent attesting to Anna's innocence in the matter to prove to the duped DuPrees that the investment was a sham, the signatures on the investment documents were unenforceable forgeries, and that she knew nothing about any of it. Fred was one of the fortunate ones. Although thoroughly chastened, he wasn't financially devastated like some of Jonathan's other victims. When she called to thank him for not suing her, he was embarrassed at having been snookered. "I'm such an old fool," he said, his voice creaking with age. "I knew I never should have invested in anything but T-Bills."

Jonathan didn't show in divorce court in late March—armed or otherwise—and the divorce was final by default. The court awarded her a worthless judgment of one hundred fifty thousand dollars, Jonathan having no assets to seize in payment.

As the spring flowers began to bloom, B&V hired an outside lawyer to help her negotiate with Newman Marvis, American CreditCorp, and whatever unknown creditors might crawl from under Jonathan's rock to infest her life in the future. Neither of the business behemoths was cooperative or willing to investigate the frauds, and both turned the DeLuca matter over to collection agencies that began to harass her on a regular basis.

A courier package from Lamar Buchanan arrived in May. In it was a handwritten note that said, "Henry Vincent told me all about what happened with you and Jonathan. I apologize for not sending you this report sooner. Regards, Lamar Buchanan." Attached to the note was an exhaustive private investigator's report chronicling Jonathan's lifetime of living outside the law with few breaks in the action. He had outstanding judgments, pending lawsuits, and criminal liability for a raft of pecuniary peccadillos: theft of services, theft by check, conversion, fraud, failure to pay on promissory notes, and failure to pay child support—among others. The total tortious amount for which Jonathan was liable topped half a million dollars.

As she read the report, she noticed that most of the court records cited a social security number for Jonathan that was different from the one she had seen on his sporadic paychecks. Even if she had tried to investigate him before marrying him, the search most likely would not have yielded anything without his second social security number. She suspected that wasn't by chance.

By June, the F-Man was back to his obnoxious, sexist ways, asking her "How could someone as smart as you fall for such a creep? Did he have a really big dick or something?"

"Excellent question and yes, very," Anna replied, setting out to find out the answer to the first question. She read the information Doug Sherman had given her again and spent her sparse free time researching antisocial personality disorder—another name for sociopathy. She learned, among many things, that the thread holding a sociopath back from crossing the imperceptible line between nonviolent sociopathy and violent psychopathy could easily be broken by some external or internal stressor.

For Jonathan, the trigger could have been another lawsuit, another criminal complaint, or another child support payment. It could have been another bottle of scotch or another bottle of pills. Any combination of psychological and chemical combustibles could have caused him to crack up, cross the line, pick up a flashlight, and club her to death with it as if she were a baby seal. The only silver lining in the whole depressing affair was that in the only way that really mattered—her very life itself—she had been miraculously lucky.

Her further search for self-understanding taught her that sociopaths are skilled predators. Like the cheetah or lion, their internal radar seeks and easily finds the weak and the lame. Once captured, the predator separates its prey from the herd, mauling the carcass at its leisure. Anna was determined to understand why she had been such easy prey, culled without difficulty from the pack of potential victims.

Instead of using her time and paychecks pursuing Jonathan for the divorce settlement or pressing criminal charges, she chose to see a psychotherapist—a woman this time. She learned a great deal about herself while talking about the things that had happened to her when she was only fourteen years old.

In December, the lawyers for American CreditCorp and Newman Marvis broke off negotiations with her lawyer, refusing to make a deal with her.

In January, she filed for bankruptcy.

* * *

Jonathan's year was also eventful. After making his way back to Dallas on his parents' dime, he spent the rest of the winter sleeping on the floor of their tiny spare bedroom. He spent the spring unemployed and wasn't looking for work because Lamar Buchanan bought him off with thinly-veiled threats and ten thousand dollars in cash to get him out of the Hibiscus Cay deal. Using that money, along with what was left of Captain Salvatore's, he leased a used ruby red Mercedes Benz convertible to drive while he lived with his parents and worked on his next deal.

By mid-summer, Ricky was dead broke from making Jonathan's child support payments and fighting lawsuits that had been filed against his son. The list was long and included David, Jonathan's former friend and lawyer, The Bargeron Law Firm, Chartrier's, Captain Barry Fogelson, Bob Peterson, a boat surveyor from Florida, a secretarial service, a florist, and Lars and Ella Bjornberg, jointly and separately.

The DeLucas were evicted from their apartment in the fall and moved to the Bedford Suites, where Jonathan slept on a cot. He and his mother were out shopping for groceries one afternoon, when Ricky came upon a loaded Browning nine-millimeter pistol in Jonathan's suitcase and killed himself with it. His devastated widow was left with nothing but his social security and disability checks, a two-year-old Cadillac, and two valid credit cards.

Jonathan's second ex-wife, Mary, called him on the day of Ricky's funeral to tell him that she had turned him into the Attorney General of the State of Texas for failure to pay his daughter's child support. The prospect of imprisonment now a real possibility, he decided to get a new start under an assumed name somewhere far, far away from Texas. He sold his mother's car and set out for warmer climes, taking a reluctant Gina with him.

Gina descended into dementia soon after her husband's suicide. Her mind was so far gone that she still thought Ricky was alive and had only gone to the bank to break the T-bill. She refused to budge, insisting that Ricky would be back any minute now. Her irrational protestations fell upon deaf ears, because Jonathan now possessed a notarized court document proclaiming that Gina DeLuca was legally incompetent. He now had sole control and power of attorney over his mother and her money.

* * *

Bob and Mona Peterson followed Jonathan in his search for a change of scenery. Mona literally had a stroke when her husband told her about the additional fifteen thousand dollars that Jonathan had borrowed from them and never repaid. Bob sued him after the Frescobaldi Prime Investments fiasco, but Jonathan's father paid him off and all had been forgotten.

Sadly, the problem of Mona's condition could not be fixed as easily as the debt had been, but Bob took solace in the fact that the climate would be healthier for Mona, and he was convinced that Jonathan's new business idea was genius. It wouldn't take long to make a lot of money, and maybe he and Mona could take that cruise one day. Having lost the ability to speak because of her stroke, Mona was in no condition to argue with her husband.

After packing his pickup truck with everything they might need, Bob sold or gave away anything they didn't. They met up with Jonathan at a gas station, and the two-vehicle caravan headed southeast and out of Texas forever.

* * *

Captain Barry was standing outside a strip mall in Delray Beach, Florida, smoking a cigar and waiting for his new business partners to arrive. Jonathan had convinced both Captain Barry and Bob Peterson that he could teach them how to sell yachts as successfully as he had once sold cars, earning commissions that would make them all millionaires.

Jonathan DeLuca may have some issues with the truth, Captain Barry mused, but he was one hell of a slick-talking pitch man who could charm the barnacles off a banana boat. Since neither Barry nor Bob were criminally inclined, they had been understandably wary at first, but when Jonathan offered to put Bob in charge of the partnership's finances, they figured they could keep him honest.

Captain Barry wished that Captain Salvatore and the Bjornbergs hadn't turned down Jonathan's offer to join the new venture as captain and crew on the yacht that Jonathan planned to buy and charter out. Captain Salvatore stayed on with Alpha Centauri after she was eventually sold to a wealthy real estate developer from Abu Dhabi, who renamed her "Moonlight over Dubai." The disillusioned Swedes returned to Stockholm after the disastrous Alpha Centauri affair and opened a catering business that had become quite successful. Then Ella had a baby, ending their seagoing careers forever.

Captain Barry glanced at the Piaget watch that Ricky DeLuca had given him—along with a pile of cash—in exchange for dropping his lawsuit against Jonathan. It was just business after all. He dropped his cigar, stubbed it out with his foot, and looked up to see a bright red Mercedes convertible and a battered blue pickup truck pull into the parking lot. Jonathan and Bob got out of their vehicles, and the three new partners shook hands all around, admiring the sign above the door of their new office that proudly proclaimed, "Frescobaldi Yacht Sales and Charter Services."

Deciding it was time for a celebratory drink, Captain Barry led the way to their temporary lodgings at the Delray Beach Residence Inn, where Jonathan used his mother's credit cards to book them two suites of rooms with lovely ocean views.

Chapter 29

Ten years later

Anna was on the rooftop terrace of her house in a small Spanish Colonial town in the central mountains of Mexico. She had retired early and built the house after suffering a "minor cardiac event" at her desk at 4:00 a.m. one morning while pulling an all-nighter on an IPO. Not wishing to work herself into a repeat performance, she sold everything she owned and moved south of the border, carving out her own little slice of Mexican heaven.

She was talking to Cindy on the phone, and as the conversation wound down, she told Cindy that she loved and missed her and asked to speak with Ken. Cindy and Ken had gotten married a few years after that fateful Christmas moving day in Dallas, and Anna had been the maid of honor at their wedding.

Ten years had gone by since the DeLuca affair, and it was time to decide whether to renew her divorce judgment or let it lapse. She had enlisted Ken's thriving private investigation firm to see what he and his minions could find out about Jonathan's whereabouts and assets, if any.

Ken came on the line and told her he and his team had picked up Jonathan's twisted trail when the Attorney General of Texas put out a notice that he was wanted by the State of Texas for felony evasion of child support. After a multi-year gap in the information, they tracked him to Florida, discovering a court judgment there against Gina and Jonathan for money owed to the Delray Beach Residence Inn. Their research also unearthed an open felony warrant for Jonathan issued by Palm Beach County for the crime of grand theft over twenty thousand dollars. There was no record of any arrests, trials, or imprisonment. Jonathan DeLuca had simply vanished.

A newspaper obituary published online a couple of years after Jonathan dropped off the radar reported that a woman claiming to be Gina DeLuca had died peacefully in her sleep in a charitable hospice facility in Miami run by The Little Sisters of the Poor. The decrepit and demented old woman had been abandoned on the nuns' doorstep in the middle of the night with only the nightgown on her back. The obituary listed no known relatives.

"Sorry, Anna," Ken said. "The man's a ghost. But cheer up, hon'. Christmas is coming."

Thanking her lucky stars that her life had turned out far better than she could have hoped, she thanked Ken for his help and clicked off. She no longer cared if Jonathan was living under a bridge in Fort Lauderdale, doing time in Tallahassee, or decomposing in Biscayne Bay. Any of those scenarios suited her just fine. She would always wonder, though, what happened to the other people who had been caught in Jonathan's widely cast net of deception.

She turned her thoughts and her gaze back to the magnificent panorama before her, watching as the sun finished its work for the day in a blazing glory of Maxfield Parrish blues, pinks, and oranges. As it dipped behind the distant mountains and winked good night, she heard a call from the living room.

"Anna, come here. You've got to see this."

She hurried down the stairs to the second floor of the house. Nicky Morgan was standing in front of her flat screen television holding two glasses of champagne. He had followed her to Mexico a few years earlier after suffering a massive heart attack while out with friends celebrating a massive business victory. One triple bypass and two months in the hospital later, he too cashed in his career chips and retired. He was currently renting a house not far from hers, and although they were still just friends, he remained optimistic that she was open to new possibilities.

"Pinkies up!" he said, handing her a glass and pointing to the television.

The 5:00 p.m. news was coming through on a satellite feed from a channel in Florida. Transfixed, she watched as a news anchor announced perkily:

In other news: Local authorities got an early Christmas present the day before yesterday when they discovered a man bound, gagged, blindfolded, and sitting on the front steps of the local police precinct. The man, who had been going by the name of Larry Jameson, was wanted for multiple felonies in two states and had been on the run for years.

He gained some notoriety here in Florida when he killed his fifth wife, the publishing empire heiress Margaret Mahaffey. Jameson shot Mahaffey with a Browning nine-millimeter handgun and stole several hundred thousand dollars' worth of jewels and cash from his dead wife's safe. He has eluded capture ever since, and authorities believed that he had fled the country, possibly by boat. The fugitive's real name is Jonathan DeLuca and he was known to have used a second alias— John Thornbury.

According to several witnesses in the area, a white panel van with blacked out windows and no license plates screeched to a halt in front of the police station. Two men dressed completely in black and wearing ski masks jumped out and dumped DeLuca on the steps before fleeing the scene.

The van and its occupants remain unidentified. DeLuca is in jail awaiting trial for his crimes and, if found guilty, faces life imprisonment without parole or execution by lethal injection.

Now here's Norm with the weather. Well, Norm, it sure looks like we're in for a sunny Christmas.

You bet it does Maureen . . .

Anna's jaw dropped and she stared wordlessly at Nicky.

A sly grin spread over his face as he said, "I forgot to tell you that I got a new van."